UNDYING MAGIC

WHITE HAVEN WITCHES

BOOK FIVE

TJ GREEN

Undying Magic

Mountolive Publishing

eBook ISBN 978-0-9951313-1-6

Paperback ISBN 978-0-9951313-2-3

Hardback ISBN 978-1-99-004778-7

Cover design by Fiona Jayde Media

Editing by Missed Period Editing

www.tjgreenauthor.com

www.happenstancebookshop.com

Contents

One

A very took a deep breath and uttered the spell that she now knew by heart. Within seconds she blacked out, and when she woke up, she found herself on the floor, her cheek against the thick wool rug.

She gingerly pushed herself upright, checked for injuries, and then looked around the room. She had no idea where she was, but the room was beautifully decorated with antique furniture, a huge bed, and expensive Persian carpets.

A moment later she heard a voice, faint but clear. "Avery! Can you hear me?"

She sighed, hating the fact that she could not master witch-flight. "Yes. I'm in a bedroom, somewhere."

A whirling black cloud appeared in front of her, manifesting into the tall, dark-haired Caspian Faversham. He raised an eyebrow. "You seem to have found my bedroom."

She glared at him. "I can assure you it was not intentional."

He smirked. "The bed would have been a softer landing." He stretched out his hand, and Avery accepted it as he pulled her to her feet.

"I'd settle for landing on my feet," she said archly.

"Perhaps you'd like me to demonstrate with you this time? I *did* suggest it was the best way to learn."

Avery sighed heavily. She had been at Caspian's house—the huge one he had inherited from his father, Sebastian—for the last two hours, and was no closer to mastering the skill than when she had arrived.

Ever since Caspian realised Avery needed help, he had offered to teach her, but she had resisted. Partly because Avery knew Alex was uncomfortable with the idea once he learned Caspian had made a pass at her, but also because she didn't really want to spend time with Caspian alone. Although, she couldn't fault him. He'd been the perfect gentleman. But he was also still Caspian, and therefore infuriating. He'd said the best way to learn was to experience witch-flight with him, but she didn't want to. Until now.

Caspian spoke again, echoing her own thoughts. "Avery, I realise you're a stubborn and independent woman, but you really are no closer now than when you first arrived." He frowned in thought. "Are you still saying that spell?" He was referring to the spell she had found in the old grimoire.

"Yes. Why?"

"Because, as I told you, I don't use one, and neither do most other witches. The spell you found was most likely for witches who are not masters of elemental Air, and was therefore designed to help them achieve witch-flight. Clearly it's flawed, and you shouldn't use it again. It's hampering your natural ability." He held out his hand again. "Let me demonstrate."

Avery stared at him for a few seconds, assessing her options, but had to agree that he was right. She extended her hand and he held it in his cool one, pulling her closer.

"What are you doing?" she asked, resisting.

"Not seducing you, just making life a little easier," he said with a smirk.

He placed his arm around her waist so her back was pulled against his chest, his chin an inch above her head. She held herself stiffly, uncomfortably aware of his closeness.

"Now, I want you to feel as I gather the air. You do what you normally do—pull it towards you, and use its energy for yourself. But you need to become a part of it, Avery."

She grimaced. "Yes I know, but..."

"But you're rushing it. You must control it. I've seen you lift off the ground before. This is a similar process. We are going to the kitchen, which I am envisaging very strongly. Do not resist me."

Avery felt Caspian's power reach out and the air begin to gather. He pulled it closer until they were wrapped within it, and then she felt its elemental force start to rush through her, her body dissolving into it. However, with the process slowed by Caspian, she was better able to feel how it worked.

With a snap, the bedroom disappeared and was replaced by a kitchen. More importantly, she was still standing and conscious.

Avery pulled away from Caspian, who still held her lightly, and looked around the room. "Wow. We made it!"

He sounded impatient. "Of course we made it! I'm an expert."

She turned to look at him and resisted slapping his arrogant face. "You're right. I could feel how to do it better with you."

He smirked. "Everything's better with me, Avery."

She snorted. "I doubt that."

He still looked insufferably pleased with himself. "Suit yourself. Now, once more. But this time, I'll do it slightly quicker."

She backed into his embrace once more, wondering at what point double-entendres with Caspian had become normal, but within seconds the room disappeared again. This time they reappeared in the garden overlooking the large lawn that spread to the shrubs and trees bordering the grounds.

She shivered as she stepped away. "Bloody hell. It's freezing! Did we have to come outside?"

He grinned. "I thought it would motivate you to get back inside again. Ready to try on your own?"

Avery nodded. "Yes. I can definitely feel where I was going wrong before."

"Good. See you back in the kitchen." And with that, he disappeared.

She took a deep breath and closed her eyes, clearly envisaging Caspian's kitchen, and then she summoned Air, dissolving her being into it. The now familiar but uncomfortable sensation overcame her, and this time, she landed in the kitchen, fully conscious, but on the floor again.

"Bollocks," she exclaimed.

Caspian was leaning against the counter, watching her. "But you're here, and awake! I really am a great teacher."

Avery just stared at him as she stood. "Can you stop being quite so irritating? I'm going to try again. Put the kettle on."

Avery drove back into White Haven after leaving Caspian's place and headed to The Wayward Son, Alex's pub, ready for some lunch.

She smiled as she navigated through the streets. It was a Thursday in mid-December, and the entire town was now groaning under Christmas decorations. A large Christmas tree had been erected in the square, shop fronts and restaurants were lit up with fairy lights, and the streets were adorned with giant baubles and snowflakes.

Avery loved Christmas. She didn't believe in God or Jesus, instead celebrating the pagan Winter Solstice, but nevertheless, she loved the way everyone came together to enjoy each other's company and to give presents.

The winding streets were full of shoppers huddled in heavy woollen coats or puffer jackets. The skies were grey and heavy with clouds, and a biting wind sliced through the streets. It looked as if it would rain, and Avery mused, it might even snow. Although, on the coast, snow never seemed to stick around for long.

As she rounded the corner onto the quayside, the view opened up and she saw the sea stretching to the horizon. The sea was as grey as the sky, and fishing boats bobbed on the heavy swells. Avery shivered, despite the warmth in her van. She pulled around the back of the pub and squeezed it into a parking spot. When she entered the pub, the chatter of the lunchtime crowd hit her, and she headed toward the bar to her usual spot.

Alex, another witch and her boyfriend, was pulling pints, and he grinned as he saw her. He was working with Zee, one of the Nephilim, and a young woman who Avery had never met before. This must be either Grace or Maia. Alex had told her he'd employed some extra bar staff for the Christmas and New Year period. The young woman was blonde, and looked to be in her early twenties. Alex had said they were both students at the university. Zee caught her eye and nodded before continuing to serve customers, and Avery smiled. Zee now had a scar running down his left cheek after his encounter with the Wild Hunt a few weeks before on All Hallows' Eve. With Briar's salves and his own unnatural ability to heal, it had already faded considerably.

Avery perched on a stool, and looked around the pub at the crowded tables. A large Christmas tree stood in the corner of the room, decorated with lights and baubles, and tinsel was strung up over the bar. She recognised quite a few faces, but there were new ones, which was unusual at this time of year. It was well out of the summer holiday season, and the school holidays were another couple of weeks off. But she knew why the place was busy. It was the same reason the whole town had been busy for weeks.

Ever since Samhain and the Walk of the Spirits, as the press had called it, paranormal lovers and ghost hunters had arrived in droves. They had booked up hotels and Bed and Breakfast places, and the whine of EMF metres sounded along every street. The event had put White Haven on the map. The footage—admittedly sketchy—had been on national news, and interviews with the locals had dominated headlines for over a week. Ben, Dylan, and Cassie, the paranormal investigators, had also been interviewed, and they were now getting referrals from all over Cornwall. National reporters had descended for a few days, and then finding that nothing else of interest was happening, had disappeared again. But the steady stream of other visitors had remained.

Avery allowed herself a smile. The Walk of the Spirits had been fun, especially after the horrors of the Wild Hunt in Old Haven Church. Although, not a single ghost had appeared in the centre of White Haven since. Except, of course, for Helena, her own witch ancestor who'd been burned at the stake. She was now a ghost who appeared from time to time in her flat. Avery strongly suspected that Helena had organised the spirit walk in order to keep everyone's focus away from Old Haven Church, if ghosts did such things as *organising*. It was a surprisingly magnanimous gesture from Helena if that was the case. Avery presumed that with the passing of Samhain, the time when the veils between worlds became thinner, the opportunity for such a mass event had gone. However, there were still spirit sightings, hauntings, poltergeists, and other unusual spirit activity in certain places.

Avery was disturbed from her reverie by Alex placing a glass of red wine in front of her. His dark brown, shoulder-length hair was loose, and as usual he had stubble across his lower jaw and chin. "Hi, gorgeous. How did your witch-flight go?"

She smiled. "Very well. I can do it! I hesitate to use the word *master*, but I don't pass out anymore."

He grinned and leaned closer. "Awesome. I knew you'd do it. And I expect you to show me later."

"Of course. How is your new staff?" Avery nodded to the blonde.

"That's Grace. She's a bit slow, but she'll pick it up. She's very charming, and I'm pretty sure very capable of telling the overeager punters to back off." He frowned, changing the subject. "How was Caspian?"

"Very helpful. I actually didn't need the spell from my grimoire, but I did need his guidance."

"Did he try anything with you?"

Avery knew Alex was annoyed at Caspian for his over-familiarity with her, and she tried to reassure him. "No. He was the perfect gentleman, and as usual, very annoying."

"Good." Alex looked relieved, and he pulled a menu off the bar. "Go and grab a seat and I'll join you in a minute."

"Are you sure you can spare the time? I don't mind if you're too busy." She looked around at the room again. "There are a lot of people in today!"

"And my bar staff are very capable of handling the crowd," he said with a wink. "Besides, I have news."

Avery headed to the small back room that Alex had spelled to remain quiet, a haven for the locals, and found a table under the window looking out on the small courtyard garden that was deserted today, except for two hardy smokers who sat under a string of colourful fairy lights.

Avery had barely had time to decide on her lunch of soup and garlic bread when Alex reappeared, placed their orders, and then sat down opposite her with a pint.

"So, what's your mysterious news?" Avery asked, thinking it was something about the pub or their Christmas plans. They hadn't decided how to spend it yet, but were debating whether to go to Reuben's, their surfer friend and rich witch who lived at Greenlane Manor.

He sighed and stared at the table for a second, and then looked up, his eyes meeting hers. "You know how we thought Gabe, Zee, and the other Nephilim had killed the two fey who broke through the protection circle?"

"Yes." Avery hesitated. "Well, not so much presumed. Gabe said they had."

"Well, he lied. One of them was killed, the other one survived."

Avery almost dropped her drink in shock. "What do you mean? A fey is alive, here in White Haven!" She looked around as if she would see it sitting in the bar, casually sharing a drink with the locals.

Alex laughed briefly before looking deadly serious. "No, she's not here. Gabe's keeping her prisoner up at that old, creaky farmhouse they live in on the edge of the moor."

"The fey is a *she*? And how do you know?" Avery's heart began to pound with worry and annoyance.

"Zee told me. He's not happy about it. He wants me to 'do something.'"

Avery frowned and took a big glug of wine in an effort to steady her thoughts. "But it's been almost six weeks since Samhain! He's been keeping her prisoner all that time? That's terrible!"

Alex shrugged. "Well, yes and no. Would you rather she was dead?"

"Well, if she was killed during battle as I expected, yes. She was attacking us! She was part of the Hunt!"

"Well, according to Zee, she's not attacking anyone anymore. She just wants to get out and try to salvage her life."

Avery's thoughts were reeling and she leaned back in her chair. "Does Gabe know that you know?"

"Not yet." Alex watched her, his dark eyes thoughtful. "But I'm going up to see him this evening, when Zee finishes his shift. Want to come?"

"Hell, yes! I've been dying to get up to their place. Gabe has been very secretive."

"That's why I'm going with Zee," Alex explained. "I want to be sure of a warm welcome."

"He still may not let us in. In fact, he may be furious with Zee."

"Zee's a big boy. I'm sure he can handle it," Alex said, and then promptly shut up as their food was delivered by a nervous Grace.

She smiled as she placed their plates in front of them and Avery introduced herself.

Grace nodded, saying, "Good to meet you, Avery. I've heard all about you! See you next time."

As she disappeared back to the bar, Avery said, "I presume she doesn't know we're witches."

Alex shook his head. "She doesn't know she works with a Nephilim, either. Not many do." He winked. "There are some things I like to keep secret."

Two

A very and Alex followed Zee up the winding country lane to the house he shared with the other Nephilim.

Zee rode on an old Enfield motorbike at unnerving speed, and Avery found herself gasping every time he rounded a corner. In the end, Alex gave up trying to keep up, and they cruised along behind him, knowing he'd wait for them before he went inside the house.

After navigating a series of winding lanes in the darkness of the crisp, cold December evening, they finally found the turn off to the old farmhouse. The road quickly became rutted, and Alex cursed as his low-slung Alfa bounced along. "Bloody stupid dirt lanes," he muttered under his breath as he slowed to a crawl.

The headlights picked out a wide, steel gate that was swung back against the wall of an outbuilding, and they entered a paved courtyard. The main, two-storey building lay ahead, but numerous small outbuildings surrounded the courtyard on all sides. It was easy to tell it had once been a working farm-house.

Zee was leaning against the wall of the house, and he pushed himself away as they exited the car. He was dressed in motorbike leathers, and he carried his helmet in his hand. A single light shone overhead, casting his features in shadow, and Avery shivered. She didn't know anything really about the Nephilim, other than they were the sons of Angels and women who had lived and died in biblical times, killed by the great flood, and unwittingly released by their magic the previous summer.

Seven of them had been released from their otherworldly plane, and they now lived in White Haven, co-existing peacefully with the town. Somewhere, magically hidden, each of them had a pair of huge wings that they could unfurl at will, and all of them were well over six feet in height, muscular in build, and had a keen intelligence. Apparently, they were reasonably impervious to magic, and had great healing powers. Avery had a feeling there was a lot more about them they didn't know. More importantly, Avery still wasn't entirely sure they could trust them. Although to be fair, they'd supported the witches when the Wild Hunt attacked at Samhain, and had given them no reason to doubt them s o far.

Gabe, short for Gabreel, seemed to be their leader, and was the only one that Alex had made a psychic connection with. Gabe was the spirit that had lurked within the Church of All Souls and had killed the verger, Harry, in order to regain physical form. Despite Gabe's leader status, Zee was clearly not happy with his current decision.

"Is he expecting us?" Alex asked as he glanced around the yard.

"No. I didn't want him to think of a good reason to stop us, or to just not be here."

Alex looked surprised. "Would that be likely?"

"Yep." Zee didn't elaborate, but he turned and led the way through the wide oak front door into a passageway lined with broad flagstones. Avery looked around and grimaced. The place was plain and unadorned. There were no pictures on the wall or rugs on the floor, and there was a chill to the air.

Avery exchanged a worried glance with Alex, and then followed them both to the back of the house and through a long, rustic kitchen to a rear passage that led to the back door and other rooms. The passageway was lined with boots and coats, and halfway along was another thick wooden door on an inside wall.

Zee shrugged his jacket off and placed his helmet on a small side table, and then opened the door. "She's down here."

"Is Gabe there?"

"Probably." Zee was trying to be impassive, but Avery detected tension around his shoulders and behind his eyes.

Alex stepped closer. "Zee, you're being very mysterious. Is this safe?"

Zee sighed and nodded. "I'm just worried about Gabe. She's safe enough."

He headed through the door, and as Avery followed him, she realised there were stairs leading down to a basement. A low light burned, and as they descended, Avery felt warmth creep towards her. The basement was heated, and was far warmer than the rest of the house.

Zee shouted, "Gabe! I've brought visitors."

Gabe's voice sounded muffled. "Who? Zee, I warned you!"

"Too late," Zee replied, completely nonplussed.

Zee led them into a low-roofed, brick-walled room with a slabbed floor. A large cage that was ceiling height took up most of the space, and in it paced a distinctly otherworldly creature.

Avery froze as her gaze met the startlingly violet eyes of a fey woman. She was slightly taller than Avery and lithe, and she paced her prison with a catlike grace. She was dressed in figure-hugging black trousers, a short jacket, and knee-length boots of soft leather. Her hair was long and shot with silver and gold, her skin was clear and almost luminous, and she emanated magic. And she was furious.

Their eyes met for only seconds, but it seemed to Avery that the moment lasted for far longer. Her gaze passed from Avery to Alex and then back to Gabe. "You invite people to stare now? Like I'm some kind of amusement?"

Her voice had a soft lilt to it, an accent that Avery couldn't quite place.

Gabe had short hair and a military demeanour. He was well over six feet and bristling with muscle, and had been sitting on a chair to the side of the room staring at his prisoner, but as soon as they entered he stood and swiftly turned, eyes narrowed. "Zee! What the hell are you doing bringing *them* here?"

Zee crossed his arms, unperturbed. "Doing what I should have done days ago. Someone needs to talk some sense into you."

Gabe looked between Zee, Alex, and Avery. "And you think these two will do it?" He frowned. "And I am perfectly in control of my senses, thank you."

Zee huffed. "You're keeping a fey prisoner in our cellar. How long do think you can do this?"

"As long as I need to!"

"I will live a long time," the fey said, sneering. "And sooner or later, I'll break out of this prison."

Gabe rounded on her, looking huge in the small room, his dark eyes narrowing. "Not from an iron prison you won't."

Of course. Folklore said the fey didn't like iron. Avery had wondered how Gabe could contain one.

Alex sighed. "Gabe, please. What's going on? You said you'd killed the two escaped fey."

Gabe grimaced. "I thought we had. And then, after you witches had left Old Haven Church, we went to collect the bodies, and one of them had gone. I decided not to tell you and find her first."

"And now you have. Well done," Alex said, looking between Gabe and the fey. "And what now? Do we open the doorway and send her back?"

The fey stepped forward, inches from the bar, looking excited. "Can you do that?"

Alex's shoulders dropped as he met her gaze. "No. I'm sorry. I was being sarcastic. That portal has long gone, and the magic that created it, well," he shrugged, "we can't create it again."

"Neither can I. And believe me, I've tried." She obviously detected his sympathy. "So, I'm stuck here, without my kind, in a world far from my own. A prisoner to this gigantic oaf." She glared at Gabe.

"I am not an oaf, woman," he growled.

Avery tried to suppress a giggle. Calling Gabe an oaf was pretty funny. "So, what *is* your plan, Gabe? Zee is right. You can't keep her locked up forever."

Gabe glared again. "I don't know what to do with her! Other than kill her."

"You couldn't before," the fey shot back. "Changed your mind?"

Avery's head was whirling with confusion. "Can you explain how you caught her, and where you found her?"

"We found her trail and tracked her for days. We eventually discovered her in Old Haven wood. She's very skilled at hiding."

"Of course I am. I am fey," she answered smugly.

Gabe continued. "While we tracked her, I had this cage made. I knew iron would contain her and her magic. Long story short, we caught her in the grove, trying to reactivate the portal in the old yew."

"And you didn't kill her. Why not?" Alex asked.

"Because I promised *you* that we wouldn't kill anyone, remember?" Gabe said, frowning. "It was part of our agreement for staying here. When I make a promise, I keep it. And besides, it is one thing to kill in the heat of battle; it is another thing entirely to kill in cold blood."

Alex smiled. "Thanks, Gabe. I appreciate that, difficult though our situation is now."

Zee was leaning against the wall. "Doesn't give us a solution, though, does it? What do we do with her now?"

Avery looked at the fey who was watching their exchange with interest. "Sorry, I hate to call you *her*. What's your name? I'm Avery, and this is Alex. We're both witches, and we're responsible for these guys being here."

"Not your finest moment then, Avery," the fey replied, deadpan.

Avery laughed. *This fey could be a handful.* "No, but they have their redeeming features."

"I have yet to see them." The fey relaxed slightly. "My name is Shadow Walker of the Dark Ways, Star of the Evening, Hunter of Secrets. You may call me Shadow."

Wow. "That's quite the name. Nice to meet you, Shadow."

Shadow narrowed her eyes. "I wish I could say the same. Maybe under other circumstances."

Avery nodded. "Agreed. You arrived here as part of the Wild Hunt. You were trying to kill us, and would have if not for our magic. And you would have killed many more if you had escaped. How can we justify releasing you?"

"I've been here for a while now, Avery. Well over a moon cycle. I haven't killed anyone since, have I?"

Avery held her gaze. "That's an excellent point. Why didn't you?"

Shadow shrugged. "There is no need. The Hunt's purpose is sport—like all hunts. It is a spectacle of courage and skill, and..." She paused for a moment. "Herne enjoys it. It releases his blood lust and reinforces his power over mortals. The witch who created the portal between worlds reminded him of his past glories, and he felt the loss of them greatly. To stride as a God amongst mortals is something in which he revels, and to retreat so soon that night would have cost him dearly. I was one of the chosen when we felt the pull of the portal. You do not refuse Herne." She stood straight and lifted her chin, her eyes flashing with a challenge. "And besides, it was a great honour. But now..." She shrugged. "Why kill? It has no purpose."

Avery looked briefly at Alex, considering Shadow's words. "I hate to break this to you though, Shadow, but you do not look entirely human. How will you survive in our world?"

Shadow smiled in a predatory manner. "I can live under a glamour. It will be easy for me once out of this cage, which restricts my magic." She turned to Gabe, who watched her speculatively. "This is a discussion we have had many times over the past few days, Nephilim. You know this. Why do you hesitate to release me?"

"Yes, good question," Zee added, meeting Gabe's grim stare.

Gabe flexed his huge shoulders. "Because it was I who failed to kill you in the first place. My failure sits heavily on me."

Shadow grinned suddenly, a flash of white teeth glinting in the dim light of the basement. "Will it help if I tell you that you wounded me? I limped away from that battle. And you have my horse."

Of course! Avery hadn't even thought to ask about them. She presumed they'd been killed, too. "Where are the horses being kept?"

"In the fields behind the house," Zee replied, admiration creeping into his tone. "They are amazing creatures—beautiful, intelligent, and fast. Faster than any horse I have ever ridden."

Alex rubbed his face thoughtfully. "Zee's right, Gabe. You can't keep her locked up forever. And, Shadow has a point. For almost six weeks she was free, and no deaths." He looked at her, puzzled. "It's freezing out. How have you survived?"

"I am fey. I can conjure magic to keep me warm, although it saps my strength. That's why *he* was able to catch me. And I can hunt to survive. My bow and arrow are over there, along with my other weapons." She pointed to the corner of the room, where an impressive array of weapons was stacked: a sword with an intricately carved pommel and hilt, a dagger, and a bow as tall as Avery, with a bundle of arrows next to it.

"And I presume your magic helps you speak our language?"

"Yes, it does. Although, our races have long intermingled, and our language is close to yours, anyway." She turned to stare once more at Gabe, whose bulk loomed over her slender frame. "Now, let me out!"

Gabe groaned. "I don't like this at all."

Zee strode forward and patted his arm. "You knew that once you imprisoned her, it couldn't last forever. You have to release her. And you," he turned to Shadow. "Behave yourself. You are superior to mortals, you know that. Don't take advantage."

She gave a shifty smile. "I'll try."

Gabe pulled a key from his pocket and reached for the sturdy padlock and chain that was wrapped around the bars and door to the cage. He unlocked them with a *snick* and pulled the door wide open. The fey quickly crossed through before he could change his mind, and took a deep breath in relief at being free.

Avery felt Shadow's magic swell around her, and stepped back a pace, watching her with curiosity. She might have been human in shape, but her violet eyes glowed from within, and her movements were swift and graceful. Her hair looked as if actual silver and gold were in it throughout. As if she was aware of Avery watching, she shimmered slightly and her magic swelled again, and within seconds the glow within her eyes disappeared, and her hair changed to natural caramel tones, soft and tumbling around her face. "Better?"

"Better," Avery agreed, nodding.

Shadow strode across the room and picked up her weapons. She attached her scabbard to her belt and sheathed her sword, strapped her dagger to her thigh, and heaved the bow over her shoulder, then turned to face them as they watched in silence. "Time to go."

Gabe looked uncomfortable. "Where will you go? It's freezing out."

"I'm inventive," she shot back.

"Stay here," he said.

"*What?*" Zee asked, stepping between them. "Are you insane? When I said release her, I didn't mean invite her to stay."

"I feel responsible for her," Gabe said, his tone short. "We have plenty of room."

Avery watched him, trying to hide her amusement. She was pretty sure Gabe had more than a passing interest in Shadow. And why not? She was seriously hot, and a warrior to boot. If Gabe had a type, Avery was willing to bet that she was it.

Shadow didn't wait for Zee's response. "Excellent. I accept."

Three

"Are you serious?" Reuben asked. He lounged on Alex's sofa, beer in one hand and a slice of pizza in the other, paused halfway to his mouth.

Avery knew that not much stopped Reuben from eating, so he must have been shocked.

"Yes," Alex answered, reaching for a slice of pizza, too.

Briar edged forward on her seat. "Really? A fey woman is here, in White Haven?"

"Yes. Staying with Gabe and the other Nephilim. It's like some twisted version of Snow White and the Seven Dwarves."

El sniggered, almost spitting out her beer. "I wish I had been there! Newton is going to be so pissed when he finds out!"

Avery laughed. It was Friday evening, the day after they had been to see Gabe with Zee, and they were sitting in Alex's flat, relaxing on his comfortable tan leather sofa and armchairs that were clustered around a blazing fire, eating pizza. The lamps were lit, candles placed in dark corners, and incense smoke drifted across the room. It had started to rain, and the steady drumming cocooned the m.

The five White Haven witches had gathered together for one of their regular catch-ups. Reuben, a tall blond surfer and Water witch, was partnered with El, a leggy blonde Fire witch with the ability to make magic-imbued jewellery. Briar, small, dark, and petite, was an Earth witch, known for her ability to heal and make great balms, lotions, and candles. She had an enigmatic relationship with Newton, their friend the Detective Inspector who had almost died at the hands of Suzanna Grayling, one of Avery's witch ancestors. It was Suzanna who had summoned the Wild Hunt on Samhain. For a while in the summer it had seemed like Briar and Newton might start dating, but then Newton declared he couldn't be in a relationship with a witch. However, after his brush with death, it seemed he might be reconsidering that idea. He'd have to be quick, however. Briar had many admirers, not least Hunter Chadwick, the Wolf-Shifter who'd since returned to Cumbria, but Avery knew he was still in touch with Briar.

Avery curled up in the corner of the couch, sipped her beer, and observed, "They could do with a woman's touch in that place. It's so stark and cold."

Alex just looked at her. "I'm not entirely sure that Shadow is the homemaking type. She was packing some serious weaponry."

"I think Gabe fancies her."

"Really?" Briar asked. "What makes you think that?"

"He had this way of watching her," Avery told her. "And why invite her to stay? That's nuts. She could murder them in their sleep."

"I doubt that," Reuben said. "The Nephilim have very heightened senses. And they're quick. I reckon they'll balance each other out."

Alex shrugged. "Well, it's not our concern. They're adults. They can sort it out."

"It will be our concern when things turn shit-shaped," Reuben pointed out as he reached for another slice of pizza.

They were interrupted by a knock at the door, and Newtown stuck his head in. "It's only me. Room for one more?"

"Talk of the devil," El said, grinning. "Come on in."

He looked suspicious as he came in carrying a couple of beers, and he joined them around the fire. He must have just finished work, because he was still wearing his suit. "Why are you talking about me?"

Alex grinned. "Well, let's just say that life keeps getting more interesting in White Haven."

Newton groaned. "Why? What's happened now?"

"A fey woman survived the Wild Hunt, and is now in residence at *Chez Nephilim*."

Newton looked like he'd been slapped. "What? Is this a joke?" He looked around at them all, dumbfounded. "It's not funny."

"Not a joke. Sorry, Newton," Avery said, patting him on the arm. "Gabe had been hunting for her for over a month, ever since Samhain, and he found her last week."

"She's one of the two who escaped? Gabe said they were dead!" Newton said, still incredulous.

"One is, but she isn't," Alex explained, stretching in front of the fire like a cat. "Her name is Shadow. But, from what we can tell, she isn't about to set out on a mad rampage across Cornwall, so she's just one more weird resident."

Newton took a long pull on his beer before he loosened his tie and took it off, opening the top button of his shirt. His grey eyes looked tired. "I can do without this right now."

"Why? What's happened?" Briar asked, looking worried.

He ran his hand through his hair and paused for a moment. "A student has been found dead on the grounds at Harecombe College."

"Oh no!" Briar said, her hand flying to her mouth.

"That's terrible," Avery agreed, feeling dread creeping through her. "What happened?"

"She was found on the campus this morning, almost frozen—her lips and skin were blue, and there were no obvious wounds."

Alex frowned. "So, how did she die? Hypothermia?"

"Nope," Newton said, and then he sighed as if reluctant to voice his next words. "As I said, there were no obvious injuries, but there were the faintest marks on her neck. Two puncture wounds."

"Puncture wounds!" Avery exclaimed.

He nodded. "The initial autopsy made it clear she lost a lot of blood."

"How much?" Reuben asked.

"We're not sure at the moment, but well over half of her body's capacity. I'll know more tomorrow."

They looked speculatively at each other, but it was El who said what they were all thinking. "I can't believe I'm about to suggest this, but it sounds like a vampire."

Newton glared at her. "Oh, don't you start. That word is being whispered everywhere at the police station."

"What do you think it is then?" Reuben asked, cocking an eyebrow. "Some weirdo who drains people of their blood for some macabre reason?"

"I'd rather it were that than a bloody vampire," Newton said, annoyed. "I've become accustomed to witches and Nephilim, and now I'm supposed to accept fey and vampires?"

"I think once you open up that particular can of worms, Newton, it just keeps on giving," Alex said with a sad smile. "You can't *un-know* this stuff."

Avery noticed Briar's eyes drop to the floor, and she realised this was another reason for Newton not to get involved with her. Not because it was Briar's fault, but because she was part of that otherworld—the paranormal world beneath the everyday. And unfortunately, whether he liked it or not, so was Newton. He just didn't want to admit it yet. He thought he was on the periphery, but he was wrong. Avery inwardly sighed. *Sometimes life was too hard.*

"Who's in charge of the case?" Avery asked him.

"Me, of course. It's already got the weird label, and we know that means me now."

Much to Newton's annoyance, he'd become the go-to investigator for what the police referred to as the strange occult happenings in Cornwall.

He sighed deeply. "I had to see her family today. It was horrible. Her mother couldn't stop crying, and her father sat there like he'd turned to stone." He looked at his beer. "I should have brought more of these, but I have to drive home."

"Have my bed," Alex offered. "That way you can have a few. I can go to Avery's."

Newton shook his head. "I have to get up early anyway and head back to the crime scene."

"Sorry, Newton," El said. "It's a crap way to welcome in Christmas."

He shrugged. "It's just the way it is. Tell me about this fey woman. Should I worry?"

"No," Alex said. "She seems reasonably well-behaved for a powerful immortal. She liked to remind us of that. And besides, if anyone has to do anything, we'll sort it out, together with the Nephilim. You have your hands full. What are you doing over Christmas? I think we've decided we're all heading to Reuben's for the day. You could join us."

Reuben nodded. "Sure, you should. Take your mind off work."

"I'll see. I might be working, if this carries on."

Briar frowned. "You already think there'll be another?"

Newton drained his bottle and cracked open the next. "There always is, Briar, you mark my words."

When Avery opened up her shop, Happenstance Books, the next morning, she tried to banish Newton's grim news from her mind as she looked forward to the day ahead.

They would surely be busy with Christmas shoppers, and they had plenty of stock to replace from yesterday. The increased traffic that White Haven was getting following the publicity from the Walk of the Spirits was translating to great sales.

After she'd been up to her flat above the shop to feed her cats and give them plenty of fuss, Avery entered the small back room and put the kettle and the coffee machine on ready for when Sally and Dan came in; surprisingly she'd arrived before Sally, who was usually in first. Sally was the shop manager and Dan was an employee, although both were good friends.

Avery then headed into the shop and inhaled with a dreamy expression on her face. The smell of cinnamon and nutmeg from the oil burner behind the counter lingered from the previous day. The strings of fairy lights that had been put up for Halloween remained, but the pumpkins, witches, and ghouls had gone, replaced with a large Christmas tree in the front window, and sprigs of green pine branches and mistletoe on the shelves and displays. Giant baubles hung in clusters from the ceiling, and the whole place sparkled with Sally's decorative touches.

She'd just arrived back in the kitchen to grab her second coffee of the day, when Sally struggled through the back door carrying two large Tupperware containers. Avery ran to hold the door open for her. "Hold on, let me help!"

"Cheers, Avery," Sally said, looking flushed. "I've been baking for today." She placed the containers on the table and shrugged off her coat. "I can't believe you beat me in!"

"Don't worry, it probably won't happen again." She peered at the boxes, trying to make out the shape of the cakes inside. "What have you made?"

Sally answered with a wicked glint in her eye. "Mince pies, baby ones, and clotted brandy cream."

"Wow! For us?"

"Us and our customers."

"Nice," Avery said, eying them appreciatively. "Have you heard about the death at the college yesterday?"

Sally nodded, her face grim. "Yes, Dan told me yesterday afternoon. Poor girl, and her poor parents. Is Newton looking into it?"

Avery nodded, but their conversation was disturbed by Dan's arrival. He appeared, wrapped in a large heavy coat and wearing a cap that he pulled from his head as he came in, revealing a thick shock of dark hair. "Ladies," he greeted, as he slammed the door behind him. "It's cold enough to freeze my bollocks off out there." He lifted his head. "Mmm, but fortunately I smell coffee, and are those your delicious mince pies, Sally?"

Sally shook her head at him. "When it comes to my baking, your olfactory senses are uncanny."

"I know. It's fortunate you're married, or I might have to woo you."

Sally laughed at that. "Idiot. We were talking about that poor girl who died at the college yesterday."

Dan's mood immediately changed. "Yeah, that's horrible. I caught up with one of my mates who teaches there. Understandably the whole place is talking about it, and it's put a bit of a damper on people's moods."

Avery nodded. "Any thoughts on how she died?" She assumed the news about the body being drained of blood wasn't public knowledge yet.

Dan watched her. "No. Why, what do you know?"

"It just sounds a bit unusual, that's all."

"Well, I presume you know more than we do, courtesy of Newton. I do know she was found sitting upright on a bench."

"What?" Avery almost stepped back in shock. "I didn't know that!"

"Yeah, very strange." Dan nodded thoughtfully as he headed to get a coffee. "I saw Dylan yesterday, too. He's pretty gutted. He knew her."

Dan was referring to his friend, Dylan, one of the three paranormal investigators that helped the witches.

Sally and Avery glanced at each other in shock, and Avery fumbled for her phone. "I'll call him. Poor Dylan. This just gets worse."

Dan stayed her hand. "Not now, Avery. I think he had a late night, a few drinks to help him sleep. Maybe call him later?"

She put her phone away and wondered if some magic would help him, but then she rejected the idea swiftly. Magic wasn't useful for anything like that. It would only mask grief, or slow the healing process. Best to let him grieve naturally. "Sure, I'll phone later. In the meantime, let's stock the shop and get ready for the day."

By mid-morning the shop was busy, and a steady stream of customers were coming in, bringing a blast of cold air with them every time the door opened. Outside the day was overcast and dark, making the Christmas lights in the shop even brighter.

Sally brought a batch of mince pies out and handed them around, cheering the customers and Avery and Dan alike. Avery was nibbling on her pie behind the counter and absently looking out the window when she saw Cassie head into the shop. It had been a few weeks since she'd seen her, and Avery left the counter to speak to her by the Christmas tree.

"Hey, Avery," Cassie said, reaching forward to hug her.

"Hey yourself," Avery replied, returning the welcome. She stepped back to appraise her. "You look different. I can't quite work out why." Cassie certainly looked the same physically; her pale brown, shoulder-length hair hadn't changed, and she wore her usual skinny jeans, flat leather boots, and a three-quarter length jacket. It was her manner that seemed different. "There's something a little meaner about you. I don't mean that in a bad way!" she stressed, apologetic.

Cassie laughed. "No, that's fine. I get that a lot. I think it's because I'm more self-confident than when you first met me a few months ago."

Avery nodded. "Yeah, that's it. You looked terrified of all those spooks and ghosts for a while, and now you look like you could seriously kick their ass."

Cassie leaned forward conspiratorially. She was of average height, a little shorter than Avery. "That's because I probably could—if they were corporeal! We've all been learning to fight."

Avery's mouth fell open in shock. "Fight! Like proper fighting?"

"Yeah. For months now, since the summer, and more in recent weeks. Facing spooks and other weird paranormal stuff needs strength of character, but you need to back that up with physical fitness, strength, and agility. Me, Dylan, and Ben have all been training together."

Avery glanced around the shop, and seeing that Dan and Sally seemed to have everything under control, she pulled Cassie to the back room, her de-facto meeting place. As soon as the door was shut, she asked, "Were you attacked or something? Is this why?"

Cassie reached for a mince pie from the supply in the second container. "Yes and no. Just the usual spirits rushing at us, falling objects, thrown objects, weird smoke, apparitions, and tricks. You have to be on your game, Avery. But you know that!"

"I guess so," Avery mused. "But I have magic to help me."

"Hence the training! We all started in the summer, a month or so after we met you guys and realised what was really out there." Cassie helped herself to another mince pie. "These are delicious! Anyway, it's been pretty intensive, but over the past few weeks, I've really started to feel the difference. I mean, clearly I'm no expert after so few months, but I have enough skills now to defend myself. With, of course, the aid of some of your magic."

"Wow! Go you. I'm so impressed," Avery said, admiring Cassie's lean form. "So, you're ready to face anything now?"

"I wouldn't say *anything*...but that brings me to what I'm here for. We've been thinking about items you could help us with."

"Go on," Avery said, intrigued. She vaguely remembered having a conversation a few weeks back about objects that could be imbued with magic.

Cassie looked excited. "We've been asked to investigate this old house in West Haven, the little village on the road between White Haven and Harecombe. The house has an occult history, and the couple who have recently bought it want us to investigate it, although I don't think anything is really happening there. We're setting up recording equipment and a few cameras in some key spots, but..." She paused, mulling over her next words. "After our initial inspection of the house, I've just got a bad feeling about it."

"The house, or the people who've hired you?"

She shrugged and frowned. "Both, really. Something's not right. We've accepted the job, and the money is good, but I was discussing it with the guys. We need magical support."

Avery was worried. None of them had ever expressed concern about an investigation before. "Do you want me or one of the other witches to come with you?"

Cassie shook her head. "No, we can do this on our own. It'll be a week or so of monitoring, and then we might stay overnight. It will be a longish job, time you won't have. Besides, we can't rely on you all the time."

"You've been pretty self-sufficient for a while," Avery pointed out. "All those spirit sightings you've been following up on."

"I guess so, but this feels different, and I can't explain it."

Avery thought for a moment. "So, going back to magical objects, you mean like a ring that could release a spell, or energy balls or fire balls?"

"Yeah," Cassie said, her expression bright. "Exactly. Alex has taught us some simple banishing spells. Briar has taught me some basic potions that I've put into these salt bomb kind of things, and El said she could definitely work some magic into jewellery or a knife. So, can you help with anything? Fire balls sound good!"

Avery grinned. "They do, if I can work out how to make them so that you can use them! Leave it with me. I'll see what I can do." And then she had a thought. "Teaching you some simple wards would also be useful—you know, to protect yourself with. I use a shadow spell a lot to hide with. I might be able to package that up in something. But that would be a onetime use. Once you release it, it's gone, until I make you a new one," she warned.

"That would be amazing," Cassie said, looking relieved.

"I'm glad you're here, anyway," Avery said, heading to the counter and putting the kettle on. "Have you heard about the death at the college?"

Cassie's face fell and she sat heavily in the chair. "Oh, that. I can't stop thinking about it. You know Dylan knew her—sort of?

"Dan mentioned it."

"She was the cousin of one of his mates, I know that much. They found her on a bench!"

Avery nodded. "Yeah, Dan told me that, too. That's just weird."

"There was a big party last night, a sort of end of term thing."

Avery pondered whether to tell Cassie about what Newton had said about the blood loss, and then decided she should. Cassie was a friend and could be trusted. "Newton said she'd lost a lot of blood, and there were two faint puncture wounds on her neck." She poured them both a cup of tea and joined Cassie at the table.

Cassie visibly paled. "Like a vampire?"

"Yep, but not exactly bite marks. It's particularly worrying because Harecombe is so close to White Haven, and I think a lot of kids from here attend there."

"Isn't that where Caspian lives?"

"Yeah, in the massive house he inherited from his crazy father." Avery realised she had no idea who Cassie lived with. "Where do you live? With Ben and Dylan?"

"Not bloody likely," Cassie said, incredulous. "Ben is so messy, it's unbelievable. No, I live with a couple of girls in Harbour Village, Penryn. Ben and Dylan live together, though, in Falmouth, not too far from me. We ended up setting up our business there, after we got booted out of that room at the Uni. They managed to get quite a big place. It needs a lot of work, but it's perfect for our n eeds. "

"I remember you saying that might happen," Avery said, sipping on her tea. She and Alex had visited their office at the Penryn campus during the summer. They had an impressive range of equipment that they used to monitor ghosts and poltergeists, as well as to test subjects who declared themselves as having psychic or telekinetic abilities. "Shame it didn't work out."

"Probably for the best. They wouldn't like all this extra attention we're getting at the moment from the Walk of the Spirits."

"I thought they'd like that!"

Cassie wrinkled her nose. "Sometimes there is such a thing as too much publicity!" She drained her cup, and then stood. "Anyway, I'd better go. I'll be seeing Dylan later. I'll ask him if he's heard anything else. Cheers for the tea and mince pies!"

Avery stood, too, and walked with her to the door. "Okay, and I'll conjure up some charms and magical aids for you. But ask if you need us. And if for some reason we can't help, we have witch friends who can."

As Avery watched Cassie leave, she reflected that she didn't want her, Ben, or Dylan getting hurt.

Four

After work had finished, Avery headed up to her flat, the smell of fresh pine from her Christmas tree soothing her senses. She breathed deeply, letting the cares of the day drain away from her. The shop had remained busy all day, which was great, but exhausting.

Night had already fallen, dark by 4.00pm at this time of year, so Avery closed all her blinds, blocking out the chill night, lit the fire with a spell, turned on a couple of lamps, and headed to the kitchen to feed the cats.

Medea and Circe wound around her legs, glad to see her, and she tickled their silky ears. Once she'd fed them, she poured a glass of wine, and then headed up to the attic, her favourite part of the house, and the place where she worked her spells. Avery had been pondering on Cassie's request all day, and she had finally decided how to capture the shadow spell. She lit the fire in the attic, too, spelling on lamps, candles, and incense, and then sat at her large wooden table and pulled her grimoires towards her.

The familiar feel and smell of the pages tickled her senses, and she sensed the spark of magic beneath her fingers, wrapping around her arms and drifting across the room. When she opened the books, it was as if a sigh escaped them, a palpable excitement at their pages being turned. A witch's relationship with her grimoire was a special one. It linked her to her ancestors, and bound their thoughts, feelings, and knowledge together. She never felt more like herself than when she was performing magic, and she knew the other witches felt the same. She smiled as she stroked the pages, softened by years of use, and protected by a spell that saved them from the ravages of time.

She flicked through the first few pages, remembering her encounter only a few weeks before with Suzanna Grayling, her witch ancestor and Helena's direct descendant, and unfortunately the witch responsible for summoning the Wild Hunt on Samhain. Suzanna had started this very grimoire and the new line of White Haven witches, picking up after Helena's death a couple of centuries before. *So much death, so much anger.* Avery sighed as she ran her hand across Suzanna's name written in her script at the front of the book. She still couldn't believe that Suzanna had managed to time-walk to the present day. The things she must have seen and experienced; Avery had never even had a chance to speak to her about them. Her spells were meticulous, annotations made in tiny writing in the margins, with corrections and recommendations. Nothing had been written in here to indicate her mindset or intentions. *What a waste.* Avery dearly hoped that whatever may happen to her in the future, she wouldn't be tempted into such rash and destructive actions.

She shivered, feeling as if a darkness has settled into her attic space, and she roused herself, turning to the shelves behind her to find a couple of black candles to ward off negativity, and a smudge stick to cleanse the room.

Once that was done, Avery returned to the grimoire and searched for a containment spell, pausing every now and again to examine illustrations, archaic writings, and the occasional journal-style entries. Realising she could search for hours, she said a finding spell, and watched as the pages started to move on their own, as if an unseen hand was searching the book. She smiled as the pages fell open at the right place. *There it is.* A spell that enabled the user to put an enchantment in a box, bottle, or other receptacle. First, she needed to find an object that was suitable.

Behind her on the shelf was a selection of bottles and jars of differing sizes. Some were made of glass, others were ceramic, and she also had a couple of small wooden boxes that might work. She decided to try a petite glass bottle with a screw cap. She placed it on the table, following the spell exactly. She needed to use wards to protect it, and she also needed wax to seal it when the spell was inside.

She worked intently, not even noticing the time until Alex called up from below. She shouted back, "I'm up here!"

He ran up the stairs and smiled, no doubt amused by her very messy workspace. The table was now strewn with objects. "What are up to?" he asked, watching her finish the spell.

Avery grinned. "I have successfully placed a shadow spell into this bottle for Cassie and the others. Something to help with their work. It's good for stealth, but now I need something with a little more punch!" She showed him the bottle. An inky blue smoke writhed inside, the lid sealed with black wax.

"Ah yes. Spells to help them with things that go bump in the night!" He picked up the jar and examined it. "Very cool. I taught them a couple of simple banishing spells, as well. What else were you thinking of?"

"Maybe an energy bomb, in something like a salt ball. Something that would smash easily when thrown to blast an attacker away." She frowned. "I'm struggling, actually. It's a different way to think of using my magic."

He kissed her as he put the bottle back on the table. "Maybe you should bottle some of that tornado wind you control so well."

Her mouth fell open. "That's a brilliant idea!" Her mind began working overtime as she started to plan how to do it.

"No, no, no. I don't mean now! I've brought Thai food, and it's downstairs waiting to be eaten. Come on. I'm starving." Alex grabbed her hand and pulled her down the stairs.

Her stomach grumbled as she followed him, and she realised she was starving, too. Alex had set out half a dozen cartons on the counter, and as she started to dish food onto her plate, she asked, "Did you see Zee today?"

Alex smirked as he loaded his own plate. "Yes, I did, and it's all fun and games at *Chez* Nephilim."

They headed to the sofa with their plates and drinks, Avery desperate to know what was going on. "Don't leave me hanging! What's happening there?"

"Fey magic can do some interesting things!" he said enigmatically.

"Like what?"

"Shadow is living in one of the outbuildings, and it's covered in climbing plants in the middle of winter." He grinned. "Sounds fascinating, but Zee didn't seem too impressed."

"Why not?"

"I have no idea. He just grunted."

Avery chewed thoughtfully. "I think we should go tomorrow. We're both off, and I'd love to see what's going on!"

He looked at her with raised eyebrows. "That might not be a good idea. They may think we're prying."

"I am!"

"You're shameless."

"I know, but so are you." Avery returned to eating, wondering how to persuade Alex they should go.

"Well, in that case, we better take the others, because Reuben dropped in today for a pint, and he wants to come, too, so I said we'd go together tomorrow morning."

Avery threw a cushion at him. "So you'd already arranged it!"

Alex laughed. "Actually, Shadow wants to see *us*."

"She does? Why?"

"I don't know, but I guess we'll soon find out."

Reuben collected Alex and Avery in his VW Variant Estate the following day. El and Briar were already with him, looking very excited. The drive to the farmhouse seemed to take far too long, and by the time they pulled into the courtyard, Briar and El had explored a dozen scenarios of what Shadow could want with them.

It was easy to tell which outbuilding Shadow had moved into. It was a long, low building set back to the left, and looked like an old stable block. The building was made of solid stone and brick, with rudimentary windows and multiple doors, but now it was smothered in a rustling wall of green leaves, and the roof was covered in moss. The greenery hadn't stopped there, either. Tendrils of growth had appeared on the farmhouse, small shrubs and greenery were thrusting their way through the flagstones, and a delicious honeysuckle smell filled the air.

Avery's mouth fell open in shock. "Wow. This place did not look like this two days ago. Nothing grew here—at all!"

Briar was wide-eyed in admiration. "Her magic must be very strong to produce so much growth in the middle of winter."

"Could you do this?" El asked.

Briar shook her head. "No way. I could make one plant bloom for a few hours, but I couldn't sustain it, and not on such a large scale. But the fey are of the Earth. It is their element."

"Very true," a voice said from their left.

They all turned swiftly, hands raised for either defence or attack. For a second, Avery couldn't see where the voice had come from, and then a tree to the side of the courtyard shimmied slightly, and Shadow stepped out from behind it, her grey and black clothes blending with the stones in the yard. She walked across the courtyard to join them, and once again Avery had the sense of how Otherworldly she was, even though she looked so human.

"Neat trick," Reuben said, watching the fey intently.

"I know," she answered. Shadow tipped her head to the side and fixed Reuben with a long, intense stare.

He glared back, refusing to give her any ground. "*What?*"

"Water. That's your element. I can sense it moving through you." She moved closer, lifting her head as if sniffing. "It is untapped, as yet. You've barely touched it."

Reuben frowned. "Yeah, well, I've avoided it for years. Go figure."

"You shouldn't be scared of it," she said, before turning to look at El, and leaving Reuben glowering at her. "And you manipulate fire—very well." She smiled at El, and if anything, it made her look even more Otherworldly. "Sister, I smell metals upon you, and jewels. You wield the old magic into weapons?"

El laughed. "And jewellery, and a few other things."

"You must show me how," she said, clearly fascinated by El.

Avery mused on how Shadow called her 'sister.' It was strange to hear, but physically they were similar, and she obviously loved her own weapons.

But Shadow was already moving on, turning to look at Briar. "And you are of the Earth. Small and grounded. It wells within you, gathering around your feet, and moving through your sinews and bones. You are stronger than you look."

Everyone was now staring at Shadow, intrigued by what she might say next, and Avery almost forgot how cold she was, standing in the courtyard with a bitter wind slicing across the moors and fields beyond.

"Alex." She turned to look up at him and closed her eyes slightly. "You have the Sight, spirit-walker. And you banish those who trespass into this realm." She shuddered. "You sometimes tread a dark path."

Alex looked startled, but Avery had barely time to react before Shadow turned to her. It was unnerving to have those violet eyes turned upon her, set within her sharp face with its pointed chin. Her little ears had a slight point to the tops, just visible behind her long waves of silky hair. Avery felt she was being mesmerised. She certainly hadn't experienced this when Shadow was in the basement only two days earlier. "Mistress of Air, and seeker of arcane knowledge. Interesting," she said, before swiftly turning, leaving Avery dazed.

"It is cold," Shadow announced to the group. "Follow me."

She marched to the door of the outbuilding, leaving the others to trundle in her wake, looking at each other, mystified and slightly confused. Alex mouthed at Avery, "*What was that?*"

She shrugged and gave him a half smile, hooking her hand into his arm, and squeezing it. The inside of the building was lined with rugs, blankets, and furs, and a few chairs and other rudimentary items of furniture had been brought in from the main house. A smokeless fire burned in a pit in the centre of the room, and Shadow gestured them to the seats placed around it. "This is my home. Welcome."

Briar sat down, warming her hands over the crackling flames. "Why are you out here instead of in the main house?"

"Here, the space is all mine, and the winged men do not trouble me."

"And why are we here?" Avery asked, and then worried she might have given offense, added, "Lovely though it is to see you!"

Shadow's eyes flashed with a challenge, but also curiosity. "You and your kind banished mine. It shouldn't have been possible. We were stronger, our magic more powerful. We were led by Herne himself, and the finest warriors of our land stood with him. I wanted to know how you did it."

"We combined our magic," Avery explained. "The High Priestess of our Coven harnessed our energies to hold you back."

"If it makes you feel better," Reuben said dryly, "it wasn't easy."

"It does not make me feel better. I am here, alone, cut off from my world and my people."

Reuben was belligerent. "Well, if you hadn't punched through our wall—injuring a witch, by the way—you wouldn't be stuck here, would you?"

A surge of magic filled the air around them, and Avery looked about in alarm, noting Shadow's hands were clenched.

"Reuben," Alex said, a warning tone in his voice.

Reuben glanced at him and nodded, dropping his shoulders and taking a deep breath to calm himself down.

"You killed one of my brothers," Shadow said accusingly.

"Not *us*," Alex answered quickly. "One of the Nephilim did, and only to prevent him from killing others. You *did* come here on the Wild Hunt, Shadow. We protected our own."

Shadow fell silent for a moment, and the tension rose.

Avery's pulse sounded loud in her ears, and she gathered her magic, ready to strike in self-defence if she needed to. *What is going on here?*

Briar spoke next, leaning towards Shadow. "I'm sorry, Shadow. No one anticipated that one of you might be stranded here. That wasn't our intention. If it was the other way around, and I was stranded in your world, I'd be terrified and very lonely. And I would want a friend, someone to trust. If that's what you want, we can help."

"I'm not terrified, I am fey," she said with an air of superiority that was infuriating. "But, yes, I am alone. I want you to open that doorway again so I can go home."

Briar lowered her eyes briefly with regret. "It's impossible. The witch who opened that doorway had planned it for years. She waited for the opportune time, used reserves of our magic, and cast a potent spell to achieve it. We cannot recreate it, and neither can she—we banished her to your world."

"We told you this the other night," Avery said softly. "It wasn't a lie."

Shadow leapt to her feet, her eyes wild. "There must be a way! I cannot stay here with these half-Sylphs!"

"Half what?" El asked, confused.

"Sylphs. They are fey who fly—creatures of the skies. That is what they are!" She gestured behind her to where the farmhouse stood.

"But they're Nephilim," Avery said. "The sons of Angels and humans, born thousands of years ago."

"I don't know these words, and I don't know what Angels are. But I smell fey magic upon them. They are part fey!"

Avery's mind was whirring with questions. "Okay, half-Sylph, fine, whatever. Isn't that good? They are half fey—part of your kind!"

"Not *my* kind. I am an Earth fey." She softened slightly. "But yes, at least part fey. But they have never known their real land. They are trapped here in this shadow-land, like me." She sat down again. "You have magic, all of you. They have not. You must help me get home."

The witches looked at each other, clearly perplexed, and El answered. "We don't know how, sister. The gateways that opened between our worlds have closed long ago."

Shadow's expression was mutinous. "But there must be something! In our world, in the Summerlands, there are special places that can be opened with words of power. And there are artefacts that possess that power, too, held within their metals or pages. That was what I did—well, one thing among many." She looked shifty, as if whatever it was had been dodgy. *Were there any laws in the Summerlands? Were her activities illegal?* Avery wondered as her mind went off on a tangent. Shadow continued, "I was a treasure seeker, a hunter of such things. Hired by others sometimes, at other times I searched for me. There *must* be some of those things here!"

Reuben looked exasperated. "Maybe there are. Through the centuries there have been rumours of arcane objects—mysterious books with unknown powers, and objects that wield incredible magic, but they are probably lost in time, buried beneath the earth. They are myth and legend only!"

"Neither myth nor legend!" Shadow insisted. "They are real, and they are here somewhere. I will find them, and you will help me."

Five

The witches sat around a table in a pub on a country lane on the way to White Haven, eating lunch and discussing their conversation with Shadow.

"She's nuts," Reuben said, sipping his pint. "I'm not going to hare off across the country looking for sodding artefacts for her to return to the Summerland!"

"I sympathise with her," Briar said, "but you're right. We have businesses to run! What she's asking is impossible."

Avery sighed as she gazed into her pint. "I don't mind doing some research for her. It might actually be pretty interesting! But, it could take ages. There are thousands of references to strange mythical objects and arcane books that hold secrets. Some of it will be utter rubbish! The difficulty will be finding the nuggets of truth amongst the crap."

"You're talking about a lifetime's search, Avery," El said, thoughtfully. "But we don't know how long her lifetime is. She's not human, her magic is different, and the fey are supposed to be close to immortal—if the myths are true. She could well have much longer to search than us."

"I think it's a good thing she's with Gabe," Alex said. "For all we know, they'll have a much longer lifespan, too. And what did she say about Sylphs?"

"They're mythological Air spirits," Avery said, frowning. "I've heard of them. I've never thought of them as fey, though."

Reuben laughed. "Well, I've never believed in God or angels. They are all part of the Christian religion, which, let's face it, none of us believe in. It's a religious construct that's all about control. And Christians hijacked all sorts of pagan beliefs and festivals. Why not Sylphs? If the borders between worlds really were so indistinct years ago, they could well have been in our world. And how weird would they have been!"

Alex shrugged. "God, angels, or Sylphs, what does it matter? They're just words at the end of the day. Whatever they are, the Nephilim are half-human, half-something. And if Shadow senses fey?" He shrugged. "I trust her to know. And what does she gain by lying? It means nothing to her."

"It doesn't help us with how to help her though, does it?" Briar said, frustrated. "Imagine that one of us had been sucked into the Otherworld? I'm horrified just thinking about it!"

"All myths suggest that we would be used as slaves. At least she doesn't have to suffer that," El pointed out. "I was wondering if I should invite her down to my shop. She seemed pretty interested in what I do."

"Yeah, she did, sister!" Reuben said, grinning. "She's going to be bored senseless. It might keep her occupied and out of trouble."

Alex drained his pint. "If Gabe's got any sense, he'll use her in his security business. That will keep her busy, too." His phone rang, and he picked it up. "Newton, how's it going?" He frowned. "Another? Where?" He nodded. "No problem. We'll meet you there." He looked at the others as he rang off. "There's been another death at Harecombe College. He wants us there now."

By the time the group arrived at the college it was nearly three in the afternoon. The sky was heavy with clouds and the day was already darkening. Avery could smell snow, and she predicted that by this evening, the moors would be covered in it.

Newton met them in the car park looking harassed. He wore a heavy wool coat over his suit and had a thick scarf, but he still looked cold. And no wonder, the wind was bitter. "We haven't got long. The coroner has, fortunately for us, been tied up with another death, and we only have one on over the weekend. So, before SOCO get stuck in, I want your opinion."

"You want us to look at a dead body?" Briar asked, her face pale.

Newton nodded. "If you don't want to, stay in the car. I know it's grisly. But I wouldn't ask if I didn't need your help."

"I'll go, if no one else wants to," Alex offered.

"No. If something weird is happening, I want to know about it," Avery said, and El and Reuben agreed.

"It's fine, I'll come," Briar said, not looking at all certain. "Just wanted to prepare myself."

"Thanks," Newton said, looking at all of them. "I really appreciate this. As soon as we get close to the scene, I've got shoe covers for you to wear. And don't touch anything!"

They followed him across the college grounds, to a building on the edge of the sport fields. He headed around the back to where a couple of big bins were half open, full of rubbish. Officer Moore, Newton's partner, was standing guard, and a uniformed policeman stood at the other end of the building. Moore nodded at them, and then walked away, leaving them to it. As usual, he said nothing.

"She's here," Newton said, lowering his voice with sadness. He handed them the plastic shoe covers, waited until they had all put them on, and then led them to the huge square bins. He pointed between them, and on the ground, sitting upright, was a young woman. Her eyes were wide open, staring into space. Her skin was pale, almost blue, and her lips were parted as if she was about to speak.

"Oh, no!" Briar said, shivering. "This is horrible."

Newton looked grim. "Yes, it is. Welcome to my world."

"What are we looking for?" Alex asked, his eyes never leaving the young woman's body.

"She's very pale, as you can see. Almost blue. It could be because it's bloody freezing, but I think it's because she's had significant blood loss. She has tiny puncture wounds on her neck, just like the other one. Can you see if there's any sign of magic? Or can you detect a vampire? Just don't move her!"

Alex looked at him. "Having never met a vampire, I have no idea what signatures they leave. And it's tricky, without touching her, Newton."

He sighed. "I know. But I just want your opinion."

Briar looked as pale as the dead girl, and El said, "Help me search the area, Briar."

She nodded, looking grateful. "Sure."

They walked away, talking softly together, and Alex crouched next to the body, Avery and Reuben crouching on the other side.

Avery looked up at Newton. "Did you say the other one was posed? Sitting up, too?"

"Yeah, but on a bench, where everyone could see her."

Avery held her hands above the girl's body, trying to sense magic, while Alex and Reuben examined her clothing and skin as carefully as they could without touching her. Avery closed her eyes to help her focus. She sensed *something*. It was hard to place, though. It was like she felt *darkness*. But it was very faint. She sighed, exasperated. "I can't feel anything. Not really."

"'Not really' sounds like something," Newton said, an edge of hope entering his voice.

"I don't know how to explain it, other than I sense darkness—almost like a void, I suppose."

"But you can see the wounds on her neck," Alex said. He pointed to the pale round marks over her carotid, almost two inches apart, the skin already looking scarred rather than raw and new.

Reuben grunted. "There's not many things that would leave marks on the neck like that."

"So, you *do* think it's a vampire," Newton said, pulling his scarf around his neck as if to protect it.

Avery had to agree. "It's possible."

"Let me see what I can feel," Alex said, frowning.

They watched for a few seconds, and then Alex jerked back, sitting heavily on the floor. "Wow. That was intense!"

"What?" Newton crouched, too, looking worried.

Alex shook his head. "I had a vision, almost a snapshot of her final moments, and it was just as you said, Avery. I felt I had dropped into a void." He rubbed his face. "Shit. I wish I hadn't done that. That was horrible. I felt her despair and confusion."

Avery reached out and squeezed his arm. "Sorry you had to feel that."

"I'm sorry *she* had to feel that," he answered.

Reuben watched silently, and then, almost regretfully, he closed his eyes and held his hands above her, too. He nodded. "Yeah, I obviously haven't had that psychic connection, but I feel the blackness, too. But that may just be death, as she loses consciousness." He opened his eyes again. "And yes, there's a lot of blood loss. I don't sense violence, though."

"How can her death not be violent?" Newton exclaimed. "That doesn't make sense!"

"It feels gentle, a sort of slipping away," Reuben said, trying to find the right words for it.

Avery nodded. "Yes, that's just like what it feels like. How do you know about the blood loss?"

"I've been harnessing my water elemental powers, practising with El. I can feel water and fluids in the body—it's something I noticed when we lifted El's curse. And consequently, I know she has less blood than she should have."

Newton stood and walked away, and the others followed him, joined by El and Briar who had completed their search. "Have you two found anything?"

"Nothing at all," El reported. "Nothing magical, anyway."

Newton ran his hands through his hair, looking weary and worried. "So, we know this must be something supernatural, and most likely is a vampire. What do you know about them?"

Avery looked baffled. "Not much."

"Well, I suggest you do some research, because if this is a vampire, I'm going to need your help in finding it, and then killing it. And if it's not a vampire, I want to know what it is."

Reuben looked sceptical. "Have you mentioned this theory to your colleagues? Officer Moore, for example?"

"No." Newton glanced over to where Moore stood chatting to the PC. "But, he knows I consult you about the occult, and whispered rumours are already circulating around the station." He looked uncomfortable. "They don't know what I do, and I want to keep it that way, so the quicker we stop this, the better."

Avery and Alex spent the rest of Sunday together at Avery's flat, talking about the two deaths and vampires.

"This is not how I envisaged spending my day," Alex said, as he looked through the books on Avery's shelf in the attic.

"Nor me," Avery said, frowning as she had a thought. "While you search those shelves, I'll run down to the shop and check my stock on the occult."

"And maybe find some books for Shadow's problem, too?"

Avery nodded. "Of course. I'd almost forgot about that."

Alex looked at her, confused. "Why are you running down? Why not use your witch-flight?"

"Of course!" Without another word and before she had a moment to doubt herself, Avery wrapped elemental Air around herself like a cloak and envisaged her shop, and within a second she was there, swaying unsteadily. But she didn't fall over, and she wasn't unconscious. *Yes!*

The shop was dark and gloomy, illuminated only by the glow from the lights on the Christmas tree in the front window. Rather than put a light on, Avery spelled a witch-light over her shoulder, safe in the knowledge that at the back of the shop and behind a large bookcase, no one outside would see.

She had a large stock of occult books, some new, but many were old, collected from house sales over the years. She started to pull books, aiming to keep her search wide. There were a few titles that she didn't remember seeing before, but Sally had been to a house sale only a few weeks before, so maybe they were from there. As she pulled a few out, a mark showed up on the cover of an old leather volume—a mark only visible because of the witch-light. She held her breath for a moment in shock. *Where had this come from?*

The book looked ordinary enough, if old. It was about the size of A4 paper, and an inch or so thick, with a worn leather cover and faded lettering that said, *Mysteries of the Occult.* Avery flicked through the first few pages and then scanned through the contents that included psychic phenomena, tarot readings, and runes and their uses. *It isn't a grimoire, but this is a witch-mark,* she mused. *Maybe there are more witch-marks inside? Maybe it was previously owned by a witch?*

After scanning through a few more books, she gathered up the pile and flew back to the attic, arriving in front of the fire. Alex let out a cry of surprise when she manifested. "Bloody Hell! I don't think I'll get used to you doing that."

"Should I ring a bell next time?" she said cheekily.

"Yes, please. I almost spilt my beer!" He handed her a glass of wine as she put the books on the floor next to the sofa. "Something to lighten our mood."

"Cheers, I think I need it." She sank down next to him, sipping with pleasure. "I found an interesting book with a witch-mark on it."

His eyes widened with surprise. "A grimoire?"

"No." She pulled it from the pile and handed it to him. "This. It looks like an ordinary, if old, non-fiction book on the occult. The mark is on the front, but there may be more inside. I didn't inspect it that closely."

With a whispered spell, Alex extinguished the lamps, leaving them only in fire and candlelight, and then with a flick of his wrist, he magicked a witch-light above them both. "*Mysteries of the Occult,*" he said, reading the title. "Not exactly exciting. But that is an interesting mark." He lifted the book closer and squinted at it.

"I don't recognise it. Do you think it means anything?"

He shook his head. "It may be just a way to mark a book of interest." He turned it this way and that, feeling the cover carefully before he opened it and turned the pages gently. "I don't feel magic on it, either." He handed it back to her. "It's your discovery. Maybe you should ask if Sally remembers where she got it from. Anyway, I'll leave it to you while I sort through these I found on your shelf. Just be careful, in case something leaps from between the pages."

"Idiot," she said, laughing.

For the next half an hour they were both silent as they searched through the books. Avery was frustrated. "There isn't one other single mark in this book."

"Maybe it needs another spell to reveal them?"

"Maybe. Have you found anything?"

"Just the usual history and lore on vampires—garlic and holy water to repel them, and a stake through the heart, burning, or beheading to kill them. I've had a horrible thought, though." He turned around to look at her. "What if these bodies *have* been bitten by vampires and start to turn?"

"You mean they become vampires, too?" She rolled her eyes. "Have you been watching old Hammer House films?"

"It's in the lore, Avery! They might." Alex looked very serious.

Avery shuddered, and the sudden flurry of hail against the window made her jump. "Now I'm spooked!"

Alex grinned and reached out to stroke her foot that was on his lap. "I'm going to go to the kitchen and cook us up a feast, something garlicky, because I'm starving, and a bulb a day keeps vampires away. You can keep reading. Will you be okay on your own?"

She threw a cushion at him. "Yes, I'll be fine!"

"Maybe you should ask Dan tomorrow if there's such a thing as Cornish vampires," he said, as he rose from the couch and headed to the stairs. "Or, of course, ask Genevieve and the coven."

Six

Dan frowned at Avery on Monday morning. "Do you go out of your way to find trouble?"

"No! Trouble just seems to find me, thanks," Avery answered, affronted.

It was just after nine, and the shop was still quiet. Outside it was bitter cold, and it was still dark, the light dulled by thick clouds. Hail lay on the ground from the night before, and the pavements were slippery. Avery had just updated Sally and Dan on the events over the weekend, and Sally looked horrified. "That poor girl. I saw it on the news. I didn't think you'd be involved!"

"Newton wanted our opinion," she explained. "And although it was horrible, we had to help."

Dan sat on the stool behind the counter, his chin on his hand as he gazed into space. "I can't think of any particular tales about Cornish vampires, but they don't have to be Cornish, do they? Say these deaths *are* caused by vampires. They could have recently arrived. Or arisen."

"Arisen?" Avery asked, startled. "You mean like it's just woken up?"

"I don't know! You're the witch. Where's it been all this time, if killings have just started?"

"That's an excellent point," Avery admitted. "Are there any other creatures that cause death by exsanguination?"

"None that spring to mind."

Sally looked at them with her mouth open. "Are you both seriously having a discussion about the real possibility of vampires?"

"Yes, we are," Avery answered. "There's a whole, big paranormal world out there. Surely you can't doubt it?"

She sighed. "No, not really. I just don't want to have to acknowledge it. It's Christmas, and I'm feeling jolly. Or was."

"Me, too," Dan said. "If I'm honest, Avery, this is not the conversation I expected to be having on a Monday morning. And no, I don't know anything about magical objects that may open doorways to the Otherworld, either. However," he said, holding his finger up. "There are many strange objects mentioned in British folklore, and in fact, world folklore. Objects that belonged to mythical beings that possessed great powers. But these are objects of myth, and if they once existed, they are long since lost."

"Objects like what?" Sally asked, clearly relieved not to be talking about vampires.

"Well, for example, there are the thirteen magical objects of Britain, commonly called the Thirteen Treasures, often mentioned in the Arthurian tales and other legends."

"What type of treasures?" Avery asked.

Dan thought for a few seconds. "There's a sword that would burst into flames all along the blade, if it was drawn by a worthy man. There's a halter that was owned by a man who could wish for any of his horses and it would appear in the halter, and there's a pot that would contain any food you could wish for. Merlin collected them all together, and placed them in his tower of glass, ready for the return of King Arthur."

Sally looked unimpressed. "Well, that's not a very exciting group of magical objects."

"They would be if you were starving and needed a horse," Dan said. "There's more, of course, but I'll have to look them up."

"What about rings of power?" Avery asked.

"I think you're confusing that with *Lord of the Rings*."

Avery glared at him. "No, I'm not. Cheeky sod. I know the difference between myth and fiction, thank you."

"I'm glad *you* do, because it's all starting to blur for me," Dan said, rubbing his head. "Have you asked Caspian, or the lovely Genevieve? Or maybe Jasper? Didn't you say he was interested in that kind of thing, too?"

"I'd forgotten about Jasper," Avery said thoughtfully. Jasper was a member of the Cornwall Coven, and one of the witches who lived in Penzance. "I'll ring him later. In the meantime, can you investigate for me?"

"Absolutely. I'm sure I can squash it in between pub and football."

They were interrupted by the arrival of their first customer, and they went their separate ways, Avery mulling on ancient objects and vampires. She returned to the stacks, wondering if she might have missed any books that might be useful. She browsed through the arcane and occult shelves, lost in thought, and nearly jumped when Ben's voice disturbed her.

"By fire and earth! Bloody Hell, Ben, you almost gave me a heart attack."

He looked apologetic. "Sorry, Avery, didn't mean to scare you." His cheeks were red from the cold, and he pulled his woolly hat off and rubbed his dark hair to stop it sticking to his head.

"It's fine, I'll live. Have you come for those spells Cassie asked for? I've only done one so far."

"No, although I'll take it if it's ready. I thought I'd show you this." He pulled an old bottle out of his pocket and shook it gently. The bottle was old, the glass a murky blue, and stoppered with an old cork sealed with wax, much like what she'd prepared for Cassie. But instead of being filled with smoke, it contained a collection of needles and nails, and some dried, dark fluid.

"It's a witch-bottle!" she exclaimed, taking it from Ben's hand. She moved from behind the shelves and headed to the window to examine it under the light, Ben following her. "Where did you find this?"

"It was found in the house we've been asked to investigate. The one the couple are renovating. They lifted some damaged floorboards, and found this. It was used to repel curses, wasn't it?"

Avery nodded, still examining the bottle. She turned it under the light, hearing the *chink* as the nails and pins turned in the bottle. She saw tiny bits of skin and fingernails shifting among the metal. A faint wisp of magic clung to it still, like the remnant of perfume on clothes. She smiled with pleasure. "Wow, this is interesting. Fancy finding one in that house!"

"How old do you think it is?" Ben asked, watching Avery turn the bottle, as fascinated by it as she was.

"A hundred years old probably, maybe older, but the witch museum could date it better than me." She looked at Ben. "How old is the house?"

"Late eighteenth-century I think. It's surrounded by an old garden, probably not half as big as it once would have been. I think the land has been sold off over time. Anyway, Rupert and Charlotte are restoring it."

"And is anything going bump in the night?" Avery asked thoughtfully.

"No. It's weird. We've never been asked to investigate a house *before* it shows signs of being haunted. Do you think this suggests it might have been in the past?"

Avery shrugged, puzzled. "This bottle protected the then owner from a curse or a hex or other negative energies. It gives protection. So, it suggests that at one point something unpleasant may have been directed at the owner in the past, but this does not tell us what."

"And the stuff that's in there is common?"

"Common enough. The nails and skin are probably from the person in the house, and the dried liquid is likely menstrual blood. It would have conferred a lot of power."

Ben grimaced. "Yuck. And how does it work?"

"By placing something of the owner in the bottle, like skin and blood, they would attract the curse away from the person themselves—sort of a misdirection—and the pins would burst the evil, or impale it. They often placed it outside, actually, or under a hearth—the heart of the house. Sometimes sprigs of rosemary were used, or urine, or wine. It depends on the witch casting the spell, the person who needed protection, and the nature of the threat. Sometimes a person would make their own to protect them *from* a witch."

"Do you use them now?"

She smiled. "This is fairly rudimentary—a simple spell. I'm using something very similar for Cassie and you, actually. A bottle that contains a spell for your protection, but much more sophisticated."

Ben fell silent for a moment. "Finding this makes me wonder if they know more about the house and the previous owners than they've told us."

"What have they told you?

"That it was owned by a medium, and her reputation suggests she was genuine. Rupert seems to think that spirits may have left their mark on the house in some way." Ben frowned, and Avery sensed he had the same misgivings as Cassie.

"You look as worried as Cassie did."

He shrugged. "I know. I can't explain why, either. Dylan's the same."

Avery was intrigued. "I'd like to check it out—just to see if I can sense something. Is that possible?"

"Certainly. I'm sure I could explain you away as a consultant."

"Great. When are you next going?"

"Tomorrow afternoon, to pick up some of the recordings. Cassie probably told you we're surveillance-gathering for now."

Avery nodded. "Great. I'll see if one of the others can come with me. I'd like a second opinion. But come and grab this spell before you go."

Avery let Sally know she was leaving the shop for a few minutes, and then led Ben to the attic in her flat. Ben looked around with a big grin on his face. "Oh, wow! Look at this place."

Avery looked at him, perplexed for a second. "Oh right, I'd forgotten you hadn't been up here before." She laughed. "It's my inner sanctum that only the privileged few get to see."

"Lucky me, then," Ben exclaimed. "It's quite the spell room, isn't it?" His gaze travelled around the room, and for a moment, Avery saw her sacred space with fresh eyes. The grimoires on the wooden table were open where she had left them earlier, revealing their archaic writing and illustrations, and were enough to give the uninitiated a thrill of the strange. Above the table hung bunches of herbs, and their gentle aroma filled the room with the promise of earthy magic. Lining the walls were several deep shelves filled with bottles of more dried herbs, roots, leaves, powders, tinctures, dark and clear liquids, gemstones, and other important ingredients for spell casting. Next to them were her books, baskets of candles, pots of living herbs, scales and bowls, a pestle and mortar, and other arcane objects. Her Athame lay on the table, next to a small, silver cutting knife and silver bowls containing salt and water. She always had something seasonal in there, too, and at the moment there were bundles of pine, ivy and holly. Yes, this was most definitely a spell room, and every time Avery came here it renewed her soul and filled her with joy.

"This is so you," Ben said, wide-eyed. "I forget when we chat downstairs and in pubs about this side of you, strange though that sounds. I mean, I know you're a witch."

Avery was amused, but she was kind, feeling his discomfort and wonder. "It's not a *side* to me, Ben. It's just me—all of me."

"I know that, really I do." He grinned again, childlike. "Go on, do your thing."

Avery laughed. "You mean this?" The candles on the table flared into life as did the fire in the fireplace, and she sent a breath of wind around the room, ruffling the pages of the grimoires and setting the herbs swinging from the beams.

"Awesome," he murmured as he wandered over to the table, his hands running along it. He paused to look at the books. "Can I touch them?"

"Of course. They're protected from wear and tear by a spell, but even so, be gentle."

He turned the pages as Avery reached for the bottle containing the spell she had made for them. "Here you go. It's for defence, not attack."

Ben turned and took it from her, watching the smoke curl lazily in the bottle. "Awesome. What does it do?"

"It's my shadow spell. When you need to hide, pull the cork and release the spell. It will last for about half an hour without me there to renew it. The wax seal is thin, so it will open easily, and the bottle is sturdy, so shouldn't break." Ben nodded and pocketed it. "I should add that it's more effective at night and in poorly-lit buildings. It will not work in broad daylight."

"Thanks. We're assembling a spell kit, so this is great."

"So I gather," Avery said thoughtfully. "I've going to bottle a mini-tornado for you, too, and a pulse of energy—enough to create a diversion. I'll make a few bottles of each, now that I know I can."

He smiled, "You're the best. Anyway, I better go. I'll text you the address."

She nodded and followed him down the stairs and out through the shop, and felt a chill settle over her that had nothing to do with the weather.

※

After work, Avery headed to The Wayward Son to spend some time with Alex, who was working behind the bar. Within minutes of her arrival, Reuben and El turned up, too, easing themselves onto barstools next to Avery. The pub was an unofficial meeting place, and most nights after work one of the witches or Newton stopped by for a drink to unwind after the day.

"Oh good, I'm glad you two have arrived," Avery said. "Are either of you interested in coming with me to the house our friendly ghost-hunters are investigating? It's tomorrow afternoon, and Alex can't come."

Alex grimaced as he placed a pint in front of El and Reuben. "Unfortunately, my new staff are sick, and we're too busy to leave the rest of the bar short-handed."

"I'm busy, too," El said, reaching for her drink. "Sorry, Ave."

"I can come," Reuben said brightly. "The business ticks along well enough without me. And I need to get out and see something new. What time?"

"About two," Avery said.

"Perfect. I'll drive—your van's a bone shaker."

Avery was mildly affronted, but had to agree. "Fair enough." She looked across to the far side of the bar where Zee was serving a customer. "Any news on our new friend?"

Alex grinned. "I think she's stirred up a hornet's nest. Apparently, she's very determined. Over the last few days, as she's observed their activities, she's realised that for now, she is very much stuck here. Gabe is busy building up his business and making money, and she knows that for now, she has to play it our w ay."

Avery frowned. "What do you mean, *our way?*"

"Jobs, money. Zee said Niel accused her of being a freeloader, and if he had to pay bills, so did she."

Avery remembered Niel from Old Haven Church. His full name was Othniel, and he was blond and bearded, with very impressive side-burns.

Reuben almost choked on his pint. "Freeloader! That's hilarious. So, she's working with Gabe?"

"For now." Alex caught Zee's eye as he finished serving and called him over. "Tell the guys what Shadow's plan is."

Zee groaned. "She's trying to recruit one of us to help her with her arte-fact-finding business. She's promised big money. It's what you call bullshit." His face creased with annoyance. "She's causing arguments."

"So some of you must be interested," El speculated.

"A couple. Barak and Ash."

"Ash!" Reuben said, his face falling. "But he works for me! And he's bloody good, too."

"Don't worry," Zee said. "Gabe is having none of it. I don't think he can bear anyone else to work with her, which is worrying in itself. And Caspian's just offered him a contract."

The witches looked at each other in shock, even Alex. "You didn't mention that! Doing what?"

Zee shrugged. "Apparently, the contract with the security team who look after his warehouses has just run out, and he decided he'd rather replace them with us. It makes sense. We know what he is."

Avery sipped her wine thoughtfully. "Wow. Yes, it does make sense, but I'm still surprised. That must be a big job."

Zee nodded. "I might have to do a few less shifts, Alex, if this works out."

Alex shrugged. "I hate to lose you, but you're wasted here. Just give me some notice."

"I'll be here over Christmas, so I'll let you know in January."

"Awesome, that will be great," Alex said, relieved.

Reuben turned, suddenly distracted, and his face fell. He nodded towards the TV screen, muted on the wall. The news had started and headlines scrolled across the bottom of the screen, stating, *Girl found dead in Harecombe.*

Their collective mood fell. "Not another," El said. "They have to be linked."

Avery voiced something she'd been wondering for the last couple of hours, ever since she'd seen Ben. "I'm hoping it's not linked to that house."

"The medium's house?"

"Yep. It's between here and Harecombe. Ben and the others all think it's weird, and they have good instincts, and well, we all know there's no such thing as coincidence."

Alex held her gaze for a moment. "Be careful when you go there tomorrow. Reuben—make sure she stays safe."

"I'm not a child!" Avery protested.

Reuben patted her head jokingly. "Of course I will! Don't worry about me, though," he said, mock-offended.

"You stay safe, too," El said, placing a hand on his arm. "No bravado, please."

Alex frowned. "Three deaths in Harecombe. I wonder if we'll hear from Caspian."

As he finished speaking, Avery's phone rang. "It's Genevieve." She answered, "Hey, how —" But before she could say another word, she fell mute and nodded. "Yes, I'll be there."

"Let me guess," Reuben said. "Another meeting?"

"Tomorrow, at her place in Falmouth. Reuben, you're coming, too."

Seven

It was a blustery day, and the wind carried the promise of snow. The moors were already covered with a sprinkling of white, and thick clouds blanketed the sky.

Avery felt the solstice creeping towards her; the longest night of the year. Another night associated with the Wild Hunt, but that couldn't happen twice, surely. But more than that, it was a time of celebration marking the symbolic death and rebirth of the sun and the turning of the wheel. Once that night had passed, summer was once more on its way. For the pagans it marked Yule. This year it occurred on the 22nd of December, and the witches would celebrate its passing together, with a fire, candles, and stories. Much like the summer solstice, it would be a time to reconnect to the earth and each other. But Avery shuddered. It was dark and cold, and girls were dying. Someone was hunting th em.

They passed a few scattered houses, and then the road turned inland. Locally, it was called the Coast Road, but that was deceptive; the village was a good way back from the closest beach. At one time there'd been a post office there, but now there were a few dozen houses, a popular pub called *The Sloop* on the main road, and a small shop.

Reuben spoke as he drew close to West Haven. "You're quiet. Are you okay?"

"I'm just thinking about those poor girls, and hoping it's not a vampire doing this."

"What else would drain blood through puncture wounds on the neck?"

She turned to face him, twisting in her seat. "I don't know what to think. It's suspicious, certainly, but there are many twisted people in this world."

He glanced at her with a small shake of his head. "Yes there are, but this is something different. Maybe it has something to do with this house. Maybe something has been disturbed. Why else would you get paranormal investigators in? It's a good thing we've been making spells for them. They could be at risk."

Avery glanced at the bag on the back seat. They had brought spells packaged in bottles, potions, salt bombs, and even jewellery. "Do you think there's such a thing as an occult black market?"

"What a weird question! Why are you asking that?"

"Well, all that stuff we've made. I bet they'd fetch good money, if someone stole them and wanted to sell."

Reuben nodded. "Yeah, they would, and yeah, there is undoubtedly one. People will traffic anything. And that stuff is solid magic, undiluted and potent. They should probably keep it all locked up. Do you know that El has spelled a knife that will slice through most things—even some metals—like butter?"

Avery was amazed. "No. You mean like rope or chain?"

"Yep. As long as the chain isn't too thick. And she's spelled a key that will unlock anything, and placed a hex inside a locket."

"Wow. She's so devious! I wish I'd thought of that stuff. What about you? What have you made for them?"

"Nothing. I'm still not as good at this stuff as you guys. I'm good at controlling water, especially when I surf—"

"Yeah, I remember that time when you raised that huge wave." She was referring to a day just after Gil's death when Reuben was so furious and grief-stricken that he'd almost drowned himself and El on the shore. It had been a dark time for their relationship, and for a while, El wasn't sure it would recover. Reuben knew it, too.

"Not my finest moment," he murmured.

"You were grieving."

"That's no excuse for my behaviour." He paused, thinking. "I'd like to re-member Gil at Yule. I know that's traditionally more of a Samhain thing, but it didn't feel right for me then. Now it would."

Reuben's brother, Gil, had died in the summer while they were searching for their grimoires. He'd been killed by Caspian Faversham—accidently, according to Caspian. Avery smiled. "That's a great idea. What do you want to do?"

"I want to head up to the mausoleum at Old Haven and wait for the dawn to rise there. It's a weird way to celebrate the solstice, I know, but..."

"But we celebrated the last solstice with him, so why not this? He'll be there in spirit. I think that's a brilliant idea." *And creepy and cold, but Reuben needed this.* "As long as we can have a fire."

"Deal," he said, throwing her a grateful glance as he pulled in front of an old house at the end of a long street, behind Ben's van. "Here we are."

Avery exited the car, pulled her coat closed, and tucked her scarf tighter around her neck. Reuben joined her, and they looked at the house that was positioned on the outskirts of the village. It had three storeys and was made of red bricks with a heavy stone portico over the front door creating a small porch. A large window was to the left of the front door, but several windows stretched away to the right, and a short tower rose from the roof on the left side of the house. The front garden was neglected and overgrown with weeds.

"It looks normal enough," Reuben said, squinting at it.

Avery nodded. "I can't sense anything weird from here." She looked down the street, and then back at the house. "Why is it bigger than the others? Has it been converted from something?"

"Didn't Ben say it probably had a lot more land before? Maybe it was built before the others." He led the way to the house. "Come on; let's get out of the cold."

Avery hesitated just before the porch and pointed towards a plaque on the stone portico. "Holy crap. Have you seen what it's called? House of Spirits."

"Didn't Ben say the owner was a medium? That's good advertising!" Reuben declared as he bounded up the steps. The front door was ajar and Reuben knocked loudly as he pushed it open. "Hello? We're here!"

Silence.

Reuben raised his eyebrows quizzically at Avery and headed inside, shutting the door behind them.

The house was warmer than Avery had expected. The long, wide hall was covered in Minton tiles, wood panelling covered the lower half of the walls, and the ceiling had ornate architrave running around the edges. Doors led to large rooms on either side, and Avery caught a glimpse of old, wooden furniture and out of date décor. Reuben walked down the hall, shouting greetings. The house went back farther than they expected, but they hadn't gone far when they heard a shout from above.

Ben appeared at the top of the stairs, hanging over the banisters. He looked dusty. "You made it."

"Wouldn't miss it," Reuben said dryly. He hefted the bag he was carrying. "And we bring gifts."

Ben grinned. "Brilliant. Come on up."

They headed up the stairs and followed him down a dimly lit corridor, passing several doors on either side. Avery was itching to see inside the rooms they passed, but Ben hurried along, not allowing Avery a chance to look around properly, until he finally halted outside double doors at the far end.

"This is the master bedroom," Ben said, pushing the doors open in a grand gesture. "It's quite impressive."

Avery gasped as she walked in. "Wow! You weren't kidding." It was a huge corner room with two big windows to the rear and side of the house, giving expansive views of the fields and garden behind them. Like the rest of the house it had all of its original features, and the walls were covered in green Chinoiserie. The furniture was solid oak, and old, worn rugs covered the floor. "This is seriously cool."

"Even the crazy bird wallpaper?" Reuben asked, perplexed.

"Particularly the crazy bird wallpaper," Avery said. "Your crazy bitch dead sister-in-law would like it." Alice, Gil's dead wife and demon-summoning witch, was also an interior designer before she was killed by her own demons. "Crazy, but she had great taste. She would *love* this place."

Cassie and Dylan were fiddling with some camera equipment by the bed, and Cassie paused for a moment. "I agree, Avery. This place is seriously cool. I feel like I'm stuck in time. Wait until we show you the rest of the place!"

Reuben adopted a sly smile as he walked over to join them. "Why are you filming in the bedroom? Is it some sort of porn gig?"

Avery sniggered as Cassie looked at him open-mouthed. Dylan winked. "I wish. No, we're just filming regular old ghost stuff. Or something like that."

Ben pointed to another camera mounted on the wall on the other side of the room. "Luckily for us, after days of experiencing absolutely nothing, Charlotte announced yesterday that she'd been having strange dreams. She thought something was in here, standing over her. Obviously we haven't been filming in here, until now."

Reuben edged closer to the camera, trying to see the screen where Dylan was replaying the footage. "Found anything?"

Dylan grimaced. "Not sure. This is a few minutes of the recording of last night. I'll examine it better once we get it home, but I just wanted to see if we'd caught anything. It's all in thermal imaging, because of course it's dark."

They crowded behind Dylan and watched some very dark footage for a few seconds, before Avery made out shapes in the thermal imaging. She could see the bed very faintly against the blackness of the room, and two shapes beneath the sheets. She heard what sounded like laboured breathing and a weird rasping noise. Avery's skin immediately erupted in goose bumps.

"Is that breathing?" she asked, alarmed.

Dylan raised his eyebrows. "Sounds like it, but then there's that horrible rattle."

"Like a death rattle," Reuben observed, frowning at the screen. "But there's nothing there. Does that mean it's a ghost?"

"But there's no spectral form, and clearly it's nothing human or we'd see *something*. You can't disguise body heat—even if it's cooler."

He was right. The Nephilim had shown up quite distinctly when they'd filmed in the church, and humans had very clear imaging.

Cassie frowned at the screen. "Well, we might not be able to see anything, but we can hear something. What is it?"

Reuben shrugged. "Maybe it's something we haven't come across before."

"Maybe it evaded this camera, but will be on that one," Ben said, pointing to the other camera.

"I'll study the footage properly later," Dylan said, changing the data card. "And I'll listen to the audio again."

"But I don't feel I'm being watched," Ben pointed out. "I've got used to spirits being around now, and it's like there's a presence lurking just at the edge of your vision. Here—*nothing*!"

"Not now," Dylan said. "But I bet if we were here all night we'd sense something."

Ben grimaced. "I'm really reluctant to be here overnight until we know what we're facing. I have a strong sense of self-preservation."

Dylan collected his gear together and placed it all in a large holdall. "We may have no choice."

While he packed, Cassie headed for the door and asked Avery, "Fancy a tour?"

Avery grinned. "You know I do!"

Reuben and Avery followed the other three through the house as they showed them the rooms. There was a thick, musty odour that permeated everything, and dust seemed to hang on the air. The wallpaper was old and peeling in places, glamorous once, but now faded and sad, and the carpet underfoot was threadbare. It was clear that renovations had started in some places, but other rooms, including the hallway and stairs, hadn't been touched at all.

"Hell! This is a massive job," Reuben exclaimed as he looked around, appalled. "The whole place needs gutting."

Cassie nodded. "I know. But it will be amazing once it's done."

"But it *is* creepy," Avery said. "I know what you meant the other day. It feels...strange."

"Madame Charron should have called it the House of Secrets," Reuben suggested.

Ben led the way, and he pushed open a door to a room at the rear of the first floor. "There are a couple of rooms we think may have been used for séances. This big one has a central table, and the wallpaper is quite opulent. It *was*, I should say."

He was right, Avery thought as she looked around. It had a faded glamour to it. The lower half of the walls were panelled, the upper half covered in wallpaper. The curtains were heavy brocade, dull now, like everything else, and full of moth holes, there was a huge floor-length mirror, and an ornate chandelier hanging in the centre of the room. "Did they buy it fully furnished?"

"Yep. Apart from some books that Joan, the housekeeper, sold off a few weeks ago, pre-sale," Ben explained. "Rupert was not impressed. He wanted *everything*!"

Avery remembered the book she had found on her shelf, the one with the witch-mark in it that she hadn't seen on her shelves before, and a strange, unsettled feeling materialised in the pit of her stomach. "Do you know who bought the books?"

Ben looked at her, frowning. "No idea. Why?"

"Just wondered," she said vaguely.

Reuben started to press areas of the wall around the fireplace. "Have you found any hidden panels in here?"

"No, but if I'm honest, we've been concentrating on the other stuff," Dylan said, watching Reuben's progress with interest. "I'm pretty sure that Rupert has searched this place very thoroughly and found nothing."

Reuben grunted with disappointment, and after some more fruitless attempts, Cassie led them downstairs to the kitchen, which like many homes, was at the back of the house. It was a building zone, with just the hob and cooker left in position, a freestanding fridge, and a basic kitchen sink under the window. Cassie filled the kettle and turned it on, rummaging for clean cups among the de bris.

Reuben grimaced as he took in the room. "Are the guys who own this seriously living here?"

"They can't afford not to," Ben said. "They sank all their money into this place."

Avery looked out of the glazed double-doors that led to a paved patio area. The garden was a mass of overgrown shrubs and weedy borders. "It's been neglected for a long time."

"There was one old lady living here for years, and one housekeeper," Cassie explained. "It was much too big for them to manage."

Avery leant against the frame, looking around the kitchen again. "What do you know about the previous owner?"

Dylan handed Avery a steaming cup of tea. "The lady of the house was the daughter of the medium. She inherited the house from her mother, and lived here alone ever since—well, except for the housekeeper. Her mother, Madame Charron, was well known for her ability to talk to those who passed..." Dylan adopted a spooky voice, *"Beyond the veil."*

"But she must have been a charlatan, right?" Avery asked as she sipped her tea, savouring its warmth.

"Not according to what I heard," Ben said, referring to his conversation the day before.

Dylan shrugged. "It's hard to know, but she was very famous in the 1920s and '30s."

Reuben leaned against the counter. "When did you find that out?"

"Rupert told us," Cassie said. She'd cleared some space on a counter and sat there, swinging her legs against the old units. "It turns out they're occultists, or rather they study it. They couldn't wait to get their hands on this place when it came on the market. Hence, sinking their money into it."

"But they love it," Ben said. "They are fascinated with every single thing—bumps in the night, witch-bottles, everything. Dynamite wouldn't move them. Especially now Charlotte has experienced her strange dreams and the feeling that someone is watching her."

Reuben looked puzzled. "So, potentially, say Madame Charron had some ability, she *could* have summoned something and now it's here, stuck in the house. Did she use a Ouija board, or a crystal ball?"

"Not sure," Dylan mused. "But I'll make some enquiries. I guess she could have been the real deal. I mean, we try to debunk this stuff, because let's face it, most people do fake it, but *you're* the real deal."

"I couldn't summon spirits," Reuben said emphatically. "I'm a witch and I can shape elemental magic, do spells, and make wicked potions if I try really hard, but I couldn't summon a spirit if I sat there for a whole year, nor could Avery. That's a different sort of skill—the type Alex has."

Avery shook her head, feeling perplexed. "We could be making too much of this. You've found nothing in the house, except for the bedroom. It could be her spirit. Or her daughter's. *Or*, Madame Charron might have summoned something deliberately, for some nefarious purpose, or summoned something accidentally and couldn't get rid of it again. Or, whatever it is, has been around for a long time, before the medium arrived."

"Bollocks!" Ben exclaimed. "So many possibilities!"

"Do you think it has anything to do with those deaths of the young girls?"

Dylan's voice was low. "Don't say that, Avery. One of those girls was my mate's cousin."

"Why should it?" Cassie asked, looking between them. "Surely that's completely unrelated."

Reuben laughed. "Avery's got a thing about coincidences. We all do, I suppose. And the deaths seem to have a supernatural cause, and here you are investigating a house with an occult history."

Avery shot him a troubled glance. "And this house is close to Harecombe and the college grounds."

Dylan groaned. "Damn it. If I'm honest, it crossed my mind, but I've been trying to tell myself I'm imagining it."

"Always listen to your gut," Reuben said. "I don't give advice often, but that one's a given. We all have a sort of second sight—a flash of knowing what's right or wrong. Don't ignore it."

"I wish we could analyse *that*!" Ben said, looking regretful.

Avery sighed. "I hope the students are taking precautions on the grounds."

Cassie nodded. "Classes are over now."

"And let's not forget the witch-bottle," Avery added. "That was placed here for a reason."

"Just more crap to confuse us. Where are the owners of the house?" Reuben asked, frustrated.

"At work," Ben said. "They trust us to come in here, and sometimes workmen are here, too."

Avery swilled her empty cup in the sink. "Show us where they found the witch-bottle."

Ben led the way to the large room on the right of the front door. The walls were covered in old, peeling wallpaper, underneath which the plaster work sagged and cracked. A large fireplace was in the centre of the far wall, and a few tiles in the hearth were lifted up. "The hearth stones are cracked, and, as you can see, they lifted some to repair them; it was under there."

Avery and Reuben crouched down and saw the hole that would have contained the bottle. Avery held her hands over it, sending out a tendril of magic, but all she felt was the remnant of an old spell. When she'd finished, Reuben reached inside as far as he could manage. Avery heard a rustle as he triumphantly pulled something free.

In his hand was a small, yellow piece of paper, dry as bone and brittle. He gingerly peeled it open to reveal a row of runes across the middle.

"What do they mean?" Cassie asked, breaking the silence.

"Something to do with the moon, and runes for protection, I think. I'd have to look them up," Reuben answered.

"I recognise them," Avery said, taking it from Reuben. "It warns against the night, as if it's a curse, and the rest is a protection spell." She looked up at the ghost-hunters. "Can we borrow this?"

"Just be careful with it," Ben cautioned.

Reuben rocked back on his heels. "I think there was something weirder going on in this house than just séances, guys. You might want to get familiar with that bag of spells we brought you."

The front door banged open, disturbing them, and a man shouted, "Ben, are you here?"

"It's Rupert," Ben said, and headed out the door, the rest of them following. "I'm coming, Rupert."

Rupert stood waiting for them in the hallway. Avery estimated he was in his late thirties or early forties, and was of average height and build, but there was an intensity to him that was unnerving. His eyes were deeply set back, with heavy lids that made him look like a hawk, and he peered at Reuben and Avery with interest as Ben introduced them. "These are my friends I mentioned. Avery owns a bookshop in White Haven, and has an interest in the occult. I thought she might know something to help us with this house."

Rupert held on to her hand a fraction longer than was comfortable as he shook it. "And *do* you?" he asked. "Know something about this house, I mean?"

"No more than you do, I'm afraid. But it is fascinating." *Why did she have the feeling that she needed to hide as much of herself from him as possible?*

He turned to Reuben. "And you? Do you work at the bookshop, too?"

Reuben shook his head. "No, I'm a friend of Avery's. We should probably go, and leave you to it." He looked at Avery quizzically, and she nodded.

They said their goodbyes, the ghost-hunters promising to get in touch, and all the while Avery felt Rupert watching them, and that feeling didn't stop until they'd left the house and were driving down the road.

Eight

"Can't we go to the pub instead of the meeting?" Reuben asked, looking hopefully at a quaint country pub on the way to Genevieve's house.

"No! Although, maybe we've got time for a quick glass of wine so we don't arrive early," Avery conceded.

Reuben grinned at her. "That's what I love about you, Avery. You're always up for a drop of the good stuff."

"Idiot! You started it," she said, smirking as she got out and almost ran to the pub. It was freezing, and twilight had fallen, bringing with it plunging temperatures.

They ordered drinks and snacks from the bar menu, and settled in a corner by the fire, surrounded by twinkling Christmas lights and the sound of Michael Bublé singing "Rudolph the Red-nosed Reindeer" in the background.

Reuben peered at her over the top of his pint of Guinness. "How much do we tell the coven about the House of Spirits?"

"I think we have to tell them everything," Avery said. "Three women have died under mysterious circumstances. We have to."

Reuben groaned. "I suppose you're right. But as soon as we say something, Genevieve and the others will be all over it. We won't get a minute's peace."

"But they'll probably know something we won't," Avery said, sipping her red wine thoughtfully. "Rasmus has a huge store of knowledge, as does Oswald. They may already have some ideas about what might be causing this."

"They may even know something about that house," Reuben said, and then fell silent as the bar maid brought them their food order. "That place must have been fairly notorious in its day. And Rasmus must be nearly a hundred by now."

Avery threw her head back and laughed. "Don't be ridiculous! He's not *that* old!"

Reuben winked. "Maybe not. But I bet he's an old gossip underneath that fusty exterior."

"You're so naughty, Reuben."

"I know. But if I didn't joke, I'd go mad. I mean, seriously, a house with an occult history, occult owners now, a hidden witch-bottle, strange noises, women drained of their blood…" He trailed off, and they both fell silent for a moment.

After a few mouthfuls of chips, Avery said, "I wonder what those runes really mean?"

"The ones on the paper? I thought you said it was a warning against the night?"

"Maybe." She shrugged. "It was a sign for the moon, but I may be wrong. We'll let El and Alex look. They're better than we are at that kind of thing."

"Vampires don't need a full moon," Reuben said, dipping his chip in mayonnaise. "That's werewolves."

"I'm pretty sure it's not a werewolf. I think they'd be messier."

"I bet Hunter could tell with that nose of his."

"I bet he couldn't. We're chasing shadows right now. They don't have a scent."

"But it breathes—albeit in a raspy, weird way. Therefore, not a shadow." Reuben pointed his fork to emphasise his point.

"Well, whatever it is, if it carries on in the same manner, there'll be more deaths this week. It's pretty terrifying."

"But Charlotte, or whatever her name is, was unharmed, and so was Rupert. What's that about? Maybe the raspy-voiced invader isn't linked with the college deaths after all."

"If we don't get any more concrete evidence, we either need to stake out the house or the college."

Avery was stunned into momentary silence. "Stake out the college? That sounds horrendous."

"But we may see something. And we're witches. We have more protection than most. There is one good thing about all this, though."

"Really? What?"

Reuben grinned triumphantly. "This has nothing to do with our magic."

Genevieve lived in an elegant Georgian house on a quiet side street in Falmouth, and it suited her perfectly. And surprisingly, it was full of toys. Avery could see toys on the floor of the hall, and a box full of them in the room to the right of the front door.

Genevieve must have noticed Avery's puzzled expression. "I have three kids," she explained. "They're in there, watching TV."

"I had no idea," Avery said, feeling terrible that she didn't know this detail about her life.

"That's because I never mentioned it," she explained, without adding any other information about them. Avery presumed she wanted to keep her private life private, and that somewhere around the house was the children's father, or she couldn't have left them alone.

Genevieve shrugged apologetically as she took their coats. "I'm sorry this meeting was called on such short notice, but it's important. And, I've only invited a few of the coven. I decided to keep numbers down, which may potentially annoy a few of our members, but it's tough. Head upstairs and take the first right. We're meeting in my spell room."

"Hey, you're the boss," Reuben said. "Sorry if I gate-crashed, but we were together all afternoon anyway."

"That's fine," she said, brushing off his apologies. "I'll grab snacks, and meet you up there."

Genevieve looked rattled, which was unusual. Avery was used to her being abrupt and rude, but this was a side she hadn't seen before. She watched her head down the hall, and then followed Reuben upstairs.

Genevieve's spell room turned out to be a long room at the rear of the house, lit with corner lamps, candles, and filled with the scent of vanilla. It was carpeted with soft coir matting on top of which were colourful rugs. The whole of the long interior wall opposite the windows was lined with shelves filled with magical paraphernalia and books, and just inside the door was a large worktable crowded with documents. At the other end of the room, next to the fireplace, were a chaise longue and a table filled with a selection of drinks, but there was no other furniture at all except for lots of large floor cushions and low, round tables. Avery felt it was like a scene from the Arabian Nights.

Rasmus and Eve were already there. Rasmus stood with his back to the fire, his hands nursing a small glass of what looked like sherry. He was again wearing one of his dark velvet smoking jackets and straight black trousers, and his shock of white hair stood up on his head. He looked grumpy, lost within his thoughts, barely acknowledging their arrival.

Eve was browsing Genevieve's bookshelves and she smiled when they arrived, clearly pleased to see them, but once they'd exchanged greetings, her smile dropped.

"I hoped Genevieve had invited you. These deaths are horrible."

Avery agreed. "The worst. We're looking forward to seeing what everyone thinks about the cause."

"I have no idea," Eve confessed. "All I know is what I've seen on the news, and they're not saying much. And neither did Genevieve."

"Newton told us what little we know," Avery said, taking a glass of gin and tonic from Reuben after he'd mixed drinks from the stand in the corner.

"The victims appear to have been partially drained of blood, which suggests something supernatural. I presume Genevieve must know that, too."

"Any ideas, Rasmus?" Eve asked, catching his eye.

"None that I want to share right now," he grunted. His face creased with lines of worry.

Avery was about to ask him more when Oswald, Caspian, and Jasper arrived, carrying in a waft of bitter cold air.

"I wish I'd known you were coming," Oswald said to Avery and Reuben. "I'd have grabbed a lift." He looked chilled and tired, dark circles beneath his eyes, and he immediately headed to the fire to stand next to Rasmus.

"Sorry," Reuben said. "We haven't been in White Haven all afternoon. Drink?"

"Whiskey, and make it large."

Reuben suppressed a grin as he fixed his drink, but then Oswald immediately fell into a hushed discussion with Rasmus, and Caspian and Jasper raised quizzical eyebrows at the others. They joined Eve and Avery, while Reuben played barman.

"It seems we must again meet while under stress," Jasper said in his low voice.

"At least we're not facing the Wild Hunt," Caspian said, accepting a whiskey.

"How's the young witch who was injured?" Avery asked Jasper.

"Mina has made a good recovery, thank you, but I will leave her out of whatever's going on here. She's not ready." He shook his head regretfully. "I think the events of Samhain have troubled many members of the coven, and that's why Genevieve has left some out of tonight's meeting."

"Very true," Genevieve said as she swept into the room, followed by Claudia, who, to Avery's eyes at least, looked like a mad bohemian in her long, flowing dress with a bold print. She caught Eve's wide-eyed expression and turned away, trying to not to giggle. Genevieve carried on, regardless. "This series of murders is not for the faint-hearted. I need witches I can rely on."

"I'm glad we meet your expectations," Caspian drawled.

"You might not be when I tell you what I think we're facing." She looked grim as she and Rasmus stared at each other for a long moment. "Sit, all of you."

They arranged themselves in a rough circle, each finding a comfortable cushion to sit on, and Avery slipped her boots off and crossed her legs as she settled herself in. This felt like things may go on for some time.

Genevieve placed a tray of biscuits and cheese on the floor within easy reach of everyone, and then also sat cross-legged on a large cushion. "I'll let Claudia explain."

Claudia began without preamble. "We have seen this before."

"What? The murders?" Eve asked, confused.

"Yes, three girls to start with, and then there'll be more—men, too."

They glanced at each other, alarmed.

"Who's *we*?" Avery asked.

"Myself, Rasmus, and Oswald. We're the only ones old enough." She closed her eyes briefly, as if to suppress a memory. "We didn't know what we were hunting then—at first—and we didn't even know if the deaths were linked. They were spread all over Cornwall, in small communities. News wasn't as instant as it is now. We were slow to act then, but now..." Her words hung on the air.

"I'm not sure I have the energy for it," Rasmus said, his gravelly voice full of sorrow. "Hunting takes energy I haven't got."

Genevieve's tone was strident. "There's nothing wrong with your magic, Rasmus. It's better than most."

He made a gesture with his hand as if to brush her off, and a wave of magic washed around the room, carrying a note of regret that hung sorrowfully on the air. "It's not my magic I doubt."

"Can you get to the point?" Caspian said, narrowing his eyes. "It's a little late in the day for games."

"I hate to say the word," Rasmus said, distaste written all over his face.

Oswald huffed impatiently. "It's a bloody vampire. I hate the damn things. They bring death wherever they go."

Avery's breath caught in her chest. It was one thing to speculate about vampires, but another to have it confirmed.

"Are you sure?" Reuben asked, leaning forward, his hand gripping his glass.

"The last time this happened, ten people were killed before we could stop it, and all ten rose from the dead."

"*Rose from the dead*?" Eve was incredulous. "But how do you know? What did you do with all of them?

Claudia answered, her tone flat. "We had to kill every single one of them."

"How?"

"A mixture of beheadings and stakes through the heart." Her voice was so matter of fact that Avery couldn't quite comprehend it.

"And I burnt one," Oswald added, looking only into his drink. It was as if he couldn't bear to look them in the eye. "Don't forget that. I can't."

The room was silent for a moment, the younger witches all wide-eyed in shock.

Genevieve took a hefty slug of her drink. "Now you know why I only need witches I can rely on."

Caspian frowned. "Was my father involved?"

"Yes," Rasmus said. "He was one of our most effective hunters. He killed four of them."

Caspian nodded vacantly, and Avery realised he was having as much difficulty absorbing this as the rest of them.

"But not mine, I presume," Reuben asked. "We were *ex-communicado*."

"No one from White Haven," Claudia confirmed. "There were other witches involved, of course, across Cornwall, but they have since died, or moved from here. And a couple of our members were killed in the fight. It was a horrible time."

Reuben looked alarmed. "Witches *died*?"

"Oh, yes. Make no mistake," Rasmus said. "Vampires are a deadly enemy. This is not *Twilight*. They do not take humans as lovers. They have no emotion.

They are killers, monsters, bloodsuckers, evil parasites—" His voice broke and he sobbed, bringing a hand to his face.

"Old friend," Oswald said, patting his shoulder and looking very tearful himself. "We should have left you out of this."

"No." Rasmus's head shot up, his expression fierce. "I will not back away." He looked at the other witches defiantly. "You should know that my wife was killed by one of these things. We had been married for only a few years. We were trying to have children." His voice broke again. "Sorry. I shouldn't have said."

Shock rippled around the room, along with the murmur of condolences, and Eve said, "I'm so sorry, Rasmus. I had no idea."

"I don't speak of it," Rasmus confessed. "It's far too painful, even now."

"Our biggest regret, and there were many, trust me," Claudia said, finally lifting her gaze from Rasmus. "Another, of course, was that we never found the vampire who'd turned them all."

"Ah," Reuben said, comprehension dawning. "And now he's back."

"It seems so."

Reuben's pale blue eyes, normally so teasing, had darkened like a stormy sea. "Apart from a stake through the heart, beheading, and fire, are there any other ways to kill a vampire?"

"Holy water will slow it down," Claudia said. "Stabbing, maiming, and shooting it will also slow it, but to my knowledge, only those three things guarantee death. I also burnt them after staking, anyway. I like to be sure."

This is a nightmare. Avery tried to imagine Claudia doing such things, but it was impossible to envisage this exotic older lady, and the very dapper Oswald and Rasmus, as being vampire killers. *I'm going to wake up and laugh about this.* But then Avery met Reuben's troubled gaze, and knew it was very real.

"How do we find it?" Caspian asked. "And why did it stop the last time?"

"Unfortunately," Oswald said, rising to his feet slowly and heading to the table to top up his drink, "we have no answer to either question."

If the mood was grim before, it now felt worse. A wind whipped up outside and rattled the window, causing every single one of them to jump.

"And the victims? Once they've been bitten and killed, is there a way to prevent them from turning?" Caspian asked.

"Not that we know of, but for us it was too late, anyway," Claudia said.

Genevieve spoke for the first time in a while. She had been listening, and Avery could see her calculating possibilities and strategies. "How long until the dead walk again?"

Claudia thought for a moment. "I think it was about four days. That's when they disappeared from the morgue."

"In theory, then, the first girl will disappear tonight?"

"Yes."

She exhaled and seemed to shrink, cowed by the news. "By the holy Goddess. This is a disaster."

"But we know what we're fighting now," Oswald pointed out, "unlike before. We can start the hunt sooner, and hopefully prevent more deaths."

"Right," Jasper said decisively. "We need a plan. Potentially, we should split up tasks to make our attack more efficient. I will do whatever you need me to. Genevieve?"

"Thank you, Jasper. I have been giving this some thought. We need to do several things, the most important being to find its lair. It cannot walk in the day, therefore it must be somewhere dark and secure."

"We are *sure* it can't walk in the day?" Eve asked. "It couldn't be disguised as something human?"

"I'm pretty sure not," Jasper said. "I have researched vampire lore, and there is nothing that suggests they can overcome their inability to walk in the sun. It will kill them instantly."

Oswald agreed. "Yes, that's what we believe, too, and nothing suggested otherwise all those years ago."

Eve looked relieved. "Good. That's something, at least."

Genevieve continued, "So, we will of course have the advantage if we can find it in the day and kill it where it sleeps. But that potentially means we have to track its movements, and that's very dangerous. At night it is strong, fast, and deadly. But, the deaths are all in Harecombe at present, on the college grounds. This suggests it's close by. The deaths must be opportunistic."

Avery put in, "We have a theory as to where it may be—or at least where it's linked to." She updated them on the house that Ben and the others were investigating. "It has a strange past, and a few recent odd occurrences there seem too coincidental not to be connected."

A palpable air of excitement lifted the room. "That's very interesting news," Genevieve said, "and definitely worth investigating."

"Unfortunately, I've never heard of the place," Oswald confessed, his brow furrowing.

Claudia shook her head, puzzled. "Me, neither."

"We're already working with Ben, so we can continue to help," Avery suggested.

Genevieve looked pleased. "Agreed. But Jasper, can you look into the background of the house, too? See if there is any chance it could be connected to those events years ago."

"Of course. Can you give me a date?" he asked.

"1979," Claudia said, immediately. "At just this time of year. Forty years ago, exactly. I will never forget it."

"Any chance you can introduce me to the ghost-hunters?" Jasper asked Avery and Reuben.

"No problem," Reuben answered. "I'm sure they'll be glad of the help. I'll call Ben tomorrow and set it up."

"Before we go on," Claudia said, "just who else in our own covens will get involved? Genevieve, you are on your own here, of course, and Jasper has already ruled out Mina, understandably."

"I will keep my other witch, Bran, out of this, too," Jasper said. "I would like to keep him free to keep an eye on Mina—and Penzance, in general. I will of course keep them both updated."

Avery leaned forward, hating to be involved but knowing there was no way anyone from White Haven would want to be left out. "All of our coven will help."

Genevieve looked relieved. "Good, I thought you would. Caspian?"

"My sister will, and possibly my cousins. I'll check." He looked grim. "If we need them, I will make them help."

"Eve?" Genevieve asked.

"Nate will help, of course. We'll do anything you need."

Genevieve's face softened momentarily. "Good, thank you. And Claudia?"

"I have two other witches in Perranporth, but I'll leave Lark out of it. She too is young, and like Mina, was overwhelmed at Samhain. But Cornell will help, if needed. He's fast and strong and to be honest, I'll have trouble keeping him out of it."

Avery had a vague recollection of Lark and Cornell. Lark was in her late teens, and certainly skilled, but yes, she was still unsure of her strengths. Cornell, however, was several years older and almost overconfident, if Avery remembered correctly.

Oswald had stood and was pacing up and down, listening, and he added, "Count Ulysses in, of course."

Rasmus looked thoughtful. "My daughter, Isolde—from my second marriage, just in case you're wondering—will want to help, although I'm not sure I want her to. But, well," he glanced at Genevieve. "You know Isolde! And Drexel will, too, although he's barely twenty. My coven is very headstrong," he muttered.

Avery smiled. She'd forgotten Isolde was his daughter. She'd met her and Drexel at Samhain, but the whole coven was there, and it was difficult to keep track of who was who. Rasmus seemed to have cheered up as everyone confirmed their involvement, and despite the risks, Avery was also starting to feel positive about the battle ahead.

Genevieve turned to Avery and Reuben. "You have good links to Newton. Perhaps you can find out more about the deaths? Access the bodies?"

Caspian grunted. "We could all do that. A simple spell will get us into the morgue."

Genevieve looked at him, annoyed. "I know that. But I want to know what the police know!"

Caspian gave a barely perceptible nod to her.

"What do you want us to do with the corpses?" Reuben asked. "I mean, if we behead them now, will it stop them rising from the dead?"

Avery's mouth fell open. "Reuben!"

He shrugged. "One less vampire is a good thing, right?"

Oswald was once again warming his hands by the fire. "It may work. But there's only one way to find out."

Reuben rose to his feet. "If the first victim will rise tonight, that means we need to go to the morgue now, and kill it before it does. I'll call Alex, El, and Briar. They can meet us there. I presume it's in Truro."

"I'll join you," Caspian said. "It's on my way home, and we'll need the numbers. We have no idea what may happen."

Reuben looked at Caspian, his expression almost unreadable. "Thanks. That would be good."

It seemed the meeting was at an end as everyone now rose to their feet, stretching out their limbs.

"Would you like me to come, too?" Eve asked.

"No. It's out of your way," Avery reassured her. "Go home and update Nate, and maybe make some preparations."

"And I will start researching." Jasper checked his watch. "It's not late. I'll start tonight, if you're sure you don't need me?" He looked to Avery, questioningly.

"No. There'll be six of us at the morgue."

"Besides," Reuben added, "if we all die, you lot will have to finish the job."

Avery swatted his arm. "Reuben!"

He rolled his shoulders. "I'm kidding. We're going to be just fine."

"I should come," Oswald said. "I'm going that way, too, and I've at least seen a vampire before."

"No," Caspian said emphatically. "You're a powerful witch, Oswald, but you're old and physically slow—no offence. I'll worry more about you, and that will distract me. There'll be enough for you to do another time."

Reuben nodded. "Agreed. You guys strategise, and we'll act. I think your battle with them last time means you get to sit this one out. And for now, that includes you, Genevieve, as our High Priestess."

Oswald nodded, a mixture of relief but also disappointment on his face. "You're right. We need to find out why it's happening now, and if there's a link to the last time. Knowing about this occult house may give us the advantage."

"Agreed," Claudia said. "We may remember something about the last time that helps us now."

Avery had a thought. "You didn't say where you caught up with the newly turned vampires. You mentioned you killed them all. Where?"

"We managed to track down a couple of places they'd used," Rasmus explained. "We cornered one and it fled to a barn as day was breaking. It thought it had lost us, but we found it, covered in hay in a hole in the floor, and we staked it. "

Oswald nodded. "We found one in a cave, hidden at the back. Again, we'd tracked it one night and struck in the day."

"And we found three in an abandoned mineshaft," Claudia said, her gaze distant. "That was tricky. The place was a death trap—fallen beams, trapped gases, twisting passageways..." She trailed off, lost in thoughts of the past.

"Gave me nightmares for a long time," Oswald admitted. "There were another couple, but I can't remember where we found those. I'm sure it will come back to me."

"Wow," Avery said, looking at them in admiration. "You're amazing."

Claudia smiled. "We had no choice, and I genuinely hoped never to face them again."

"You'll need weapons," Rasmus said, all business as he picked up a holdall next to the bookcase and placed it in the centre of the room. He rummaged in it for a moment and produced a stake with a flourish. It was about one foot long with a long, sharp point. "Take the bag. There are about half a dozen of these in it, and a mallet."

Reuben took it from him, twirling it in his hands like it was a drumstick. "You're a dark horse, Rasmus. We'll take three. Keep the rest for yourself—just in case. We can make more later."

Rasmus straightened his shoulders, as if squaring for a fight. "Fair enough. I'd better start practising."

"I think we all should, and begin finding spells that could help. Our magic will give us an advantage, but..." Claudia looked intently at Avery, Caspian, and Reuben. "Do not underestimate the strength and speed of a vampire. They are superhuman, preternaturally strong, and vicious. Never forget that. I hope to see you all at the next meeting."

Hope. The word hung on the air.

Reuben said, "I'll get El to bring a sword, too. And besides, there'll be plenty of knives in the morgue."

"Be careful! Wear gloves—you may be witches, but we still leave finger-prints—and do not take risks," Genevieve warned. "If it escapes, so be it. I'd rather have you all alive, and we'll get our chance again. And protect your friends and family—and that applies to all of us. There are tough times ahead, and there'll be more blood spilt before this is over."

Nine

As soon as Avery and Reuben got in the car, Avery called Alex to update him on the plan, and she asked him to call El and Briar. She could hear the shock in his voice, but he didn't hesitate. The last thing he said was, "Don't you dare go in without us," and then he rang off.

"I'm going to call Ben, too," she said to Reuben, as he steered them out of Falmouth and on to the A39 to Truro. "They need to know the danger they're in. They *cannot* stay at that house overnight. What if that was a vampire standing over Charlotte?"

He nodded. "Using her as a regular blood bank? Agreed. But it makes me wonder why they're still alive, if it's linked to this business. "

"I'll worry about that later," Avery said. She was relieved to find that Ben and the others were not at the house, and made them promise not to go at night until they had more information.

She glanced over to the back seat and pulled a wooden stake out of the bag, feeling its weight. "You need a lot of strength to drive this into someone's heart."

"Hence the mallet."

"But they'd need to be sleeping for that to happen—in the day. It would be tough if you were fighting one."

"Buffy managed it," he said, grinning.

"Yeah, well, I'm not Buffy. She was a Slayer."

"But you're a witch. You can punch it in with a well-timed blast of wind."

She considered his suggestion. "That might actually be possible."

"Of course it is. You just need practice. "

"There are many things I need right now. Maybe I should ask for a mannequin for Christmas."

"What I need right now are directions to the morgue. Can you look it up?"

"Of course," Avery said, reaching for her phone again. "All I can think about is what to do when we get there. I can't believe we're actually going to face a vampire—*tonight*!"

"Hopefully we won't. Hopefully all we'll encounter is a dead girl that needs beheading. Maybe three dead girls that need beheading."

"We should tell Newton."

Reuben sounded alarmed. "Not bloody now, we shouldn't! And I hope Briar doesn't, either."

Avery quickly found the directions to the Cornwall Coroner. "Bollocks. It's not in Truro. It's just outside, off the A39. And there are a few buildings onsite, including a crematorium. I'll tell the others." Behind them she could see the lights of Caspian's Audi, so she phoned him first before telling Alex. "My hands are shaking," she confessed to Reuben.

"It's the adrenalin," he reassured her. "You'll be glad of it when we get there."

They arrived at the Coroner's office all too quickly. It was in a secluded area of countryside, surrounded by fields, and it was bigger than Avery expected. The place was in darkness, apart from some security lights, but Reuben pulled into the rear of the car park and killed the lights, and Caspian pulled next to them.

A heavy frost covered the ground, and rather than wait outside, Caspian joined them, getting in the back of Reuben's car. "I don't like it. It's isolated, and the vampire could be out there, watching us right now."

"On the plus side," Reuben said, twisting to speak to him. "It's well away from public places and from where people could get hurt. Although, if the girl rises and gets away, there's no way we'll find her out here."

Caspian grabbed a stake, hefting it much as Avery had done. "I've done many things, but I've never encountered a vampire before."

"Did your father ever tell you what happened all those years ago?"

"Never." His eyes glinted in the dim lights of the car. "And I have no idea why he never spoke of it, either."

"Maybe," Avery suggested, "it was such a nightmare that none of them ever wanted to think of it again. Rasmus lost his wife!"

"We should work in pairs tonight," Reuben said. "No one should be alone."

Caspian and Avery nodded, and then they fell into an uneasy silence, waiting for the others to arrive.

It was another fifteen minutes before they saw the headlights approach in the distance, and Alex phoned to check where they were. A minute later, El pulled up in her Land Rover, and they all piled out of their cars, stomping their feet for warmth, their breath billowing around them in clouds.

Alex leaned back against El's Land Rover, arms crossed in front of him, leather gloves on his hands. "What the hell happened today? Avery's given me some details, but why are we at the morgue?"

Reuben twirled the stake. "We have a vampire to kill."

Briar's eyes were wide with surprise. "Really? Because when Alex called, I thought he was joking. The whole journey here, we've been debating what you found out at the meeting."

"It's not a joke," Avery reassured her. "I'm going to make this quick, because it's freezing and I don't want to stand in the dark, knowing we could be attacked at any moment. Claudia and the others are sure that this is a vampire, because it's happened before. We think that the first girl who was attacked and killed will turn into a vampire too, tonight, and we need to stop it happening."

El, Alex, and Briar regarded them silently, looked at each other, and then back at the other three. El gave a dry laugh. "You know you sound nuts, right?"

Caspian huffed with impatience. "I can assure you, if you heard what we did, you wouldn't question this. And when Avery tells you everything later, you'll understand. In the meantime, let's get on with this. If she turns tonight, that big ol' vamp that turned her could be waiting for her. Out there!" he jerked his head to indicate the surrounding fields.

"Right," Alex said decisively. "Do we know where her body is being kept?"

"No idea," Reuben said, shaking his head. "Mr Google does not provide online maps of the facility."

Briar was clearly struggling with their plan. "Hold on. How will we know which girl is which? It's the Cornwall morgue. There could be dozens of dead bodies in there. And when we do find her, what if she's lying there, looking completely normal? Are you actually suggesting we desecrate her dead body? That's appalling!"

"Can we address this issue once we're inside?" Caspian asked, growing impatient, and he turned and led the way across the car park.

"Brought your sword, El?" Reuben asked, as they followed him.

She patted the scabbard strapped to her left side. "Two swords. One for me, and Alex is carrying the other one. Briar declined. Why do I need it?"

"You may have to behead her."

El stopped dead, and Briar walked into the back of her. "I might *what*?"

Reuben paused, too. "I only said *might*."

El sighed and started walking again. "Maybe you should carry the sword, because I'm not sure I can do that."

Reuben nodded. "I'll do it if we need to."

As they closed in on the main building a security light activated, but within seconds it was off, shorted out by Caspian's magic. He quickly turned to the other lights over the entrance and on the far corner and spelled them off, too. Avery noted the security cameras and quickly deactivated them, and then the group huddled together in front of the glass doors.

Caspian suggested, "Before we go in, I want to scope the perimeter."

"Agreed," Reuben said. "I want to know our exits, and the general layout."

Avery nodded. "The only thing I could make out on the map is that the crematorium is to the right." She pointed to a square building with a separate entrance a short distance away.

"This place is bigger than I thought," Briar said, hugging herself for warmth. "I'll come with you, Caspian. Are we sure her body won't be in the hospital morgue?"

"Very. I checked," Caspian answered. "Only those who die in hospital will be in the hospital's morgue, and that's just a holding place. She'll be here. They all should be. Reuben, if we go right, you go left. We'll meet around the back. There'll be a rear entrance, and we'll get in that way. Alex and Avery, are you happy to go in through the front?"

"Anything to get out of the cold," Avery said, starting to shiver.

"It'll be just like the museum, Avery," Alex said softly.

"Let's hope there aren't security guards here." She remembered when they shorted out the security system at the Truro museum, and guards had arrived to investigate.

Alex nodded. "With a bit of luck, there won't be."

Caspian checked his watch. "Ten minutes should cover us. We'll see you inside. Phone us if you need to explain where the morgue is. And don't do anything rash."

"Nor you," Alex said, resentment creeping into his voice.

Within seconds, the other four had disappeared, leaving Avery and Alex alone. Alex deftly released the lock on the door, and they slipped inside, the heated air warming their chilled skin.

The silence surrounded them like a blanket, and it was completely dark, other than the alarm system blinking to their left on the wall. Alex took care of it, and the lights winked out.

"Where now?" he asked, his voice low.

Avery could just make out a reception desk on the left, a long corridor leading to the back of the building, and doorways to the left and right, but she was reluctant to send up a witch light because the door behind them was made of glass.

"I'm sure the morgue must be toward the rear of the building, but we should check every room as we go," Avery suggested.

"Agreed." Alex quickly checked the door to the right, and Avery to the left. "It's an office," he called, softly.

"Here, too," Avery answered.

Alex moved down the corridor, past the reception desk, and Avery sent up a witch-light as soon as they were out of sight of the entrance. The corridor arrived at a T-junction, with another corridor running from left to right.

Avery whispered, "It would be logical for the morgue to be close to the crematorium, in which case we should try right first."

Alex nodded and led the way, and Avery listened intently for any noise, but it was still silent, and that made it creepier. They passed several offices, but there was no sign of the morgue until Alex found a door leading to another corridor. Satisfied they hadn't missed anything he headed down it, and quickly came to a door with swipe card access and a sign saying *Morgue*.

"Bingo," he said, running his hands across the panel and whispering a spell. The door released with a *click*, and they entered a small anteroom with a desk and a large whiteboard. Numbers ran down the side and columns were next to it, listing names, investigations, time arrived, and other details. There was a door in the rear wall.

"What was the first girl's name?" Alex asked as he searched the board and then opened the other door. The witch light illuminated another short but wide hallway with a couple of doors to the right.

Avery quickly pulled her phone out, searching for a news report. "Bethany Mason, aged eighteen." She looked up, searching the board. "There. Number 4b."

"That must coincide with the storage number. Come on." He continued down the corridor, lined with stark white tiles. The first room on the right was very long and filled with stainless steel work surfaces and cupboards, and had three gurneys in the centre of the room. Various jars and stainless steel objects were laid out on the counters. "This must be the autopsy room," Alex guessed.

The next room was also large, but on the right-hand side were rows of doors, three short doors to each row, and each numbered. There were no windows in any of these rooms, so Alex flicked the light switch on; they both blinked as a bright white light banished the shadows.

Alex pointed to a square door situated in the middle of the fourth row. "There's 4b. She must be in there."

"There's no way you could get out of that on your own," Avery said. She patted her backpack, double-checking the stake was there. "It locks from the outside. Even if she turns, she couldn't get out."

"Maybe you could if you had superhuman strength," Alex said, grimly. "We should wait for the others. Let's see if the other girls are here, too."

Avery searched for their names in her phone again, while Alex headed back down the corridor. Avery followed him absently, half watching him while searching in her phone. He found a few more offices, a room lined with lockers, sinks, showers, and toilets, another wide anteroom, and a set of double doors. "That must be the rear entrance," he murmured. He quickly checked that all the alarms and cameras were disabled, and then pulled the door wide open. The cold night rushed in from the parking bay. A couple of vans were parked out the back, but it was otherwise empty.

"Where the hell are they?" Alex muttered, and stepped out to look around. A black shape swooped past the entrance, and Alex disappeared.

Avery blinked, thinking she'd missed something. "Alex?" She ran to the back door and looked out, but nothing moved, and Alex was nowhere in sight. *Shit.* Avery's heart thumped and her mouth went dry. She wanted to shout, but she bit back the urge, instead pocketing her phone, dropping the backpack, and pulling the wooden stake free. Her magic rose instinctively, surging into her hands.

An explosion of bright white light emanated from the corner of the building and Alex dropped onto the floor, landing in a crouch. Avery heard a shout, and Reuben and El ran around the corner. El had drawn her sword, and the blade flashed with white fire, the only thing illuminating them in the darkness. There was another swoop of blackness, a deeper shadow against the night sky, and Avery rocked backwards as a wave of air buffeted her, bringing the stench of death and rotten meat with it. She had barely time to look up when a figure collided with her from the left. Caspian. She landed on the floor, winded, with

Caspian sprawled across her. She peered over his shoulder and saw Briar running towards them, throwing a ball of fire into the air.

Caspian rolled away and threw a jagged bolt of lightning up towards the swooping figure, and it disappeared.

"Get inside, now!" Reuben yelled, as he, El, and Alex pelted down the side of the building towards the rear entrance.

Avery jumped to her feet, stepped just inside the entrance and grabbed the door, ready to pull it closed. Caspian waited outside, searching the skies. Briar ran through the door first, followed by El, Reuben, and then Alex, and Caspian whirled in after them. Avery pulled the door shut with a resounding *thud*. A shudder passed through the door as something hit it from the outside. She shot all three bolts across at once with a wave of magic, and sighed with relief as she leaned against the wall.

Avery was happy to see all of them in one piece, but particularly Alex. "Are you all right?" she asked, concerned. "What happened? Did it pick you up?"

He nodded, his face pale under the witch light. "Shook up, but unharmed. I never even saw it coming. It's quick and strong." He felt his neck. "I can still feel its grip, and its smell—ugh! It certainly didn't expect me to fight back." He looked at the others. "How are you?"

"Annoyed," Reuben said, brushing himself off. He'd skidded across the floor as he entered the building, colliding with the opposite wall, almost taking down El in the process. "That thing is bloody quick."

"And it *stinks*," El reiterated, wrinkling her nose. "But I'm fine."

"Briar? Caspian? Are you okay?" Avery asked, turning to them.

"Just about," Briar said, still breathless. "It ambushed us by the crematorium. Caspian witch-flew us out of there with mere seconds to spare."

Caspian looked as annoyed as Reuben. "I didn't even hear it! I could only bring us as far as the corner of the building—I had no idea where we were going!"

"It bought us precious time," Briar said, reassuring him.

Another *thud* on the outer door interrupted him, echoed by an answering *thud* from down the hall.

They fell silent, listening with dread, and then heard another *thud* and a blood-curdling scream.

"Shit. She's awake," Alex said, drawing his sword and racing back down the corridor without a backward glance, El and Briar hard on his heels.

"I'll hold this door," Caspian shouted. "Reuben?"

Reuben nodded, gripping the stake firmly in his right hand. "I'll stay with you. Avery, go with Alex. We'll shout if we need you."

Avery skidded into the morgue seconds after the others to see the door labelled 4b being dented from the inside, crumpling as if it were a cardboard box.

Great. A vampire outside, and one inside. We're trapped.

Before any of them could act, the door burst open and a snarling Bethany dropped onto the floor, squinting in the bright light. Her skin was pale, almost blue, and her bloodless lips were pulled back, revealing two long, curved canine teeth either side of her mouth. Her eyes were like dark pits, and for a brief second she was unfocused, but as she saw them, her mouth opened, her jaw unnaturally wide.

Everything became chaotic, Avery barely able to register what was happening, it was all so quick.

The newly-turned vampire leapt at Alex and he threw her back against the wall where she crashed to the floor, before jumping again to her feet. Briar hurled a stream of fire towards her, but Bethany ran at her, evading the fire with catlike reflexes. El and Alex slashed at her with their swords, but she dodged effortlessly through them.

The vampire wrapped herself around Briar, the force of her lunge carrying them both to the floor, Briar underneath, her arms pinned. Briar looked terrified as Bethany opened her jaw wide, revealing the long curve of her teeth, ready to strike her neck. Avery ran forward, braced herself, and plunged the stake into the middle of the vampire's back. The vampire rolled off Briar and lunged to the doorway, effectively blocking them in. She hissed and snarled, the stake hanging uselessly from her back.

How the hell had that happened?

Despite being in shock, Avery noticed the girl moved in an odd way, her limbs stiff, and her hands grasping like claws. Her lack of humanity was startling. She reached behind her and wrenched the stake out of her back, throwing it to the side,

A series of shouts sounded from the corridor, followed by a tearing, groaning sound, and then they heard plaster falling, along with noise like a roaring wind. A lean creature landed on its feet behind the girl, and rose to its full height of over six feet. Its shoulders were broad, and it wore the semblance of dark clothing, but its skin was grey and leathery, and its eyes glinted like dull metal. It scooped the former girl towards it, encasing it in his scrawny limbs, and then it was gone, leaping up through the hole it had made in the roof, and silence fell.

Ten

Reuben and Caspian skidded to a halt, and Reuben stood under the hole in the roof, looking up. "I didn't see *that* coming."

"So much for blocking the entrance," Caspian said angrily.

Alex turned quickly towards the freezer storage doors. "We haven't got much time. We need to kill the other two girls before we leave." He hesitated. "Not kill, they're already dead. You know what I mean. But that *thing* may come back, and I do *not* want to hang around."

"I agree." Briar patted her neck with a trembling hand, clearly shaken, although she was trying to hide it.

Caspian nodded as he stepped into the storage room. "There's an excellent chance of it returning if it has somewhere close by to store its new friend."

"Did she hurt you?" Avery asked Briar, struggling to call Bethany an *it*, despite her lack of humanity.

Briar shook her head. "No. You saved me."

"We all saved each other," she answered.

Reuben was still standing in the corridor. "I suggest three of us get the cars and bring them outside the rear entrance while we still have time. I don't want to be attacked again."

Caspian immediately volunteered. "I'll go."

"So will I," El said, joining them. She too looked shaken, and that was unusual for El. "I know what I've just seen, but I can't behead someone. Yet."

"I can do it," Alex said, looking at a second whiteboard on the wall. "Names, Avery?"

Reuben answered instead. "Amy Warner and Clara Henderson. I checked earlier."

"5c and 3a," Caspian noted, eyeing the doors warily, especially the one that was dented and hanging loose. "Are you sure we should go?"

"Yes." Alex's dark eyes met Caspian's, and he glanced at Reuben and El beyond. "Be quick, and be safe. We'll deal with this."

They nodded and ran, leaving the other three to stand staring at each other bleakly for a few seconds. If Avery was honest, beheading a dead girl was the last thing she wanted to do, but it had to be done.

"Plan?" she asked, the stake once again in her hand, poised to strike.

Alex looked decisive. "Briar, grab the gurney, and we'll slide the next body straight out and onto it to give us plenty of room. Then—" He paused and swallowed, looking at the floor as if strength would flow from it to him. "I will use the sword to cut her head off." He looked up at Avery. "Stand ready with the stake—just in case."

They had only one stake between them as Caspian and Reuben had taken the other two.

They nodded in agreement, and while Briar fetched the gurney, Alex opened the freezer door. 3a was in the section at the top of the freezer, and the body was covered in a white sheet. As soon as the gurney was in position and raised to the correct height, they slid the body clear of the freezer on a long, white tray and then rolled the gurney to the centre of the room, lowering it to waist height. Alex peeled the white sheet back, revealing the victim's head. She'd already had a post-mortem as they could see the stitched incision that ended at the base of her throat.

Briar looked at the young girl's pale face and sighed. "What a way to go."

It was the first time—other than seconds before, and Avery didn't really count that—that she had seen a dead body. She felt overwhelmingly sad more than anything else.

"Well, at least she's not moving," Alex observed. He raised his arms high above his head, sword extended, and took a few deep breaths.

"Are you sure we have to do this?" Briar asked, looking between Avery and Alex.

Alex didn't hesitate. "Yes." He brought the sword down so quickly that there was a *whoosh* of air and then a solid *thunk* as he sliced through the girl's neck, beheading her in one, clean sweep. Her head rolled to the side, turning towards Avery, and even though she was expecting it, she jumped.

She met Alex's eyes across the body. "Well done."

He looked pale. "One more to go."

They pulled the sheet back over the girl, slid her body back into place, and shut the door, before turning to the next. They worked quickly, listening for any sign of movement from outside or in, but all was still silent.

This girl was as young as the others. Her dark hair was swept back from her head, her skin was an icy blue, and her eyes were closed. Alex once again raised his arms high, ready to bring his sharp blade down on her neck, but without warning her eyes opened, revealing pupils as black as night. She snarled low in her throat and started to rise, her right hand shooting up to grasp Alex's arm.

"Shit!" Alex instinctively tried to jump back, but he couldn't. She was too strong, and he couldn't bring the sword down, either. "Avery!"

Briar was standing at the end of the gurney, and she leaned forward, her hands on the girl's legs to stop them from kicking up. She whispered a spell, momentarily pinning her down.

Avery's heart was in her throat, but she leapt forward and brought the stake down over the girl's heart, thumping into her body with a sickening *crunch* as she hit the rib cage. She used her magic to force it down harder than her normal strength would allow, and the stake plunged through her body with such force it went through the plastic tray beneath her, as well. The dead girl loosed her grip on Alex and tuned to Avery. Her black eyes focused with a hungry intensity, and she snarled again, showing her sharp, white teeth and her extended canines. Alex didn't hesitate.

"Get back," he yelled at Avery and brought the sword down, severing the girl's head, the sword's tip missing Avery by inches only.

The head rolled to the side, eyes frozen open. In seconds her eyes reverted to their normal human state, her teeth retracting.

"Holy shit!" Alex exclaimed. "Let's get the fuck out of here."

Briar ran to the doorway. "The cars are here—I can hear them. And something else."

A howl carried on the still night air.

"We haven't got time to put her back," Alex said. "They'll know what's happened soon enough, anyway. Let's go."

Avery hurriedly pulled the stake free, and Alex swept the room, ensuring they had gathered everything, and then they ran to the back door, wrenching it open.

The cars were lined up, engines revving, ready to flee. Reuben leapt out of his car and ran to El's Land Rover. "I'm going with El. Alex, you take my car. Caspian will make his own way home."

"No!" Briar said immediately, running straight to Caspian's passenger door. Caspian leaned half out of his window, peering into the sky above. "I'll go with Caspian. He may need me. You can find me a bed, right?"

He looked grateful, even if he didn't voice it. "No problem. Jump in."

Alex slid behind the wheel of Reuben's car, and Avery had barely shut the passenger door when he revved the engine and raced across the car park, following the other two past the Gardens of Remembrance and onto the country lane.

Alex glanced over at Avery. "Are you all right?"

"As much as I can be after encountering three vampires in one night." She noticed Alex's hands were gripping the wheel, his shoulder's stiff, as he concentrated on the road. "Are you?"

"I'm not sure I'll ever forget cutting someone's head off, but I'll survive. Better that than being bitten."

All three were driving fast—too fast for these lanes—but it was now well after midnight, and hopefully no one else would be on these back roads. A howl sounded again, and Avery saw a blurred figure as something leapt out of the fields to the right, over the hedge, and onto the top of El's car. It crouched, gripping the sides, and then started to punch the roof as El's car veered across the road.

"What the—" Avery's voice trailed off as she wound the window down, wiggled halfway out of the car, and aimed a blast of wind towards the vampire. Alex put his foot down, bringing them closer.

Avery's aim went astray as El's car kept veering across the road, but an explosion of light from within the car pulsed up through the roof, knocking the creature off balance. Avery aimed again, directing a vortex of swirling air at the dislodged vampire and tossing it high in the air. She grinned to herself. *I've got you now!*

She slowed her breathing and focused, trying not to let her underlying panic throw off her natural control. The wind whipped the vampire around and around, turning it in the air, where it hung helplessly for a few seconds. Avery raised her hands, lifting the creature higher and higher before sending it spiralling to the right, far over the fields.

Alex had slowed down, keeping the car steady, and Reuben had done the same, all three cars moving together and staying close. The main road was ahead, the lights of the junction bright against the night sky. *Safety...hopefully.*

Avery made sure the vampire was still being carried on the fierce wind and then ducked back in the car, just as they reached the junction. Barely slowing, they turned left and headed towards Harecombe and White Haven.

"Do you think we've lost it?" she asked, peering behind them.

"I think so." Alex took a deep breath in and out. "Well done."

"Do you think it can fly? Like a bat, I mean?"

"Isn't that Dracula?

"I don't know! My vampiric lore is shaky."

"Maybe it can. Can they change into smoke or something? You should call Genevieve, let her know what happened. She'll be worried. But I think we're safe. For now."

"For now," she echoed ominously as she stared ahead, vacantly. Just how long would *for now* last?

Eleven

appenstance Books seemed unnaturally bright and festive after the events of the night before, but Avery was glad for it.

She'd had a bad night's sleep—they both had. Images of dead girls and snarling vampires filled her head, and even Alex's warm arms couldn't dispel those. Before sleeping they'd reinforced Avery's protection spell, but they'd agreed they would need more—something more specific to the undead. The others had also arrived home safely, but they'd agreed to meet again later that day, and invite the ghost-hunters. They would catch up with Genevieve and the others another time.

Sally took one look at Avery over their morning coffee and asked, "What happened?"

"You don't want to know."

"Yes, I do."

Avery fell silent for a moment, thinking. Sally was right. She did need to know, if she was to protect herself. But equally, this would terrify her, and did she really want to inflict that on her—and Dan—before Christmas?

"Spill!" Sally insisted, cradling her cup of coffee as she leaned against the shop counter. "I can cope."

"What's going on?" Dan asked warily, as he joined them.

Avery looked at him and sniggered. "What the hell are you wearing?"

He looked down. "What? It's my Christmas t-shirt. I'm being festive!"

His t-shirt was bright red with white lettering and it read, *I'm not Santa, but you can sit on my lap.*

He grinned. "I have several that I shall wear from now until Christmas. Hope you approve, boss."

"Of course—as long as you don't offend anyone too much."

Sally interrupted. "Don't distract her, Dan! Something has happened. Look at those bags beneath her eyes!"

Avery grimaced. "Thanks!"

"Ah. More mayhem in White Haven." He bit into a mince pie. "What now?"

Avery glanced around, checking the shop was empty. "We encountered a vampire last night. Well, two actually, and *almost* a third."

Dan almost spit out his pie. "Are you serious? I foolishly assumed that conversation we had the other day was purely theoretical. "

"Yes! And it wasn't. I wouldn't lie about that."

"So those girls *were* killed by a vampire?"

"Yes. Without a doubt." Saying it now, in the cold light of day, sounded ridiculous, but last night had been only too real.

Sally visibly paled. "Is it here? In White Haven?"

"No, not quite. We think it's halfway between here and Harecombe. Close enough." Avery looked sheepish. "We broke into the Cornwall Coroner's office last night and it attacked us there."

Dan whistled. "Wow, Avery, you just keep surprising me. And what did you do that for?"

She filled them in, and noticed them both looking at her, slack-jawed. When the door chimes rang to announce a customer, they all jumped. The customer nodded in greeting and headed to the shelves, browsing the stock.

Avery concluded in a low voice, "I need to enhance my protection spells, for this shop, and you two, so I'm going to spend a few hours doing that today, if that's all right."

Sally and Dan exchanged an uneasy glance, and Sally said, "That's fine. Do I need to start wearing garlic bulbs?"

"Maybe. I'll let you know when I've done some research. Hopefully I can think of something more sophisticated than that."

Dan waved her away. "Go now. I'll call you for elevenses. And you better have made progress!"

"Yes sir!" Avery saluted him and headed up to her flat.

Avery laid out her grimoires and started hunting for spells to specifically protect against vampires. In order to cheer herself up she put on some Christmas music, lit the fire, burned some incense, and turned on the fairy lights that she'd placed around her walls and across her shelves.

Satisfied she'd banished some gloom, she began searching her grimoire methodically. She found all sorts of interesting spells that she'd missed before, some of them quite unpleasant. There was one to give someone warts, one to cause uncontrollable sweating, and one to cause 'the pox.' She shuddered. Her ancestors seemed really quite unpleasant sometimes. She could only hope they hadn't really used them.

One spell made her pause, excited. A spell to bottle sunlight. That would be perfect—not only for them, but for the ghost-hunters, too. She marked the page, and started to list all those she thought would be useful.

She found another spell that detailed how to make a wooden stake. It specified the type of wood to use, suggesting that ash or hawthorn were the most effective. The stake she had from Rasmus was made of hawthorn. It sat across the table where she'd left it the night before after cleaning it and blessing it, banishing the negative energies. The newly turned vampire might not have bled, but nevertheless, the stake had been covered in gore, the point dented from where she'd driven it through the plastic tray beneath the body.

She turned back to her grimoire and found several spells that used garlic. One made a useful potion, and there were herb bundles that incorporated it and other protective plants. That was a brilliant idea. She could make Christmas wreaths for the all the doors and windows, or she could just bundle the plants together to make posies. And maybe she should see James for holy water. While she didn't believe in the value of it, clearly a vampire did if the lore was to be trusted.

Avery had a hawthorn hedge at the rear of her garden, and plenty of holly and bay. All offered protection. She'd already brought in branches of holly to decorate the shop and her flat. If she visited Old Haven Church, she could cut some yew and oak, as well. And they'd need ash to make more stakes—the more the better. She picked up her cutting knife, grabbed some garden gloves, and headed outside.

The day was dark, the sky full of heavy grey clouds, and it was bitterly cold. Most of the garden was bare, as all of her summer flowers had died back, but the shrubs still struggled along, and there were bright berries in places. She'd only been working for an hour when she heard a shout, and looked around to see Newton marching towards her, looking furious.

Avery braced herself as she turned to face him, and dropped her cuttings of hawthorn into the wheelbarrow next to her.

He didn't bother with pleasantries. "Are you responsible for that horror show in the Coroner's building last night?"

"I'm afraid so."

"You beheaded young, dead girls! Do you know what that will do to their parents?"

She squared her shoulders. "Better that than they become vampires! I presume you've noticed that one of the girls is missing?"

He paused. "That wasn't you?" He looked around suspiciously, as if he would see the girl propped up in the corner somewhere.

"By the great Goddess, Newton!" Avery glared at him. "I'm not a bloody body snatcher! She turned last night and became a vampire!"

He looked apoplectic. "Why the hell didn't you tell me?"

Avery took a deep breath in an attempt to calm herself down. Sometimes Newton was infuriating. "By the time we left the morgue—pursued by a vampire, by the way—it was very late. I presumed you wouldn't want to be disturbed. I phoned early this morning, but it went straight to voicemail. Don't you check your messages?"

He looked slightly chastened. "I was called into the morgue at six. I went by Briar's house, actually, but she didn't answer." *Interesting!* Avery raised a quizzical eyebrow, but Newton rushed on. "I was worried. Is she okay?"

This should be fun. "She should be. She stayed at Caspian's last night."

Newton's face darkened. "Caspian's? Why?"

Avery explained what had happened at the morgue and on the way home. "It was probably a good idea to go with him, not only to have two of them in the car, but also to save Briar sleeping at home on her own."

Newton nodded, and a calculating expression settled behind his eyes. "I could stay at hers for the next few days, or weeks, until this is over."

Avery crossed her arms in front of her and glared at him. "What are you *doing*, Newton? Stop messing her about! You seemed to make it very clear a few months ago that whatever you two had going on was over, and now you seem to be hedging your bets! Either walk away and stay friends or actually commit to a relationship! You can't have it both ways."

"I am not trying to have it both ways!" he protested poorly.

"So what are you doing?"

He seemed to deflate, like a popped balloon. "She saved me, and I liked it." His hands moved to the scar on his neck, caused by Suzanna's blade on All Hallows' Eve. Newton had been seconds from death, and only Briar's magic had saved him. She hadn't moved from his bedside for over 24 hours, and had been tending him for days afterwards, helping to reduce his scar and regain his strength. Up until then, Briar had been blisteringly impatient with him for months after the summer when he'd backed away, but now she'd calmed down, and Avery had the sense that she was waiting, again—for him.

"So *do something*! Ask her out, take her for dinner, or make it clear you're just friends. Briar is hot! She doesn't deserve to have to wait for you to make your mind up. I don't even know why she *is* waiting! I bloody wouldn't." Avery's exasperation came flooding out. "Hunter fancies her, and he's still in touch! He may even be coming down over Christmas. I hope they get together."

Newton looked like she'd slapped him. "He's coming back?"

"He might be."

Newton abruptly changed the subject. "Are you all meeting again for a debrief?"

"Yes, tonight, at my flat. You're welcome to come. Just don't be a dick." She turned her back on him and went back to her cuttings, and she heard Newton leave. *Men!*

By the time she'd finished gathering wood from her garden, she was cold and hungry, and her cheeks were glowing. She staggered into the small kitchen behind the shop carrying an armful of branches, dumped them on the table, and went back for the rest.

Dan was waiting when she brought in the last load, and he handed her a cup of steaming hot chocolate. "You've been busy."

"I'll be making wreaths and posies. Lots of them. It will take me a few hours, but magic will help speed up the process. You can have a couple to put by your front and back door. By the end of the day I'll have something basic for you to take home."

He looked worried. "This is just a precaution. Right?"

She started sorting through her cuttings, not meeting his eyes. "Right."

"I bet you haven't heard the news."

Her head shot up. "No. What's happened?"

"A young man has been reported missing. He was last seen outside a night club in Truro, and his jacket has been found in an alleyway behind it."

Avery closed her eyes briefly, as if she could block out the news. "Crap."

"Didn't Newton say anything? He was here earlier."

She shook her head thoughtfully. "No, he didn't, but maybe he didn't know." She rubbed her face, exasperated and overwhelmed by what they faced.

"This isn't going to go away, is it?" he asked, sadly.

"No. It's only just beginning."

As soon as Avery had finished her hot chocolate, she headed to Old Haven Church.

As usual it was deserted, which gave it a haunting beauty. Frost lay thick on the ground, and clung to the branches and decaying vegetation, and as she crunched along the path to the wood behind the cemetery where they had encountered the Wild Hunt, she found her gaze drifting to the mausoleum where Gil lay. So much had changed since he died. She wasn't sure Gil would have liked the changes at all, but he would have enjoyed being part of the coven.

She plunged under the trees and made her way to the clearing and the huge, old yew tree in the centre. There was nothing left to remind her of that terrifying Samhain. The space had been cleansed of the ritual blood magic, and once again it was a peaceful place, the silence broken only by the occasional bird song.

And there was something else. A flickering movement on the edge of her peripheral vision caused her to whirl around, hands raised, her heart beating wildly in her chest. Shadow stepped out from behind the trees, as if out of thin air.

"Shadow! You scared the crap out of me. What are you doing here?"

Shadow gave a slow, calculating smile that chilled Avery's blood. "I always come here, human. It's where I arrived, and where I keep trying to return to the Summerlands."

Avery kept her distance, taking a pace backwards, and summoning her magic. Shadow was dressed all in black: skinny jeans, black boots, and a fitted leather jacket. *Where had she got them from? Not her problem.* "But you can't return, you know that. The doorway is closed."

"Maybe I should try some blood magic."

Was that a threat? "You'll fail." Shadow stepped forward again, and Avery raised her hands. "Take one more step and I'll freeze your faery blood until you explode into shards of ice."

Shadow gave a hollow laugh. "I'd like to see you try."

"Take one more step and you will."

She held her hands up in surrender. "Sorry. It was a joke. I was wondering what you'd do if I threatened you, and now I know."

Avery narrowed her eyes. "I don't think you understand the word *joke*. Besides, you asked for our help. I won't be much help if I'm dead."

"True. Does that mean you've found something to help me?"

"Not yet. I've been a little side-tracked." *Understatement of the year.*

"With what?"

"A small matter of the undead."

"The undead? Spirits or night-walkers?"

"Vampires."

"What's that?"

"They were once human, but now suck human blood to survive. They are fast and deadly."

Shadow walked towards Avery, her threatening posture gone. "So, what are you doing here?"

"I'm collecting supplies to make a spell," Avery said warily, still not trusting Shadow.

"I'm no threat to you. Maybe I can help?"

"I can manage just fine on my own. I just need some branches of the yew, oak, and rowan, and then I'll be gone."

Shadow pulled a long, thin knife out of the scabbard on her belt. "I can help. I will feel useful." She nodded behind her to where a couple of oak trees stood. "I'll get some oak." She ran over to the tree and began to climb it nimbly and effortlessly, and Avery turned to the yew.

The sooner I do this the better. She laid her hand upon the yew's trunk and blessed it, asking to take only what she needed. She worked quickly, until she had a small pile of skinny branches covered in tiny needles at her feet, and then found the rowan tree and did the same, cutting some branches that still had a cluster of bright red berries on them.

She'd just finished when Shadow reappeared with her arms full of cuttings, and a swath of mistletoe on top. "What do you need these for?"

"Protection. All of these plants have special properties."

Shadow shrugged. "I'm not a healer. I'm a hunter, a treasure seeker. Are you hunting this creature?"

Avery nodded, wondering where Shadow was heading. "Yes, we need to stop it as soon as we can."

Shadow flashed a huge smile. "Good. I can help."

Twelve

Avery's open-plan living area was full of people. The White Haven Coven was there, the three ghost-hunters, Newton, and Caspian had arrived last with a bottle of wine, as if attending a meeting to decide how to hunt vampires was something he often did on an evening after work. They were seated on the sofa and chairs, around the dining table, and others were standing and talking.

Avery had gone back to work for a few hours after meeting Shadow in the wood, mulling on her offer, but it was something she wanted to discuss with everyone else, and she'd told her that she would be in touch. She'd spent most of the afternoon in her attic making wreaths and posies for protection, and sent Sally and Dan home with two each, and then started to prepare food for everyone—platters of cheese, ham, fresh bread, olives, pickles, and a tray of mince pies.

By the time the other witches started to arrive she felt exhausted. Alex greeted her with a kiss. "Busy?"

"Too busy. Especially after last night. How have you been?"

He headed into the kitchen to deposit a six-pack of beer, and she followed him. "Exhausted and depressed." He popped a cap and took a long swig of beer before he spoke. "A bloody vampire! I keep trying to tell myself I imagined last night, but then I remember how that sword felt, and well, it makes me feel sick."

Avery tried to reassure him. "You did what you had to do. What we couldn't."

"But I feel like a monster."

"You're not the monster."

"I know, but—" He shrugged, unusually despondent.

"You're sleep-deprived and tired. Come and eat," she said, leading him back to her dining room table that groaned with food. "You'll feel better."

The news was on the TV, and Reuben stood watching it, absently eating. "That vamp must have gone hunting as soon as you threw it off our tail, Avery."

"You think the vampire's behind the missing man, then?"

"In Truro? Last night? Sure. The timing's right."

Newton nodded. He was still in his suit, but he'd pulled his tie off and opened the top button of his shirt. "I agree. I mean, I have no proof, but you did deprive him of two victims."

"We had to," Avery said, feeling guilty.

"I know. It would have probably done it anyway if what your coven says is true." He sipped his beer, half an eye on the TV. "Is he making some kind of undead army?"

"It takes more than two to make an army," Reuben pointed out.

Newton sighed. "I think there have been more victims."

They all looked confused, and Briar paused mid-bite to ask, "More disappearances?"

He nodded. "My colleagues have been investigating some for weeks. All adults, nothing suspicious, other than they have just gone!"

"Doesn't that automatically raise questions?"

"People go missing all the time, for all sorts of reasons. Often they're alive, but are hiding from domestic abuse, parental abuse, or are using drugs, or there's trafficking at play. It's huge. You have no idea. But these particular disappearances are clustered together," he admitted.

Alex exchanged a worried glance with Avery and asked, "If the disappearances are linked, why would the vampire overtly kill some, while others have just disappeared?"

Newton sighed. "Maybe he's stronger now, and wants to scare people. Vampire psychology is not my thing. Cassie? Isn't that your area of study?"

"Not exactly," she answered, dead-pan. "But killers thrive on power, and the more they get away with the more confident they get. I'm not sure if that's a useful comparison, but it's all I've got." She shrugged apologetically.

"Hold on!" Ben said, holding his hand up. "Before we all start speculating, can you recap us on everything that happened last night? All we've been hearing are terrifying snippets. Remember, some of us weren't there."

"Thankfully," Cassie added, her face grim.

Dylan agreed. "From what I've heard so far, I'm wondering if we should drop this job."

Ben looked shocked. "No way! This will be the biggest thing we've done—for money, at least!"

"My life is worth more than money." Dylan was annoyed, and it sounded like their conversation was the continuation of an earlier argument. "Remember, my mate's cousin was one of those girls."

The six witches glanced at each other, a warning in their eyes. *Shit!* Avery had forgotten that. They were going to have to tell him that she was the one who'd turned.

Alex sat heavily in one of the chairs next to the table. "Actually, we really need your links to this house. We think this is all connected. Everyone settle in, we have a lot to share."

For the next fifteen minutes, Avery, Caspian, and Reuben updated them on the meeting with the coven, and then the other witches joined in and shared what had happened at the morgue.

Dylan looked at them all, stunned. "Are you seriously telling me that *dead* Bethany escaped the morgue?"

"I'm afraid so," Briar said. She was sitting next to him on the sofa, and she squeezed his arm in sympathy.

He flinched. "Are you sure it's her?"

"Very sure," Alex answered. "We'd just identified which freezer she was in."

Dylan fell against the back of the sofa and closed his eyes. "This is a nightmare. Beth is a *vampire*."

Ben looked sceptical. "Seriously?"

"I've never met one before," Reuben answered sarcastically, "but yes, I think so. I don't know anything else that causes people to rise from the dead."

"It could be a zombie," Cassie said, as if that might be better.

Reuben was emphatic. "It's not a zombie. It had big canines, perfect for sucking your blood!"

Cassie shifted uncomfortably in her seat on the sofa, glancing at the others in a way that made Avery think they knew something they hadn't yet shared. "And you still think it's linked to the house we're investigating?"

El nodded. "It seems too much of a coincidence. But maybe we're wrong. What have you found out?" she prompted.

Dylan exhaled, opened his eyes and sat up. "Lots of weird shit. I'll start at the beginning. The House of Spirits was built in the early nineteenth century, but was bought by Madame Charron, as she became known, in the late 1920s. Her real name was Evelyn Crookshank. Her husband had died in 1923 by suicide, after his experiences in World War One, leaving her with a daughter, Felicity. She'd have been about two at the time. Suicide was pretty common, unfortunately, for war veterans. At about the same time there was a resurgence in interest in the spirit world and mediums. There's lots of research about it. People speculate that it stemmed from a need to contact their loved ones, and charlatans took advantage of that. It seems Evelyn became interested in spiritualism just after his death, and in a short time became a medium."

Avery leaned forward, fascinated. "Was Evelyn a charlatan?"

"Hard to know for sure. That's partly why we're investigating the house. I think I told you that Rupert and Charlotte are fairly obsessed with this kind of thing, particularly Rupert. Apparently, he's wanted to buy this house for years."

"How do you know?" El asked.

Ben shrugged. "He told us. He develops this fervent glint in his eye when he talks about the house. Makes him look feral."

"Anyway," Dylan continued, "from what I could find out through various sources, she bought the house in 1928. By then she had a reputation, she'd made good money, and she moved in. It's big and imposing, good for impressing people, as you saw. It wasn't called the House of Spirits at the time. She named it later, had renovations done. For years the business did well, up until about 1938, and then something happened." He paused dramatically.

Caspian had been silent for a while, listening intently, almost an outsider in the group, but then he said, "She disappeared."

"Sort of. She retreated into solitude with her daughter. She stopped all her séances, all her private work, and wasn't ever really seen again."

"And her daughter?" Caspian asked.

"She'd have been a teenager by then. But no one saw her much, either. They dismissed the servants, and apart from the daughter who went out for shopping, they pretty much became recluses. They both died in the house—several years apart, of course."

"Wow," Avery said, feeling sorry for them. "Imagine living in a house for so long and never going out!"

Briar looked shocked. "Felicity never moved out? Never got married, never did anything?"

Dylan shook his head, looking as perplexed as Briar. "No. She inherited the house from her mother, who died in 1979, and just stayed there, letting it decay around her."

"She'd have been, what—97, 98 when she died?" Reuben speculated. "Living on her own?"

Cassie stirred from where she'd been listening in the corner of the sofa. "She had a cleaner for the last twenty years or so. She inherited *everything.*"

"But," Dylan said, "she sold the house as soon as she could—to Rupert. It was a very quick sale."

"What was the cleaner's name?" Newton asked, pulling out his notebook.

Ben looked frustrated. "Joan Tiernan. We've tried to contact her, but she hasn't responded to our calls, yet."

"She could know quite a few things about that house," El speculated.

Ben nodded. "That's what we think, too."

"Have Rupert or his wife, Charlotte, spoken to her?" Alex asked.

"It doesn't sound like it," Cassie said. "They only dealt with the estate agent for the sale. They're just focusing on renovating the house, and finding out its secrets."

Briar frowned. "Secrets?"

"Hidden panels, mechanisms, tricks—anything that could indicate Evelyn was a fraud. Or better still, the real deal," Ben explained.

Newton stood and paced the room, looking very policeman-like. "I need to get this straight. Felicity dies, leaves the house to Joan, and she sells it to Rupert, Mr Occult. At what point do they employ you?" he asked Ben, Dylan, and Cassie.

"Right after they start renovating," Ben explained. "We were on the news because of the events at Samhain, and they thought we could investigate the house—even though nothing was really happening, as far as hauntings go. We agreed...the house sounded interesting."

Newtown stopped pacing and stood, deep in thought. "But what links the house to these disappearances and murders?"

Ben gave a wry smile as he looked at Avery. "Witches don't like coincidences. And now there's timing. From what you've just said, the disappearances started at the same time as Felicity died. And then Charlotte told us that she's been experiencing strange dreams about someone standing over her in the night—for a while, by the way—not just the last few nights. She came clean about that today."

"Did you have a chance to examine the footage?" Reuben asked.

Dylan nodded. "Yes, and it's looking really odd. At about two in the morning she gets out of bed and heads to the window, opens it, and returns to bed. Then for a few minutes we lose part of her image as something comes between her and the camera. We can hear a strange breathing noise, and a rasping sound, but we can't see anything on thermal imaging. *Nothing*. And then we see her again. And that's it." He spread his hands wide, perplexed. "We'll keep filming, obviously."

Avery had a horrible thought. "Is she wearing a scarf around her neck?"

Cassie met her eyes, fear lurking behind them. "All the time. Silk ones, of varying designs."

"Holy shit!" Reuben exclaimed, looking at Avery. "We talked about the possibility of that in the car. The vampire has his own blood bank."

Cassie almost shrieked. "And she lets it in?"

"Just like Dracula," El murmured. "He was very persuasive."

"And there's nothing in the rest of the house?" Avery asked.

"No. But we found something else," Ben added.

"What?" Newton asked.

"All that poking about with panels has paid off. Rupert found a panel that opens to a hidden staircase that leads up to the tower room, and there's all sorts of weirdness up there!"

At that point, anyone who wasn't paying full attention was now, edging forward on their seats.

"Go on," Alex prompted.

Dylan elaborated. "Well, from the outside it's a square tower, but inside there are painted wooden panels that make the room circular instead. There are sigils and signs on the floor, too."

Avery shuffled in her chair. "What kind of paintings?"

"Demons, and what look like tarot images," Cassie told her.

"We need to see it," Reuben said immediately.

Ben nodded. "Yes, you do. I'm wondering if the attic is the seat of power in the house, actually."

"Although," Dylan added quickly, "there are no EMF readings up there at all at the moment. We checked it out today."

"That reminds me," Reuben said, reaching into his jeans pocket. "We found this yesterday afternoon." He pulled an envelope out and then from inside that, the yellowed scrap of paper with the signs of the moon on it. "When we were at the house yesterday, we found this under the hearth where the witch-bottle was found."

Caspian took it and examined it, and then passed it to Alex. "I didn't know there was a witch-bottle."

"Ben showed it to me," Avery said, and Ben nodded. "I presumed Evelyn had felt threatened and needed to protect herself from some curse or something. I must admit, I thought it was older, initially—maybe a couple of hundred years, but I must be wrong."

Caspian looked at her speculatively. "Maybe not. The house is old. It could have been there from a long time before. Maybe there's always been something about that house. Maybe something that predates Evelyn. Was there anything unusual about the bottle?"

"Not that I could tell. It contained nails, sharp objects, blood, skin, human nail cuttings—the usual." She turned to Dylan. "Did you film in the tower?"

"No, just ran the EMF metre around it."

Newton huffed impatiently. "Did you test the walls?"

Ben looked disappointed. "We did, but they all sounded the same—hollow. But that's not surprising. There must be a gap between the panels and the walls."

"Maybe they hide a passageway?" El suggested.

Reuben grinned. "You need to get us back in the house."

Thirteen

By unspoken agreement they took a break, some refreshing drinks and topping up on food, while others clustered in small groups to discuss their findings.

Alex was in the kitchen getting another beer, and Avery was bringing more cheese out of the fridge. "Before we do anything," Alex said to her, "we need to do some more homework. I don't think any of us should be blundering into that room without knowing more about that house or vampires."

"Agreed," Caspian said, joining them to refill his red wine. "There's a vampire out there—well, two now, that we know of. I do not want to stumble into their resting place unprepared."

Avery sighed and rolled her shoulders to try and release her tension. "I agree, but we haven't got a lot of time. I mean, the deaths and disappearances have happened so quickly, to wait even a couple of days will inevitably mean someone else will die."

Alex nodded. "Then we divide up, cut the work in half, just like Genevieve suggested to the coven. Come on, let's get this done with." He turned and led them back to the living room.

Newton was partway through a conversation with Reuben and looked agonised. "Well, yes and no. But, that thing has kidnapped someone, for all we know. It could be out again tonight. We have to stop it quickly."

"I agree," Reuben said, leaning against the wall, looking nonchalant despite the risks they faced. "But we need a plan." He called over to Ben, "Did you hear from Jasper today?"

Ben straightened up from where he'd crouched, talking to Briar and El. "Yes, sorry, meant to tell you. He's coming over to our place tomorrow. He and Dylan are going to get geeky over research."

Dylan wagged a finger at him. "That research may just save your miserable ass, my friend!"

Caspian frowned. "Check as far back as you can. If that witch-bottle is old, then maybe something dark has been happening around that house for a long time."

"And what can I do?" Briar asked, looking around the room. "I feel useless at the moment."

"You're far from useless," Newton said, his eyes shadowed. "You weren't useless last night."

"I wasn't the one beheading vampires-to-be. That was Alex."

"And I'll never forget it," Alex said, regretfully. He smiled at Briar. "Don't worry. There'll be plenty to do when the time comes. Ben, when can we get in that house?"

Ben rubbed his forehead. "I don't know. I'm not sure Rupert will want you in there. He was a bit annoyed to find Avery and Reuben there, actually."

"We've glamoured people before," Reuben reminded them. "We glamoured Stan out of White Haven for a few days before Samhain, and I'm sure we can do the same with Rupert."

"No," Newton insisted. "Not a chance."

"Spoilsport," Reuben said, looking annoyed. "You like us breaking the rules if you need us."

Cassie brightened. "I know when! They're away this weekend—don't you remember them saying so, guys? Charlotte told us they have to go to her sister's birthday party. They leave Saturday morning!"

"That's right," Dylan agreed, excited. "They're back on Sunday. They know we'll be in there checking the cameras, so you could come with us. They'd never know."

"Excellent," Reuben said, stretching to his full height and grinning like the Cheshire cat. "We have three days to find out the secrets of that house—well, you do," he said, looking at Dylan. "And we have three days to try to figure out what we're facing, and to track missing, newly-turned vamps, and one lair."

"Or several lairs," Alex reminded him, looking thoughtful. "We could check out likely dark and secure places within a reasonable radius."

"Three days to hone my vampire hunting skills and spells," El said, not looking half as excited as Reuben.

"By the way," Avery said, "Shadow wants to help with this. I haven't given her an answer yet."

Alex shook his head. "I don't want her help. I don't trust her. I don't *know* her!"

"I'll call her," El offered. "My *sister* may be able to help make vampire-killing equipment. That way I can get to know her, and suss out her motives."

"Have we missed anything?" Newton asked, pacing again.

"Yes," Caspian said, as he put his glass down and pulled his coat on. "Get us the autopsy report, and check Rupert and Charlotte's background. I agree with Avery. He sounds dodgy."

Newton rubbed his hands through his hair, and absent-mindedly stroked the scar on his neck as he did so. "Yes, I could see if they have a record of any sort, or check where they came from. It shouldn't be too difficult."

Caspian frowned and paused. "What happened when the people at the morgue discovered the mess this morning?"

Avery had been meaning to ask that all evening, but had become distracted by everything else, and so had the others by the look of their reactions. Everyone focused on Newton.

He exhaled heavily. "There was utter hysteria from a couple of people, a few who thought it was a sick prank, but most were just shocked. We shut the whole place down for the day while we investigated. They'll have to get the roof repaired, and that freezer door, and we've all had to have some horrible conversations with family members. It was like a horror show in there."

"You should have been there last night," Alex said. He'd sat down again and was watching Newton with tired eyes.

Newton nodded. "The morgue has a 24-hour police watch on it now, and will have for the next few days—until we can decide if it might happen again."

"Is anybody linking the deaths with vampires?" Caspian asked.

"Only in a jokey, unbelievable kind of way. No one really thinks there's a vampire on the loose. Although, as you can imagine, there have been a lot of questions as to why someone would behead dead girls and steal a body. And it hasn't gone unnoticed that the freezer door was kicked off from the *inside*."

"And the press?"

"I give it until tomorrow," Newton answered. "That Sarah woman from Cornwall TV will be all over this, I guarantee it."

"No links to us, though, right?" Reuben asked.

"None. And it will stay that way." He looked around at them all, frowning. "I still wish you'd told me what you were planning."

Avery tried to reassure him. "There was no time. And besides, you can't get involved in this. You know the rules. You're a policeman. We're protecting you...your job."

"I know." Newton sighed. He looked across at Ben, Dylan, and Cassie. "Make sure you don't go anywhere alone at night, especially around that house."

Cassie shuddered. "Don't worry, we won't."

"Take some of my protection wreaths with you." Avery walked over to the table where she'd stacked them up. "Hang them on your front and back doors, and don't let anyone in that you don't know."

Alex agreed. "That thing we saw last night looked distinctly inhuman, but it could have a sort of glamour to look human when it wants to."

Briar looked up, her face drawn. She'd been in quiet conversation with El. "What if it tracked us after last night?"

As one, they all looked towards the windows. Avery had drawn her blinds against the night, but they were all aware how cold and dark it was outside, and the night was a vampire's friend.

"You can stay with me again tonight if you want," Caspian said to Briar, pausing by the door.

Ever since Briar and Caspian had teamed up to save El from the curse, they seemed to have reached a new understanding. Briar hadn't hesitated to help Caspian the night before, and he didn't have a problem with her staying at Faversham central. Avery couldn't believe how things had changed since the summer and after Sebastian's death. Apparently, Newton couldn't either, because he released a barely-suppressed huff of annoyance at the suggestion. He needn't have worried, as she declined.

"Thanks, but I need to stay at home tonight. I'll be fine."

"I pity the vampire who tries to attack you," Caspian said, laughing briefly. "I'm going to investigate the area for possible places for them to hide. I'll be in touch." And with that, he left.

Dylan started to get ready to leave, too, addressing his partners. "Come on, guys. I want to go home and try to sleep. I have a feeling that sleep is something I'm going to miss over the coming days."

"I'll be interested to hear what you find out about that old place," Reuben said, reaching for another beer.

Cassie rose to her feet, grabbed her coat, and headed to the door behind Dylan. "Me, too. I'm starting to wonder what we've got ourselves involved in. Thanks for the food, Avery, and good to see you all again. We'll call with updates."

Newton picked his jacket up from the back of a chair, and as he followed the ghost-hunters out the door, he looked back at the witches. "Don't take any chances. And please, try not to behead any dead bodies again."

Avery wondered if she was reading too much into how he looked at Briar, and how she returned his glance, but she decided that whatever was going on between them was none of her business.

Once the witches were alone, Avery started to feel the weight of their situation sink in. It felt huge. A vampire on the loose that was killing and creating new vampires; they could all be at risk.

Reuben had been energetic during the meeting, standing for most of the time and leading much of the discussion, but once everyone had left he sank into a chair, his shoulders bowed.

"Are you all right?" El asked, sitting next to him.

"I'm fine, just daunted at what we're facing."

She squeezed his arm. "It's no worse than what we've faced before, it's just...different."

Briar laughed, dryly. "That's one way of putting it."

Alex and Avery joined them on the sofa, and Avery felt herself relax finally, comfortable with her coven. It had taken her a while to acknowledge the other witches as that, but tonight, finally, she felt they were, and she trusted them with her life. She turned to them, smiling shyly. "I'm glad I got to know you all properly. My life is better because of it."

El grinned. "Thanks, Avery. So is ours."

Reuben snorted. "Snowflake."

"Sod off, Reuben," Avery retorted.

He laughed. "Kidding. So is mine, although it took Gil's death to make me see it."

"You're my family," Briar said, tearing up slightly. "I love you all, and I'm terrified that something will happen to you. This thing has got me genuinely scared. It's like nothing we've ever faced before."

Alex looked at all of them, one by one. "We're not all going to die, you depressing bunch of gits! We're facing a vampire here. We're bigger, badder, and more powerful. And we're going to kick its scrawny, undead ass. We gave it a serious setback last night. Don't underestimate what we did."

Avery looked at him, wishing he were right. "But, Rasmus lost his first wife to one. They were young and powerful, just like us. One of us could die, too!"

"No, we won't. I won't allow it." He looked stubborn and annoyed and Avery loved him all the more for it. "Evelyn and Felicity would have known exactly what was going on. That first attack in 1979 coincided with Evelyn's death. What if Felicity was the one to stop it? You said Rasmus and the others never found the original vamp. Maybe her death has released whatever hold she had on it?" He started to get excited. "They both lived there for years, and although their spirits may not be roaming the house, they must be there *somewhere*. I want to speak to one of them. Whatever secrets that house holds, whatever they know, I aim to find out."

"On Saturday?" Reuben asked.

"Yes. I'll check with Ben first, see which room will give me the best chance, and that will be the room I'll try. In the meantime, I'll have a think about the best way to connect."

Fourteen

A persistent scratching sound woke Avery from a restless sleep. For a few moments she lay quietly, trying to discern what the noise was, and trying to work out the other noise that was competing with the scratching. She realised she could hear her cats growling, their throaty rumbles coming from deep within their chests.

Avery sat up, trying not to disturb Alex, and in the pale light that filtered through her blinds, she saw Medea and Circe sitting up at the end of the bed, staring at the window on the far side of the room. She followed their gaze, mystified. *What were they fixated on? Why were they growling?*

She edged forward to reach the cats, stroking them to try and reassure them, but their fur bristled, and they ignored her, transfixed.

The steady *scratch*, *scratch*, *scratch* perplexed her. There were no trees by the window, nothing natural to scratch in such a persistent manner. She slipped out of bed, heading to the noise, and the cats increased their deep, throaty rumble as if in warning. As she reached towards the window, a shudder ran through her. *Something was on the other side of the window, something strange. Something that shouldn't be there.*

As if she couldn't control her movements, she reached forward and raised the blinds.

A face was pressed against the glass, and fingernails tapped and scraped downwards. Avery faltered and stepped back, almost stumbling, a cry caught in her throat. The figure on the other side of the window was clearly Bethany

Mason. Her long hair floated around her head in a halo, her face was pale, and her dark eyes were fixed upon Avery with a fierce intensity.

This shouldn't be happening. Avery was three floors up, and there was no way to her window other than climbing up a straight wall or by flying. And yet Bethany was there, her fingernails scraping the glass. Avery made the mistake of looking into the dark abyss of her eyes, and she was lost.

She needed to open the window. Bethany was cold. She must come in.

Avery reached forward towards the latch, ready to release it and let her inside. Alex slept next to her, unmoving, his sleep almost unnaturally deep.

With an unearthly howl, Circe leapt towards her, launching on to her arm and sinking her claws deep into her skin, and at the same time, the door to the bedroom flew open, banging against the wall.

Pain cleared Avery's head. She backed away from the catch and clutched her scratched arm, retreating as the reality of the situation dawned. She turned to the door of her bedroom where Helena stood, a spectral wind whirling about her. Her eyes blazed with fury, but she couldn't come in; Avery had cast a spell that banned her from the room. But it wasn't Avery that she was glaring at—it was Bethany.

Avery stepped back again, terror rising. Bethany locked eyes with Helena and for a few seconds neither of them moved, and neither did Avery, frozen with fear. And then Medea howled, spurring Avery into action. She uttered a spell that banished Bethany from the window, causing her to skitter away down the wall like a lizard. Avery ran to the window, watching her leave, her stomach twisting with horror at Bethany's unnatural movements, just like the night before in the morgue. She glanced up once, giving Avery a malicious look that suggested she would be back.

Avery shuddered and turned back to Helena, who watched with her equally dark and hollowed-out gaze. "Thank you."

Helena nodded, her expression softening, and then she vanished.

Medea had returned to the end of the bed, next to Circe, and both watched the window more placidly, their tails swishing across the quilt. Alex was still in a deep and soundless sleep. *How could he have slept through that?* She considered waking him, but in the end, Avery decided that it was pointless. There was nothing he could do now. At least one of them would get some decent rest.

When Alex finally woke the next morning, he was groggy and heavy-headed. "I feel like I have a hangover, and after only a couple of beers, that really seems unlikely."

Avery rolled over to face him, watching as he squinted in the dim light of the room. "I think your groggy head is because you had some weird, vampire mojo on you last night."

"*What?*" he turned to her, frowning. "Are you kidding me?"

"No. I had a visitor, and Helena and the cats saved me." She told him what happened, and Alex's expression changed from confusion, to worry, to complete panic.

"But I didn't hear a thing!" He propped himself up on an elbow and stared at her. "Nothing. I was in a really deep sleep."

"Yep, vampire mojo." She was making light of it, but she wasn't fooling anyone.

Alex pulled her towards him, his arm around her waist. "Are you sure you're all right? You should have woken me."

She reached up and stroked his cheek, feeling his stubble beneath her fingers. "There was no point."

"Yes, there was. That's what I'm here for, to look after you."

"I'm a lucky girl."

"Yes, you are," he said, grinning. And then his smile faded. "But what if Bethany tried the same on Briar or the others? They haven't got a helpful ghost or cats to save them." He sat up and reached for his phone.

Guilt flooded through Avery. "Sorry, I didn't even think of that. The whole thing had me so freaked out." She sat up, too, watching him call, reassured only when they all answered and confirmed they were okay.

"I need to put those bundles of protection around my windows," she said, getting out of bed. "I didn't consider that vampires could scale walls like Spiderman."

"Dracula did," Alex pointed out as he pulled his clothes on. "You must have read it. Poor old Jonathan Harker watched him crawling the walls in the castle."

Avery headed into the bathroom for a shower. "Great. Transylvania has come to White Haven."

Avery was not looking forward to updating Sally and Dan on the latest events, but she had to. Dan had entered the shop that morning reeking of garlic, and wearing another Christmas t-shirt that was painfully unfunny. Sally had arrived with mince pies.

Sally's hand flew to her neck as Avery told her of her encounter the night before. "She was here!"

"I'm afraid so. I don't want to panic either of you, but you need to know to take this seriously. With luck she will only be targeting us, but who knows where the main vampire is, and who he is—rather, *was*." Avery shook her head perplexed. "I never know whether to call them an 'it' or a he or she. They're so inhuman they seem to have lost their gender. Anyway, you need to be careful."

"And that's why I'm already taking steps to protect myself," Dan said, sipping his coffee.

"With garlic, yes, I can tell." Avery wrinkled her nose, keeping her distance. "Did you put the protection bundles up?"

Dan mock-saluted. "Yes ma'am." He looked around the bookstore and dropped his voice. "I even made a stake last night. Just in case. Not that I want you to involve me in any other way."

"Wow! Good to know you're prepared. Which reminds me, I need to prepare some stakes, too. I have the wood. I'll put in a few hours here and then head outside, if that's okay with you?"

"No problem," Sally said. "As far as I'm concerned, that's your number one priority."

Later that morning, Avery headed out to the garden with the harvested wood from Old Haven and a sharp knife, and using a combination of magic and the sharp edge, fashioned several stakes. As she worked, she cast a spell into them, too, something to enhance the accuracy of the user when it came to finding the heart. As she'd found out only too well, the stake was hard to use, and to combine strength with accuracy was difficult. She'd only managed it the other night with the aid of her magic.

She looked around the garden in the bleak winter sunshine and again found it hard to believe that only the night before Bethany had scaled the wall of the building. She looked up to her attic window and shook her head. *Unbelievable.*

And then she thought of something else. *They needed holy water.*

The Church of All Souls was decorated with pine branches, holly, ivy, poinsettia, and candles. Not only did it look pretty, but the pine scented the air and Avery inhaled deeply, enjoying the refreshing smell.

She hadn't bothered going to the vicarage as the church doors were wide open, inviting parishioners in, and quite a few people were sitting quietly in the church, praying or enjoying the colours of the light through the stained glass windows, and the Christmas cheer.

Avery passed them all, heading to the sacristy where James, the vicar, wrote his sermons, hoping he would be there. A new verger had started since Harry's death in the summer, and Avery passed her doing some Christmas preparation by the altar.

The last time she had seen James was at Samhain, when he had taken the press to Old Haven to watch him take down the witch-signs that had been hanging in the trees. The magic they contained had blasted him off the ladder, and he'd broken his arm and suffered a concussion. The cameraman had also been injured, as had the reporter. Avery and Alex had visited James at home and shown him the true nature of their magic. It was an attempt to warn him of the dangers of other witches in the hope that he'd be more careful, but she knew they had scared him, and if anything, the knowledge had made him unsure of Avery. She hadn't seen him since.

The door to the sacristy was open, and James was at the desk under the window, writing. He turned at the sound of her footsteps, but when he saw who it was, an undisguised apprehension filled his eyes. He stood and came to meet her at the door. "Avery. It's been a while. What can I do for you?"

She pondered how to broach this request, and knew he would leap to assumptions, but there was no way to ask this any differently. "It's a strange request, but important. I need some holy water."

He flinched. "Holy water? I presume it's not for a christening?"

Was that an attempt at a joke? Doubtful. "No, not a christening."

"You're not converting to the faith?" His tone was light, but scathing.

"No."

He watched her for a few moments, silent, and she could tell he had a million questions he was trying hard to push to the back of his mind. "Should I know why?"

"Probably not, but I'll tell you if you want."

His eyes dropped to the floor, and when he lifted his face again, his lips were pursed. "I think that if I'm to supply you with my services, then I should know what they are being used for."

"Then I should come into your office and close the door."

His eyes flickered with fear for the briefest of seconds before he backed away, allowing Avery inside. He retreated to his desk, and she shut the door behind her and leaned against it, giving him lots of space.

"Are you sure you want to know?" she insisted.

He folded his arms across his chest, resolute. "Yes. If I'm to protect my flock, I need to know from what. And there's only one thing I know of that can be defeated with holy water."

Here goes. "There's a vampire in Cornwall—well, two now, actually—and potentially there will be more."

His hands flew to his neck, in that unconscious gesture she'd seen a few times now. "Here? In White Haven?"

"Close enough," she said, "and one paid me a visit last night."

"A visit?"

"At my window, on the third floor. Fortunately, I was able to send it away."

He paled. "*Vampires*! And what do you plan to do about them?"

"Kill them, of course. Holy water will be one of our weapons in the fight."

He straightened his shoulders and nodded. "Yes, of course. The church will be a safe haven should any need to come here. It is open to all, regardless of faith."

She smiled, relieved by his support. "Thank you, James, I appreciate it. How does this work?"

"You bring me a large container of water, and I will bless it. Then you can use it as you see fit."

"Thanks. I can get one now, if that's okay?"

He nodded. "Yes, that's fine." He sat in the chair and despite the chill in the stone room that was inadequately heated, a light sweat broke out on his forehead, and he wiped it with the back of his hand. "I never expected to hear that word here, especially in the quiet, small towns of Cornwall. Vampires are more associated with big cities."

Avery's mouth dropped open. "Big cities? Has this happened before in somewhere you know?"

"Reports of suspicious deaths and disappearances are common in towns. Sometimes people choose to disappear into the underbelly of places, some reappear after a while, changed, older, worn out by poverty and crime. Others have no choice, and they are taken by drink, drugs, traffickers—you know." He looked at her, his eyes dark. "But there are those that return in unexpected ways. My colleagues in other parishes report such things, and well," he hesitated, summoning his strength. "They sound suspiciously like vampires. They love the underbelly of cities. The crowded streets, the anonymity. It's hard to track who is where, or what has happened to them."

"Wow. You're actually admitting they exist? I did not expect to hear you say that." She sank into the only other chair in the room, feeling her legs go weak beneath her.

He smiled, breaking the tension in the room. "So, finally I have surprised you."

She laughed, grateful to have him actually talking to her like she wasn't a monster. "Yes, you have. Although, I am pretty disturbed to hear about vampires elsewhere, like it's a normal thing."

"Oh, I wouldn't say normal."

"You must have tips about how we can get rid of them."

"No more than you already know, I'm sure. Holy water, a stake through the heart, beheading, burning. The church and vampires have a long history. They cannot cross consecrated ground."

"But why?" she asked, leaning forward. "I don't understand."

He shrugged. "They are the undead, and as such reject the rules that govern everyone else. Call it God's will, or your elemental magic—the magic of the wind, the rain, the sun. All of it is natural. The undead are not. Maybe that's why holy water and consecrated ground burns them. I'm sorry, it's only conjecture. I believe the real reasons will lie in the mists of time, because they have been around for that long. As have witches, spirits, and other things that exist which are considered abnormal."

"Witchcraft is not abnormal," Avery corrected him. "It's just unconventional. And some of us happen to be more skilled than most." She frowned. "If you were aware of the existence of vampires, why was the existence of witches such a shock to you?"

"I have known that vampires exist for a long time. They are associated with the church, in an unnatural way, but to acknowledge their existence as something other than abstract is something else. It's the same with witches. Of *course* I know about them—Wiccans, that is. But your type of magic, the covens you talk about, seem darker to me, more frightening," he explained. "Even though I know that was not your intent."

"But lots of people call themselves witches now. It's accepted."

"But they're not witches like you are, are they?" he asked gently. He considered her for a moment. "I confess I was wary of you for some time, Avery, especially after Samhain and the strange events there. And of course when you revealed your skills. I've been avoiding you."

"And I, you. But I was trying to protect you from the witch at Old Haven. I needed you to know how dangerous magic can be."

"When wielded by someone with dark intent." He nodded. "I understand. But, seeing you again today, I know that's not you. And I know you protect others like you, which is sensible. I can live with that."

Relief flooded through Avery. She hadn't realised how important it was to hear that from James. He was a good man, and while they had their differences, both had good intentions. "Thank you. I appreciate that."

"Which means," he said, rising to his feet, "that I will help you in any way I can to get rid of the vampires. If you need me to bless a swimming pool, I will."

"Not necessary yet," she said, grinning. "I'll be back with a few litres for now."

Fifteen

Avery lined up several large bottles of holy water in the back room of the shop, and then returned to work to spend the last few hours of the day chatting to Dan and Sally. Dan had changed the music from Michael Bublé's Christmas album to pop Christmas specials, and the 1970s band Slade rang out around the shop.

Stan, the local councillor and pseudo druid was leaning against the counter. He was middle-aged and balding, and took great pleasure in all the town festivals. "Once again, you've outdone yourself." He looked around the shop with pleasure.

"Sally has," Dan corrected him. "This has nothing to do with me."

Sally grinned. "Thanks, Stan. And how are the Yule Parade preparations going?"

On the day of the solstice, a Sunday this year, there would be a Yule Parade through the town, ending at the harbour. Lots of schools and local businesses took part, and everyone dressed up. There'd be a mixture of Christmas and pagan figures in the procession, and all of the costumes were elaborate, some macabre.

"Exhausting," he said, but there was still a twinkle in his eye. "This will be the biggest year yet, and the most visitors to watch, too. White Haven is becoming quite the place to visit! Especially after Samhain."

"How's Becky?" Avery asked, referring to his niece who had been visiting at the time of the last major celebration.

He wagged his hand. "So, so. Not coping well with her parents' separation. She'll probably visit for a few days. Anyway, must press on." He grabbed a mince pie and headed for the door. "One for the road."

They watched him head to the shop next door, and Dan said, "He'll have doubled in size by Christmas day if he has a mince pie in every shop."

Sally smirked as she watched Dan help himself to a chocolate. "Look who's talking."

"But I have youth on my side," he pointed out.

Avery checked that the shop was still quiet, and customers were nowhere close by. "Any idea of suitably dark and secure places that our new friends may like to stay in during the day?" She sipped a strong coffee while perched on a stool behind the counter.

"Tin mines," Sally suggested. "There are plenty of abandoned ones around, and they stretch for miles underground. Didn't you say you found the Nephilim in one?"

Avery nodded. "Yeah, but I don't know which one. However, they would offer a good, safe place, especially as most of them are unsuitable for visitors. I could ask them, hopefully they'd remember."

"I can't see them holing up in the Poldark Mine." Dan was referring to the tourist attraction a few miles away. "But I think your best bet are caves. I'm sure there are some beneath Harecombe and White Haven, leading to the sea. Old smuggling routes that lead out of cellars."

"True. And there might be a passage beneath the House of Spirits. They've found a hidden panel that leads to the tower, and it sounds really odd."

"Wow!" Sally said, looking excited. "So there could be a hidden passage down through the house, behind the walls! That would make sense, if she was a fake."

"You're right. It would explain how she would have performed tricks and illusions!"

Dan reached for a mince pie from the plate on the counter, took a meditative bite, and then said, "But that doesn't make sense. You can't build hidden passages into a house that's already been built. The work would be extensive!

Whatever passages or hidden panels there are would surely have been put in by the person who built the house in the first place."

Avery's excitement completely disappeared. "Damn it, you're right. I didn't think of that."

"If anything, though," Dan continued, "surely that's *more* exciting. It means that house was built for a purpose—not just for a medium who wanted to trick her punters."

"You think the house keeps an older, darker secret?"

He shrugged. "Maybe. Why else build hidden panels and passageways? But, I know nothing. I'm just trying to be logical."

"They found a witch-bottle, is that right?" Sally asked.

Avery nodded. "Yeah, under the hearth, which already suggests something was happening years before Madame Charron."

Sally looked doubtful. "But does it really link the vampire to the house—originally, I mean? I still can't see that they're related."

"But when Evelyn died in 1979, the vampire killings started," Avery explained. "And again when Felicity died. You know I don't do coincidences."

"I'll be interested to see what Dylan and Jasper find out," Dan said, dropping his voice as a couple of customers came in. "Sounds like that place should have been called the House of Secrets, instead."

Avery perched on her usual stool in The Wayward Son, her cheeks glowing after her brisk walk down through White Haven. It was already dark, and the streets glowed beneath the Christmas lights, filled with the hustle and bustle of visitors and locals alike.

Zee greeted her with a glass of mulled wine, and she took the opportunity to ask him about Shadow. He rolled his eyes. "She's nothing but trouble."

Avery laughed. "I get that. What's she done now?"

"What hasn't she done? Gabe watches her like a hawk. He's trying to get her involved in the business, particularly with security for Caspian's business, but she's obsessed with finding a way back to the Summerlands."

"And some of you are still interested in helping her, I suppose."

He raised an eyebrow. "Yes, and Gabe's starting to get interested, too, ever since she pitched it as a side business."

"A side business?"

"Recovery of rare artefacts, for a high price. Let's face it—we have special skills that most don't have. It would help a lot."

"You're starting to sound interested, too, if I'm not mistaken, Zee." She sipped her wine and watched him over the top of her glass. There was energy about him that she hadn't seen before. An air of excitement.

He shrugged. "To be honest, it sounds far more interesting than endless security jobs and bartending forever."

"I don't think anyone expected you to bartend forever. We all know it's a side gig until you all get on your feet. Reappearing after years in the spirit world, a few thousand years after your past life, was never going to be easy." She thought for a moment. "But you're right. This could be a great business for you, if risky. And probably illegal."

He frowned. "Why illegal?"

"Buried treasure or found treasure normally goes to the government or museums, with a finder's fee. If you declare it. I think, anyway. It's not something I know a lot about. There would be a lot of black market interest. But I have a feeling you wouldn't care about breaking the law."

"Maybe not. But it could compromise the security business."

"Well, you'd have to keep them very separate, wouldn't you? And besides, I'm sure there would be times when for a certain customer, those jobs would go hand in hand," Avery suggested.

A speculative gleam entered Zee's eyes, and he looked into the middle distance, transfixed. "You know, this could actually be a good idea."

Avery laughed, nervously. "Oh, dear. What are you going to get up to? It was only a couple of days ago I wondered whether there'd be a black market for magical objects." *Was it really only two days ago? It felt like a lifetime.*

"You want to sell magic?" Zee asked, confused.

"No! Not at all! That would be a terrible idea. I was thinking about how to keep magical objects off the black market, actually!"

Over Zee's broad shoulder, Avery saw Alex emerge from the kitchen behind the bar, and noticing her, he joined them.

He looked between them, frowning. "Why do you two look as if you're up to no good?"

"*Zee's* up to no good," Avery corrected him.

"It was your suggestion," Zee said.

"Oh, no. You're not blaming that on me. It's Shadow's suggestion that I merely speculated on, and you got excited about."

"Now I'm really worried," Alex said.

"No need, boss!" Zee turned and nodded to a woman who was looking at him with a speculative gleam in her eye, and Avery was pretty sure she was thinking about more than her next drink. "I'll let Avery fill you in, while I serve a few customers." He headed to the other side of the bar, leaving them alone.

Avery laughed and filled him in on the conversation. "I wonder what they'll call their new business."

"I'm not sure I want to know," he said, leaning over to kiss her. "How was your day?"

"Interesting! I talked to James today, and he's blessed lots of water for us."

Alex looked surprised. He'd been with Avery when they revealed their powers, and they'd both worried that they had shown him too much. "Really? He talked to you?"

She nodded. "We seem to have come to an understanding. And guess what? He's not shocked that vampires exist—only that one is here in Cornwall. He says his colleagues have long believed they are dwelling in cities. It's easier to hide."

Alex leaned on the shiny wooden counter that ran between them. "Is there no end to the unexpected behaviours of people today? Zee wants to become a treasure hunter, and James knows about vampires. I feel something has shifted in my world."

"I haven't," Avery reassured him. And then she noticed Newton heading through the door, Briar next to him. "But Newton is here with Briar. It *is* a day of surprises!"

They both turned to watch the pair approach, Avery wondering what had brought them here together. She didn't have to wait long. As Briar slid onto a stool next to Avery, Newton leaned on the bar and said, "I collected Briar on the way here, so I wouldn't have to tell you all what I've found several times. A pint of Doom and a chardonnay, please."

"You look pleased with yourself," Alex noted as he poured the drinks.

"And he's keeping quiet about it, too," Briar said, taking her glass from Alex. "We have to wait for El and Reuben."

Avery looked hopeful. "At least give us a clue."

"It's about Rupert, nothing too exciting, but that's all you're getting. Any chance you can put the footie on while we wait?" he said to Alex, nodding to the TV mounted on the wall.

Alex switched the channel over and then headed off to serve some more customers, while Newton sipped his pint and silently watched the highlights of the mid-week matches, refusing to be drawn.

Briar turned to Avery and kept her voice low. "How are you after last night? It sounds terrifying."

"Ah, my vampire visitor." Avery shuddered. "It was, actually. I was mesmerised by her, and I knew it, but all I wanted to do was open the window. I'm lucky the cats and Helena saved me. I've hung my protection bundles outside the windows now. I suggest you do the same."

Briar looked shaken up. "Already done. Another reason for me to get a cat."

"You could always take Caspian up on his offer to stay there again."

Briar shook her head. "No, I'd rather not. He was great, but his sister wasn't, and I'd rather be in my own home, anyway."

Avery whispered back, although she probably didn't need to, Newton was so transfixed by the football. "Maybe Newton could stay with you?"

Briar narrowed her eyes. "No, definitely not. We're friends, and that's the way it's going to stay."

Avery was surprised. "Really?"

"Yes, really."

"You don't look sure," Avery persisted.

Briar appeared suddenly coy. "Hunter has called again. He wants to come down after Christmas. I said sure, why not?"

Avery let out an undignified squeal. "Go, Briar! He's staying at your place?"

"Yes, I have a sofa bed."

"Sofa bed! Yeah, right."

Briar looked prim. "That's all I'm saying. We were talking about vampires."

Avery snorted. "No, no, no! Has he been phoning a lot? He must have. You're a dark horse, Briar."

"Yes, he's phoned, we've chatted, he's coming to visit. That's it! So, vampires. Discuss."

"Don't think this subject is dropped for good. It's merely on a hiatus," Avery warned. "Moving on, you tell me, have you done any vampire-related stuff?

"Not really. I've been busy in the shop. Everything's selling out. Which is great, but keeps me busy restocking. And Eli is side-tracked by Shadow, which means he's not as onto it as he usually is."

"Did Eli tell you why he's distracted by Shadow?"

"He's the strong, silent type, but he did say something about treasure hunting services." Briar looked at Avery, amused. "Do you know more?"

"It seems Shadow's expanding on her idea for searching for something to get her back to the Summerlands, and she's trying to persuade the Nephilim to help. I think it's working."

They chatted quietly for a few more minutes until Reuben and El arrived, striding through the now crowded pub to their side. Alex lifted the hatch that was set into the counter and joined them. "Let's head upstairs, away from prying ears," he suggested, and he led the way up to his flat.

As soon as they were through the door, Briar burst out, "Come on, Newton, don't keep us waiting."

Newton pulled his notebook out of his pocket and flicked through the pages while the others settled themselves. "It seems Rupert has a reputation."

"For raising vampires?" Reuben asked, looking surprised. He'd dropped into the closest chair, his legs hanging over the armrest.

"No, idiot," Newton answered scathingly. "Buying creepy old houses, and doing them up. Houses with their own reputation."

He had everyone's attention now.

"What sort of reputation?" El asked.

Newton referred to his notebook. "Houses that have had people killed in them. Over the last fifteen years he has bought six houses, all of them old, large, and with an unusual history. But, that's it, Nothing has happened, nothing macabre or occult, and no other deaths."

Reuben groaned. "Nothing! Well, that's boring. So, he's just a nutter who likes creepy houses."

The witches glanced at each other, confused, and El asked, "There's nothing to suggest he's on a vampire hunt? That he's raising an undead army?"

"No!" Newton looked annoyed. "I think even the police with no paranormal background would have noticed something like that!"

El glared at him. "No need for sarcasm."

"Now, now," Briar said, trying to smooth troubled waters. "It seems as if he's interested in the occult, just as Ben suggested. Ghosts, poltergeists maybe, vampires, troubled spirits of some kind that may be easy to manipulate. He sounds harmless." She paused for a moment, thinking. "To me, this suggests a man who maybe likes using Ouija boards and trying to summon spirits. Maybe his lack of success was what made him involve the ghost-hunters."

"And if he was hiding something, he wouldn't hire Ben, would he?" Avery asked. "Plenty of people like the occult, there's nothing wrong with that."

El mulled over Avery's suggestion. "He hired them before Charlotte's strange dreams, right?"

"Right."

Alex lay flat on his back on the rug in front of the fire, and stared up at the ceiling. "He's interested in the House of Spirits because of Madame Charron's reputation. But, unbeknownst to him, there's something *else* attached to this house. He thinks it's all about spirits. It's not."

"And now they've discovered the tower room," Reuben said. "I wonder what that hides."

Newton's phone started to ring, and he headed to the kitchen to answer it, his voice low.

Avery watched him for a second, and then said, "I'd love to know if Dylan or Jasper have found out something about that house. I was thinking about hiding places for vampires earlier, and I think they must be hiding in old smuggling caves. There are no mines that are that close to White Haven or Harecombe, but they both have a smuggling history. There's probably a warren of tunnels that everyone's forgotten about."

"Or the sewers," Reuben suggested, wrinkling his nose. "That will be a fun place to hunt them."

"Excellent suggestion," Alex said.

Newton finished his call and stated to pull his heavy wool coat back on. "I have to go. There have been two deaths in Harecombe. A couple found together on a side-street in the middle of town." He looked grim. "Their throats were ripped out."

All five witches sat up, alarmed.

"Ripped out?" Briar asked, eyes wide.

"Yep. This will be a long night." His phone went again, and he picked up. "Newton here... *Another* one? Give me half an hour." He hung up. "And another at the Royal Yacht Club Marina. Those bastard vampires are hunting, right now, in Harecombe."

Reuben jumped to his feet. "Then we'd better come, too. This could be our chance to kill them. And we should tell Caspian."

Sixteen

The centre of Harecombe was busy, with holiday crowds still milling about the streets as Reuben navigated them through the main roads towards The Royal Yacht Club Marina. It was private, and the largest of Harecombe's two marinas, sited on the west of the busy harbour that Kernow Shipping, Caspian's business, overlooked.

Bars and restaurants were busy, and the streets looked bright and festive, but it was hard for Avery to appreciate it as they were discussing strategies, and the most effective spells to use to fight vampires. There was a bag of stakes in the boot of the car, along with bottles of holy water.

Briar sighed. "I don't feel prepared at all."

"Nor me," Avery agreed, "but we have to try. Three people are dead in one night."

"Three people who may become vampires," El pointed out.

Alex turned around to look at them from the front seat. "I doubt it. Their deaths are more violent than the others, their throats ripped out. The others didn't die like that." He shrugged. "I don't know anything about vampire motivations, but the viciousness of their deaths suggests to me that they won't transform."

"I agree," Avery said, meeting his worried gaze.

Briar looked at the crowded streets with sorrow. "Maybe that's one positive thing to take from tonight."

"What did Genevieve say?" Reuben asked, glancing over his shoulder. Avery had phoned her before they left.

"She agreed that they're unlikely to turn from their injuries, but she can't help us tonight. I told her that was okay and that Caspian will help."

For the past few days Avery had kept her up to date with their findings, and Genevieve had been coordinating with the older witches, too. But so far, she hadn't had much to share.

"I'm going to park at the back of the marina," Reuben said as he slowed down to navigate the lights. "This is where Newton said the last body was found."

Newton had left a good half an hour before them, as they had needed to gather equipment.

"I wish the shifters were still here," Alex said, twisting to look out of the window. "If anyone could sniff out a vampire, it would be them. It might give us the upper hand."

Avery glanced at Briar, who returned her glance slightly sheepishly and said to the group, "Hunter is going to come and visit after Christmas, but I could see if he's free before."

El leaned forward to look at her. "Really? That's great! You kept that quiet."

"There's not much to say," she said nonchalantly, but looking pleased.

"Sounds bloody brilliant," Reuben said as he parked. "I like Hunter. If you can ask him to come, why not?"

Briar nodded. "I'll call him tomorrow."

They all exited the car and clustered around the boot, each of them taking a stake, and Reuben pulled out a large water gun loaded with holy water.

El stared in disbelief. "I cannot believe you've got that."

"You'll be glad when it works. I think I should get you all one."

"Give them to the ghost-hunters. I'll stick to my sword, thanks," El answered as she patted the scabbard that hung at her side.

"Good idea," Reuben said, slamming the boot shut. "I spot Caspian, over there on the corner."

Caspian's tall, distinctive profile was highlighted against the streetlights, his shoulders hunched against the cold.

They crossed the road to join him, Avery calling, "Caspian, thanks for helping."

He looked pale. "This is bad news for all of us. Unfortunately, my family is out of town on business, so it's just me."

"Six are better than five," Reuben told him.

"Maybe. But our chances are better in the day. Tonight will be ugly."

"It's already ugly," Briar said, looking at the police cars lined up along the road, their flashing lights garish.

Alex shouldered his backpack. "We should split up. We'll cover more ground that way."

"I'll scope out the marina," Caspian suggested, "or as much of it as I can get to." He pointed to the uniformed officers patrolling the area. "They'll be crawling all over this place for hours."

"Which means the vampires will have moved on. It's too bright and busy here now," Avery put in. "They could be prowling the back streets of the main centre, or they could be in the harbour. There's too much area to cover and not enough of us."

Alex was eager to get moving. "We have to try. Me and Avery will head to the square by the harbour, all the main streets join that, and we'll check out the smaller Clearwater Marina while we're there. Briar, you search this marina with Caspian. El and Reuben can head to the harbour. We'll check in with each other in thirty minutes."

They separated, and Alex and Avery hurried down the dark streets, their stakes hidden in their backpacks. There were less people around once they left the quayside, and they were alert and watchful as they walked.

"This is insane," Avery said. "I don't know what we're thinking."

"We're thinking that we don't want any more people to die," Alex answered.

Avery zipped her jacket closed, and wrapped her scarf tightly around her neck. She had decided to wear her leather jacket rather than her wool coat, but it wasn't really keeping her warm. The night was clear and cold, the stars above bright pin pricks in the sky. She considered using the warming spell she had used before, but the brisk walk soon warmed her.

They entered the square and gasped. The square was surrounded on most sides by large, wooden buildings that contained shops and restaurants, the space in the centre reserved for bands, markets, and other gatherings. Tonight a Christmas Market was in full swing. Lights glowed and customers strolled through the narrow aisles between the stalls. She could hear a brass band playing somewhere, and delicious smells filled the air. Had they not been hunting vampires, Avery would have liked nothing better than to stroll and shop, but Alex pulled her to the edge of the market as if reading her mind. "No time for shopping, Ave. We'll come back next week when we're not in danger of being di nner."

They walked to the less well-lit areas looking for anything unusual, and then on through the square to the streets on the far side where Harecombe Museum sat. It was quieter there, and Avery could hear the sea. They explored around the museum but again saw nothing suspicious, and headed towards Clearwater Marina. The entrance was secure but they passed through it, unlocking the gates easily with magic as they headed to the yachts bobbing on the water. Lights illuminated the area in patchy spots, and for a moment Avery stood silently, watching the shadows, hoping to see or hear something. However, all was still, other than the gentle lapping of the waves against the wall.

Alex waited behind her, staring at the wharf over the water, part of the main harbour. He called softly, and pointed. "Avery. I can see something moving along the quay. Over there."

She ran to his side, and saw he was right. "Are you sure it's not a dog?" The creature looked low down, but they were too far away to see details.

"It's keeping to the shadows around the shipping containers. A dog or a cat wouldn't care. We need to get over there."

"We'd have to walk right around the quay, and by then we might have lost it," Avery pointed out. "There's no direct access from here. But I could fly us there."

"Witch-flight?" Alex asked, glancing at her briefly, unwilling to take his eyes from the creature. "Can you take us both?"

Avery hesitated. She'd been practising a lot, and had no problems on her own now. She travelled without nausea or passing out, and had landed where she wanted to all the time. From here, she could see exactly where she was going, too. *But could she manage Alex?*

"I think I can. We should let the others know what we've seen before we go." She pulled her phone out and called Briar first. "Have you found anything?" she started without preamble.

"Nothing," Briar said. "We've seen Newton, discretely, but there's nothing in this marina now. We had to break in around the back just to make sure."

"Head to the harbour," Avery instructed. "We think we've seen something. We'll liaise when you arrive." She described the spot as best she could, and then phoned El and Reuben, who should already be there.

"That wharf is big," Alex said as she was waiting for El to answer, "and very secure. They might have had trouble getting in." And then he paused, worried. "Shit. I can't see it anymore. I think it's moved further in. We have to go."

Before Avery could respond, El answered, her voice low. "They're here. We can see Bethany. She seems to be stalking a couple of dock workers."

"We're on our way," Avery said, starting to panic. "We'll find you, stay safe."

"Alright we'll—"

El's voice broke off with a muffled cry, and the line went dead.

"Bollocks," Avery said forcefully as she pocketed her phone. "Something's happened. We need to go now. Hold on tight."

Alex looked like he was going to protest, and then he hugged her close, pulling her so that her back rested against his chest as she gazed out across the dock. Avery tried to remain calm. *This will be fine. Absolutely fine.*

There was a rushing sensation as both she and Alex were swept up into a vortex of air. She was aware of his presence next to her, part of her almost, and then it was over and they landed next to a huge container, both falling into a heap as Alex dragged them both down.

Avery struggled out of his grip. "Alex! Are you all right?"

He lay on the floor, white and breathing heavily. "I feel as sick as a dog."

Avery glanced around nervously, aware they should be running to find El, not crouched on the ground, vulnerable to attack. She grabbed Alex's hand. "Can you stand?"

"Give me a minute."

Sweat beaded on his forehead, and she knew exactly how he felt, but when Caspian had transported her before she had felt fine, and so had Briar on Samhain. She must be doing something wrong.

A scream broke the silence, making her skin crawl. "Alex! Get up!"

Alex dragged himself to his feet, and leaning on her arm, they ran as best they could down the dark passages between the stacked containers. Echoes of their footsteps reverberated around them, and when the scream came again, Avery froze at a junction, unsure of which way to go. It was a maze. Another shout resounded to their left, and they ran again, finally stumbling to a halt as they came upon carnage. A man lay on the ground ahead of them in a space formed on three sides by the containers, the fourth by the sea. Blood poured from his neck, and in front of him Bethany snarled, like a cat over its prey. El stood a short distance away, her sword raised and blazing with a fiery white light, while in her left she held a fireball. She hurled it at Bethany, who easily dodged it, leaping out of the way with inhuman speed, before running towards El.

El crouched, ready for the attack.

Alex turned to Avery, his voice low. "Bethany hasn't seen us. Call Briar, and I'll distract her."

Before Avery could protest, Alex sent a force of white-hot energy at Bethany, which slammed into her back and smacked her against the side of one of the containers. Bethany slid onto the ground, dazed.

Avery called Briar, glancing around to make sure another vampire wasn't close by.

Briar answered, "We heard a scream, where are you?"

"Over on the far side of the harbour, behind some containers and next to the sea. I'll send up a witch light. Come as soon as you can."

She hung up and sent half a dozen lights high into the air, not caring who else would see them at this moment. Hopefully the area was poorly staffed, although no doubt that scream would get someone's attention.

Bethany was already rising to her feet, as if smashing into a container was nothing, and she raced at Alex. He and El sent more fireballs towards her, but she rolled with freaky agility, dodging all of them.

From her position in the shadows, Avery saw a coil of rope lying on the pavement. She lifted it with a gust of wind and hurled it at Bethany. The vampire didn't see it coming and it dropped on her, sending her sprawling.

Alex still looked pale, but he pulled a wooden stake out of his pack and ran towards Bethany; she didn't stay down long enough. She threw the rope aside and leapt to her feet again.

Where was Reuben? Avery glanced around anxiously, and saw him crumpled against a wooden crate on the edge of the harbour, a large cut on his head. Just as she was considering how best to reach him, he struggled to his feet, and raised his ridiculous water cannon to his shoulder.

Bethany leapt at El, but she defended herself by slashing the vampire's stomach with her sword. Unfortunately, it was as if Bethany hadn't been stabbed at all. She side-stepped and snarled again. For the first time, Avery could see the vampire's face clearly and her breath caught in her throat. Her skin was white, almost translucent—what she could see of it anyway, beneath the smears of blood over her chin and cheeks. Bethany's eyes were dark pits, devoid of any humanity, and her jaw opened wide to reveal long canines that dripped with bl ood.

Before her courage faltered, Avery sent a blast of wind at the vampire that swept her up and pinned her to the side of the container. She extended her power, closing her hands like a vice, and the vampire struggled to break free. Reuben followed up with a blast of holy water that he enhanced with his magic, the water spreading like a fan. It hit her face and body, steaming and hissing as it bit into her skin. The vampire screamed and writhed, but still couldn't break free of Avery's grip.

Alex hurled the stake, and it arced through the air, his magic holding the aim true, but inches from its target another vampire leapt over the side of the container, moving so fast it was a blur of motion. It snatched the stake out of the air, landing on its feet with unnatural strength and grace. It turned to face the group, grimacing and snarling, its long teeth exposed.

There was a momentary pause in the fight as they all stopped in shock, assessing each other for the briefest of seconds.

It was the vampire from the other night, the older, male vampire. Tonight, the monster more closely resembled a human, dressed in a black shirt, trousers, and a three quarter-length coat. It was old-fashioned clothing, from a century or so ago at least, although the clothes themselves did not seem old or damaged. The vampire's hair was dark, falling over its face, making its pallor more marked. Its skin was stretched across its skull like a cadaver, and its limbs looked equally thin, but with the strength of steel. It stalked up and down in front of Bethany, guarding her, and assessing them.

Avery's hand was still outstretched, pinning Bethany to the container several metres above the ground. The old vampire focused on Avery, and she felt as if its cold, dark eyes penetrated her soul. For a moment, it felt as if time stood still, and then it hurled the stake at her. In order to protect herself, she raised her other hand to knock the stake away with magic, but the distraction was enough for her to lose her hold on Bethany, who dropped to the floor in a panther-like crouch.

Two of them. We can take two, she reassured herself. And then a third vampire entered the fight, slipping out of the shadows like a nightmare incarnate, and Avery's blood ran cold. It was a young man; it must be the man who'd gone missing. *They couldn't cope with three.*

The older vampire smiled at her with a strange, rictus grimace, and then charged across the ground so quickly that she barely had time to respond.

Neither did the other witches, as Bethany raced towards Alex, and the other male vampire charged at Reuben and El.

Avery hardly knew what happened next, other than she saw movement as Briar and Caspian ran around the corner of the farthest container and joined the fight.

Powerful blasts of magic surged across the space as they fought to repel the attack. Avery raised a wall of fire in front of the old vampire who was closing the distance between them, but it passed through unscathed, threw her to the ground, and straddled her with its powerful legs as it pinned her down. It opened its mouth, its teeth bearing down upon her neck. She could smell its foetid breath, foul with the stench of rotting meat and the metallic smell of blood.

No one could help. They were all fighting for their own survival. Avery couldn't throw it off, but she could use witch-flight, and in a flash she vanished, re-appearing on top of the closest container. The vampire squirmed on the ground, bewildered at her disappearance. While it was still confused, Avery pulled the stake from her backpack, smothered the point in fire, and hurled it towards the creature, using her magic to make the blow more powerful. It pierced its back and it screamed with anger, flailing wildly as the stake immobilised its body temporarily. She followed it up with a huge, swirling fireball, and it ignited in flames, screaming with an inhuman howl.

The scene below was chaotic. Bursts of fire and pure energy zigzagged across the space, but as the old vampire howled and burned, the other two vampires immediately disengaged from the fight, their eyes narrowed with hate and confusion, and running to the side of the burning vampire, they all fled down a narrow passageway.

Avery had no urge to follow; she was exhausted and injured. Her chest ached from where the vampire had straddled her, her shoulders felt bruised, and her head throbbed from where it had hit the ground. She looked down on the other witches and saw they were all bleeding and dishevelled, too. The concrete had been torn up by Briar's magic, and ropes, oil drums, and tools were strewn around as if a tornado had hit, water sloshed across the ground from where Reuben had pulled it from the sea, and the sides of the containers were dented where the vampires had hit them.

The dead man still lay in the shadows at the edge of the area, a pool of blood beneath him.

Alex looked around, shouting, "Avery?"

She materialised at his side. "I'm here."

He jumped as he saw her. "I don't think I'll ever get used to that. Are you all right?"

"Bruised and battered, but I'll survive. You?"

Alex's hair was wild and tangled around his face and his pallor had gone, his skin now flushed red with cold and action. "Annoyed as hell, but fine."

Shouts and running footsteps sounded in the distance. "Time to go," Caspian said, running a dirty hand across his face. "We snuck in, and can leave the same way. Follow me." He ran, and the others followed without a backward glance.

Although they used magic to escape, and were deeply cloaked in a shadow spell, it was still a close call. The witches emerged on to the busy road outside the harbour, breathless and nervous. They took a moment to gather themselves, and then slowed to a walk, stakes stashed back in their packs, looking as if they were out for an evening stroll. Police cars were already whizzing past them, the darkness broken with bright blue and red lights.

Avery wanted to go home, but Caspian headed to his business headquarters, calling, "Follow me."

They entered the warm, dark lobby and backed away from the glass doors, watching the scene of chaos outside. While some people seemed oblivious to what was happening, others were running away, looking panic-stricken.

Alex's eyes narrowed. "They probably think there's been a terrorist attack."

"I'm not sure what would be worse," Briar answered.

Caspian turned to them, his shoulders bowed. "There's no point in searching for the vampires. They could be anywhere by now. Besides, they're too strong to tackle at night—by choice, anyway. I just hope they're not searching for us."

"You're closer than we are," El pointed out.

"I'm well protected. Don't worry about me," he reassured them. "I've got tricks up my sleeve and magic traps all over the house." He looked at Avery, his glance too intense to be comfortable. "I feel we were lucky back there. If you hadn't managed to set the oldest one on fire, Avery, I don't think they'd have retreated."

Avery shuddered. "No. It was close to ripping my throat out. Just promise me that we'll stick to hunting them in the day."

"I'll call Jasper tomorrow," he answered. "Let's hope they've found something out about that house."

"Are you coming to the House of Spirits on Saturday?" El asked him.

"Yes. And we better tell Genevieve in case she wants to come."

"I can do that," Avery said, trying to stifle a yawn. "And now I want to go home and sleep for a week. If I ever sleep easily again."

Seventeen

"Please tell me you've found some good news out about that house," Avery said to Dylan.

It was Friday morning, and Avery had risen late, exhausted by the fight the night before, and she hadn't long been in the shop. For the millionth time, she thanked her lucky stars that Sally and Dan were so understanding.

Dylan leaned on the counter of Happenstance Books, his expression both pleased and perplexed. "Sort of."

"What's *sort of* mean?"

"It means," he said, his voice weary, "that weird stuff has been associated with that house for a long time, well before Madame Charron, but there's nothing concrete—although Jasper is looking into another couple of things today."

"Bugger," Avery said, groaning. She sighed, stretched, and winced. "Ouch."

Dylan frowned. "Why are you *ouching*?"

Avery hadn't told him what had happened the night before. She guessed now was as good a time as any. She lowered her voice as she described the battle, and Dylan's eyes opened wider and wider with shock.

"You set it on *fire*?" he hissed. "Did you kill it?"

"I doubt it. It ran off, trailing flames, smoke, and the stench of burnt skin. Although, its breath stank like death, anyway."

Dylan looked around to make sure no one was close by, and then glared at her. "You should have called. We'd have come."

"I know you would have, but it was too dangerous. Only our magic got us through unscathed."

"Not completely, Ms Ouchy. You know we've been training?"

"Yes, Cassie told me."

She assessed Dylan's frame. He was tall and lean, and although he'd always had an edge that Cassie hadn't, he held himself with more conviction now, a threat lurking behind his eyes. She wondered if they all had that, a result of knowing about the paranormal world and the threats they faced.

"And so?" Dylan looked very annoyed, and Avery knew he was desperate to do more than just monitor paranormal activity.

"Dylan! It was very dangerous. They killed four people last night! *Four*! Their throats were ripped out and they were left on the road like litter." Avery started to get angry, and wind whipped up around her, making Dylan step back. She took a deep breath and calmed down. "Sorry. I don't want my friends to die. And besides, you might not have liked what you'd have seen. Bethany was there."

Dylan's shoulders dropped. "She's hunting now?"

"She is a fully fledged vamp, and needs blood to survive. When we found her, she was crouched over her victim."

"Bethany's a killer." Dylan slumped against the counter, his fight gone. "This is horrific. There's no way back for her—er, *it*—is there?" He looked agonised. "Is she a *she* or an *it*?"

"She's whatever you want to call her. And no, there isn't."

They were suddenly interrupted by Dan, who knew Dylan from Penryn University. "What's up, Dylan?"

"Everything," he said, shaking Dan's hand. "Good to see you again. You know all about what's happening, I presume?"

Dan nodded. "Need a drink? It's my lunch soon. We can head to the pub."

Dylan brightened. "Yeah, that sounds good."

Avery smiled. That was just what they both needed. Dan made light of her magic, but she knew that underneath it all he must be worried by the supernatural weirdness that was going on. He and Dylan could support each other.

"Boss?" Dan said, raising an eyebrow at Avery. "Now okay?"

"'Course it is. Take your time. And Dylan, we might be meeting tonight. I'm waiting to hear from Genevieve."

"I'll hang around, then, and let Cassie and Ben know."

Avery watched them leave, wondering how she could advance their investigation and protect her friends. Her gaze drifted to the shelf under the counter where she'd stacked a few books in case she had a spare moment. She pulled out one called, *Cornish Smugglers: Truth is Stranger than Fiction*, and settled down to read, disturbed only by the occasional customer.

When she finally looked outside again, she was shocked to find snow was falling. No wonder it felt cold, and no wonder the shop was so quiet. Dan hurried past the window alone, and burst through the door, shivering. "God's bollocks, it's freezing out there."

"No Dylan?" Avery asked.

"Nah, he's gone to my place, actually. He's a bit upset about Bethany." Dan looked worried. "I've never seen him like this before."

"He's never had a mate's cousin become a vampire before," Avery pointed out with a sigh. She placed her book back beneath the counter, thinking she was no further forward than she'd been hours earlier. "I'm heading for lunch, and I'll be back soon."

During her break, Avery received two calls. The first one was from Briar, her voice heavy with tiredness. "You sound as shattered as I feel," Avery said, putting the call on speaker as she pottered in her kitchen and made lunch.

"I dreamt of vampires last night," she answered. "And every time I heard the slightest noise I woke up, convinced a vampire was at my window. I got up at five. It was pointless trying to sleep."

"You should have stayed at Reuben's." Reuben had almost begged Briar to stay at his place with him and El, but she'd refused.

"I like my own bed, as lovely as Reuben's place is. And it's handy for work." Briar lived within walking distance of her shop, in a lovely old cottage full of vintage charm. She hesitated for a moment. "And Newton called just after I got home."

Avery fell silent for a moment. "Just a call?"

"He dropped by at about half past two."

"In the *morning*? So it wasn't just vampire dreams that kept you awake. How was he?"

"Shattered. Four deaths in one night. Everyone is depressed and frightened. And he's angry. We need to stop this, Avery."

"I know," she said, feeling the weight of responsibility settle even more heavily on her shoulders. "Did he stay?"

"No. He was just checking that I was okay."

Avery could hear the tightness in Briar's voice, and was that regret she could hear? She softened her tone. "What's going on with you two?"

"Nothing. *Absolutely* nothing."

"That's not true. He wouldn't be around if he didn't care about you," Avery remonstrated.

"He's conflicted."

"Hunter isn't."

She started to protest. "Avery—"

Avery cut her off, very frustrated. She took it out on her toasted sandwich, slicing it in half with a vicious cut. "You know I'm right. You could be waiting forever, and as much as I like Newton, that's exactly where he wants you—waiting and hoping while he works his shit out. Hunter is a threat, and Newton's trying to buy himself time. Don't let him." Briar was silent, so Avery continued. "You know I'm right."

Briar groaned. "I know."

"And as much as Hunter is a cocky Alpha, literally, he likes you—*really* likes you! Prepared to drive seven hours to see you-likes you. What does that say to you, Briar?"

"I know," she repeated softly. "And I like him, too. But Newton's stuck in my head, and I'm so annoyed with myself, because I know that what you've just said is right. *I know it.*" Her voice rose with frustration. "I'm an idiot. A hot, male shifter wants me, and what am I doing? Pining after someone who can't move past the fact that I'm a witch. And I want what you have with Alex, and what El has with Reuben. I want someone to be there for me. To hold me when horrible things are happening, and to laugh with me when things are great."

Avery could have whooped with joy. Finally, Briar was opening up. "Yes, girlfriend! What are you going to do about it?"

"I don't know."

"Liar. What are you going to do?"

"Call Hunter?" she asked tentatively.

"With conviction, please."

Briar's voice got stronger. "I'm going to call Hunter and ask him if he wants to visit earlier, maybe stay over Christmas."

"Yes!" Avery shouted, startling Circe, who was cleaning herself with great thoroughness on the floor. "He'll be down by tomorrow."

"Don't be ridiculous. It's almost one already."

"Next round's on you if I'm right—which I am. You *will* owe me a drink."

"He might say no."

Avery snorted. "Bollocks he will. He'll break land-speed records to get here."

"He might. He does call a lot." Avery could hear a smile creep into Briar's voice.

"Oh, you are so going to get lucky this Christmas."

"Avery!"

"Once we get rid of the vampires, of course."

"You know, I didn't actually ring to talk about this at all," Briar said.

"You so did. But what else is on your mind?"

"Have you heard from Genevieve? I wondered if we might be meeting with the coven tonight?"

"No, not yet, but I'll let you know. If anything it would make more sense to meet tomorrow, when we're at the house."

"Good point. All right, I'll leave you to it. Speak soon."

"And ring Hunter now!" Avery shouted quickly before Briar hung up. Then she'd gone, leaving Avery hopping with excitement about Briar's love life.

She immediately rang Alex, and he answered quickly, the noise of the pub in the background. "Hi, gorgeous. Are you okay?"

"I just wanted to hear your voice, and tell you I love you."

His voice was warm and velvety, even down the phone. "I love you, too. What's brought this on?"

"I'm lucky, that's all. I wanted you to know."

"You are lucky, I am awesome," he teased. "But what else?"

"Briar's inviting Hunter down today."

He laughed. "I knew it, you gossip. Good for Briar. Any news from Gen?"

"Not yet."

"Okay. I better go—it's insane here. See you tonight at yours?"

"Please."

He rang off, and within seconds, Genevieve phoned.

"You've been busy," she said brusquely. "I've been trying to get through for the last ten minutes."

"Just chatting to Briar," she explained, trying not to be annoyed. She did have a life outside of vampires.

"Jasper has some more leads to chase up, so he wants to see us tomorrow. I told him to meet us at the House of Spirits. Ten o'clock okay? Ben assures me that Rupert and Charlotte will have left by then."

"Sure," Avery said, pleased that her Friday night would be uninterrupted.

"Fine. Tomorrow then," Genevieve answered, and hung up.

Before Avery did anything else, she texted Dylan in case he wanted to leave Dan's place and go home, and told him they'd meet tomorrow instead, and then she turned the TV on, watching it absently as she finished her sandwich that was almost cold. The news was on, and it was filled with reports on the four brutal murders. Sarah Rutherford, the news reporter who had been in White Haven over Samhain, was on the broadcast, managing to look simultaneously Christmassy and grim all at the same time. She wore a bright red coat and deep red lipstick that highlighted her blonde hair and pale skin, and she stood on the main street in Harecombe, with shoppers hurrying past her. She talked with sorrow about the deaths and how the police had no leads, but she also speculated that the attacks looked as if they were caused by an animal, and said there would be a press conference later.

Avery turned the TV off. Although the news had depressed her, it also spurred her on. She had research to do.

By late afternoon, Avery had read everything she could about smuggling on the Cornish south coast.

She knew the names of the pubs that were known to store smuggled brandy and gin, as well as silk, muslin, china, and tea. Some of those pubs in Harecombe still existed now. The ships that anchored off the coast usually came in carrying coal, with casks of brandy and gin hidden in the hold. There was no mention of hidden passages, though. Maybe they should try to investigate some of those pubs after they'd been to the House of Spirits the next day. Or maybe try to access the sewers. The vampires could be sheltering down there. *In fact*, she mused, *there was a strong possibility the passages and the sewers now intersected.*

Avery thought back to the summer when they were still searching for their missing grimoires. Gil and Reuben had found a smugglers' passage beneath their glasshouse and had hoped their grimoire was hidden there. The passage had led to caves and then out to Gull Island off White Haven coast; it was the cave that

Gil had died in, when they were attacked by Caspian. The fight had eventually led to Faversham Central, their nickname for Sebastian's house, where Helena had killed Sebastian and they had reclaimed Reuben's grimoire.

After all of that, they were almost friends with Caspian now. He had saved El from Suzanna's curse and taught Avery how to use witch flight, and offered Briar shelter at his house. She wasn't sure if she should feel regret for all of their actions, or ashamed for making a truce, or whether it was a good thing they were now working together. And Caspian had made a pass at her, but that was something she wasn't going to think about, *at all.*

The sounds of jazz lulled her thoughts, and she drifted over to the window of the shop to look at the street. It was almost dark, and the snow had stopped, leaving a light covering over the road and footpath that reflected the Christmas lights. The shop was quiet, and she'd sent Sally and Dan home for the day. She should be looking forward to Christmas, but all she could think about was vampires, necromancers, and mediums.

Avery sat behind the counter again and opened another book, wondering if it was too early to close the shop up, when the door chimes jingled. She looked up in surprise, and then felt a stone settle in her stomach. It was Rupert from the House of Spirits. He wore a short jacket over a jumper and dark jeans, and his shaved head was bare. In the light she could see faint pock marks on his skin, old acne scars.

Avery forced a smile. "Hi, Rupert. What a surprise to see you here!"

For a moment he didn't answer, instead pausing at the entrance of the shop to glance around, his hooded eyes taking everything in. It was a cool gaze that assessed and judged, and Avery became acutely aware that they were alone.

He turned to her finally, and headed to the counter. "Avery, isn't it? Good to see you again. Where is everyone? Your customers, I mean."

"I think the snow has kept them home, but my shop assistant's out back, cataloguing books," she said, lying. "I'm surprised you're here." She glanced at the windows and the snow beyond.

"Oh, the main roads are not too bad," he said, fixing her with an uncomfortable stare. "Besides, I really wanted to see you today. I went to see Jean, who sold us the house. She tells me she sold the books from my house to your shop. I'd like them back, please."

Avery was completely flummoxed. She'd been meaning to ask Sally all week about the book with the witch-mark in it, and where it had come from, but with everything that had happened, she'd completely forgotten. In fact, she'd even forgotten to examine the book again.

"I'm sorry, Rupert. I have no idea which books are yours. From what I understand, you said they were sold months ago. I'd have to ask Sally, my manager. And besides, we bought them in good faith."

"I'll rephrase it," he said, still pinning her under his gaze. "I'll buy them off you."

"But as I said, I don't know which ones are yours. I'll have to check with my manager, and she's not here right now."

"I thought you said she's out the back?" He glanced across the room toward the door to the back room, as if he might march over and find out for himself.

"I said my assistant was in the back room, not Sally."

"Can you call her?" He stood immobile and implacable, and it infuriated Avery.

Who the hell did he think he was?

"No, I'm afraid not. She's finished for the day." Avery refused to be intimidated. "And besides, we buy lots of books. She might remember the purchase, but she won't remember the inventory. Fortunately, she keeps excellent records, and we can check them tomorrow. But of course, it's likely we'll have sold some."

He narrowed his eyes, annoyed. "Do you keep records of who would have bought my books?"

"No, there's no reason to." *And they're not your books. In fact, for all she knew, the book with the witch-mark wasn't from his collection.*

He leaned over the counter, intruding on her personal space, and watched her silently for another moment. Avery stared right back. If he took one more step, he'd find himself the victim of a very unpleasant hex.

As if he'd sensed her annoyance, he stepped back and looked around once more. "This is an occult shop."

"Sort of," she admitted. "We're a book shop that sells some occult things, but we have a wide range of all kinds of books."

He swept his hand up and around. "But the incense, tarot cards, divinatory equipment, and witchcraft items all suggest the occult. Not common objects for a book shop."

"I'm not a common book shop owner."

"No, you're not." He frowned. "Remind me why Ben wanted you to see my house again? And that big blond man you arrived with? Reuben, was it?"

Shit. What had Ben said she was? A consultant, that was it.

"I have an interest in the occult, as you've noticed." She gestured around vaguely. "Ben knows this. He, Cassie, and Dylan often visit, and Ben wanted my opinion on the witch-bottle found under the hearth. I suggested a site visit might be useful." She smiled, trying to be as charming as possible. "Thank you for agreeing."

"And what did you think of my house?"

"It's fascinating. I think its name references its history. What do you think?"

His lips were tight with annoyance. "It's the most likely explanation, I agree. But the spirits of the house are keeping their secrets very close."

What a strange admission. "Do you speak to spirits? Are you a medium?"

He blinked as if he'd said too much. "No, not really. I meant as in, I can't find out much about Madame Charron and whether she was real or a fake."

"But you employed Ben. What are you hoping he will find?"

"Something that proves Madame Charron was authentic." He looked excited, fervent almost. "I'm so tired of fakes, and now with Charlotte experiencing strange dreams, we hoped it might indicate something was awakening... That she might be there in the house, waiting to speak to us. But so far, things are proving elusive."

Avery persisted. "And is that good or bad? Most people don't want ghosts in their house."

He smiled, but it didn't reach his eyes. "I like old houses because of their ghosts, so no, it doesn't bother me. Anyway, I must go. My wife will be waiting for me. Please speak to your manager and let me know how much you want for those books. It's very important. I suspect there may be personal items in those books that could be relevant to my research." He held out a business card. "Call me as soon as you can."

Avery went to take the card from his hand, but his hand closed over hers with a vice-like grip. "Don't let me down, Avery."

She resisted the urge to blast him through the window, and instead settled for a mild magical current that made him release her hand immediately. His eyes opened wide with shock.

"Must be static electricity," Avery explained blandly. "I'll be in touch."

He narrowed his eyes at her and then turned and left the shop, leaving the bells jingling in his wake. *Wanker.*

Avery hurried to the door and locked it. She checked that the bundle of herbs and wood above it was intact, and uttered another protection spell on top, and then she lit a sage bundle and walked around her shop, cleansing it of Rupert's very negative energies. Meeting him again confirmed her earlier suspicions. He was odd—dangerous, even. She could sense it. Was he a necromancer? Necromancers raised spirits with the intention of controlling them. Surely he would have been able to raise the spirits in the house easily if that were so. Maybe there was another level of protection on the house that was stopping that. And how did this connect to vampires? Were they wrong? Were the house and the arrival of the vampires completely unconnected? She needed to speak to Sally.

Sally answered the phone after half a dozen rings. She could barely hear her above the shrieks in the background. Sally's kids were either in deep distress or having the best fun ever, and she couldn't quite work out which. "Is everything all right, Sally?"

"Oh, God. It's mayhem here. The kids are so excited. I wish I'd stayed at work. Are you okay?"

"Yeah, fine. Look, I have a quick question. You bought some books from a house sale a few weeks back, a house in West Haven. It turns out they're from the House of Spirits, the one Ben is investigating. Do you remember what books we bought?"

The sound dulled as Sally obviously moved rooms. "I do vaguely remember, but check the online inventory for August, maybe September. I'd have noted it there. I don't think there was anything that I thought you'd be particularly interested in. You know I flag them for you if I do."

"Thanks, Sally, you're a star. Remind me what file the inventory's in again?"

As Sally talked her through the electronic filing system, Avery headed to the back room and sat at the computer. When she found it she rang off, leaving Sally to her chaotic household, and then started to scroll through the list. Sally had grouped the books together under general fiction, and then detective novels, thrillers, and romance. *A lot of romance.* Avery presumed that Felicity had developed prolific reading habits after living alone for years. Sally didn't name the titles for these, just added the numbers. After these were the arcane and occult books, of which there were about a dozen in total. Sally did add the titles and authors for these, because they were of interest to Avery. She recognised a couple, especially *Mysteries of the Occult*, the book with the witch-mark on it; the book that was now in her flat. She printed the list off and headed back to the shelves in the shop. It was fully dark outside now, and the only light in the shop came from the coloured Christmas lights that were strung up around the shelves. Of the books they had purchased, only four were left, five including the one upstairs. *The others must have been sold*, Avery thought.

There were three books on witchcraft, one on runes, and another on divination. The missing books were of a similar mixture. Avery decided to pull all of the ones she still had and take them up to her flat. Alex was coming around later, but not for hours. That would allow her time to research.

Once she'd fed the cats, turned the lights on, and made the place cosy, she spread the books out on her attic table and threw a couple of witch lights above her, and then started to methodically examine them.

An hour later, she'd still only found one witch-mark, the original one on the first book. The witchcraft books contained simple spells, nothing that you couldn't find in many books on the craft, or at least variations on themes. The book on runes was more interesting. There were notes along some of the pages in scrawling script, and the pages about runic divination were heavily marked, which was curious.

She was so absorbed that when her phone rang in the silent flat, all outside noise muted by the snow, she jumped, startling the cats who slept beside her. It was Sally.

"I've just remembered something," she started breathlessly. The noise behind her was still deafening. "I found a book that wasn't a book in that collection."

"What? I don't know what you mean." Avery said, puzzled.

"You know, a fake book. The spine looks like a book, the cover looks like one, but actually, it's a box. I found it and put it aside for you."

Avery's heart started to race with excitement. "Where?"

"I'm not sure. I think it was under the kitchen cabinet with the biscuits. I wanted to make sure it didn't get mixed up with the other books and I think you were busy hunting Mermaids at the time. I'm really sorry."

"No, it's fine," Avery said, getting ready for witch-flight. "Was there anything in it?"

"A little pouch of something. I didn't look. I left it for you."

"Great, thanks, see you tomorrow." Avery hurriedly ended the call, and within seconds she was down in the kitchen. She ferreted in the kitchen cupboard, pulling biscuits and teabags out of the way, and then she saw it. *A book that was a box.*

At the same time that she pulled it free, her protection spell on the building started to toll like a bell, and a deep reverberation ran through Avery's body. Someone had triggered her protection spell.

Within seconds, she threw the book back under the cupboard. Now she could concentrate.

She pushed out her magical awareness, trying to feel where the threat was coming from. If it was the windows, it could be a vampire, but immediately she found it. Someone was trying to get in through the back door.

Avery knew her protection spells by heart, and as the reverberation grew stronger, she added to the strength of her spell, uttering the words with power and conviction.

She hadn't got time to be afraid. Instead, she was furious.

She turned the lights off with another whispered spell, plunging her flat and shop into darkness, and simultaneously cast a shadow spell and cloaked herself. She opened the door to the small hall that led to the rear entrance. The external door had small panes of milky white glass in the top half, but nothing was discernible through them at all as it was pitch black outside, and her security light hadn't come on.

She stood still, listening intently. The door handle rattled slightly, and she smiled. She ran back into the kitchen and grabbed a handful of chamomile teabags. They weren't as effective as the bundle of chamomile in her attic, but they would do. She ripped them open and threw them in the air, whispering a spell that sent the chamomile spinning in a gentle vortex towards the door. Avery whispered the final incantation meant to lull and confuse, and the chamomile vanished through the door to the other side. There was a muted cry outside and the handle stopped moving, and then she heard footsteps retreating down the alley behind her house.

She raced through the shop to the front window, hoping to see someone emerge onto the street, but it was snowing heavily again, blurring everything into swirls of white and muting all sound. With a sinking heart she realised she had no idea who her attacker was, but she strongly suspected it was Rupert.

He was annoyingly persistent, and clearly naïve as to her powers, but was he a threat?

Only time would tell.

Eighteen

Avery spelled the Christmas lights back on, and walked back to the small kitchen to retrieve the box disguised as a book.

She checked to make sure everything was locked and her wards were in place and then headed upstairs. She walked instead of using witch-flight, needing the security of seeing her home intact rather than heading straight to the attic. The Christmas tree glowed with light in the corner of the living room, and her jumble of scarves, throws, cushions, and books made the place look warm and chaotic, but nothing seemed out of place. Reassured, she carried on to the attic, stoked the fire, and placed the box on the worn wooden table.

It was quite obvious that it was a box, but if she'd looked at the spine in the midst of a row of books, it wouldn't have stood out at all. The title was the *Esoteric Mysteries of Divination*, and the box was made of wood covered in thick paper, but when Avery lifted the lid, she found the interior was lined with black velvet. A cloth of soft white linen was folded at the bottom, and a pouch of black silk lay in the centre. She held her hand over the box, feeling for any magic, but instead she felt a presence. It was faint, but it was there.

She picked up the pouch and pulled out an old, well-used pack of tarot cards, and then unfolded the square of white linen, thinking that it would likely be for reading the cards on. *These must have belonged to Madame Charron.*

Just as she was wondering why they were in a box disguised as a book, she heard the door open below as Alex arrived. He shouted hello, and within a minute arrived in the attic, covered in a fine sprinkling of snow. He stood behind her, wrapped his arms about her waist, and nuzzled into her neck. "You smell delicious."

She leaned into him. "Thank you. You smell of snow."

"That's because it's snowing, smarty pants." He dropped his head on her shoulder. "What have you got there?"

"Tarot cards."

He laughed. "Er, yes, I can see that. Where did you get them from?" He released her and picked up one of the cards. "These are nice. Unusual. And I feel a little bit of magic in them."

"Me, too, although I thought it was more of a presence than magic."

Alex placed the cards down, and slipped his jacket off. His cheeks were flushed from the cold, and he headed to the fire to warm his hands. "Where did you find them?"

"It's a long story." She told him about how Rupert had visited, prompting her to call Sally.

Alex's hair was pulled back into a half-ponytail, but he released it and ran his hands through it. "So, they're from the House of Spirits?"

"Yes. They must be Madame Charron's. But I can't decide why they were tucked away in this box."

"Maybe for safety," he suggested.

Avery looked at them, frowning. "This case just gets weirder and weirder."

"Case? You sound like a detective," he said, laughing. "Do you think Rupert knows these exist?"

"I doubt it, but even if he did, how would they help him? And what the hell have these got to do with vampires?"

"God damn blood sucking vampires," he exclaimed, quoting the 1980s film, *Lost Boys*. "I must admit, I've never worried about walking through White Haven before, but I did tonight. Every sound made me think one was behind me. I hate feeling like that. Your protection charms feel stronger tonight. Is it because of the vamps?"

"No." Avery didn't really want to tell him about the attack, she knew he'd worry, but equally, she couldn't lie. "I think Rupert hung around and tried to break into the shop when it was closed."

"What?" He'd been absently gazing into the fire, but now his head whipped around to look at her. "Why didn't you phone?"

"There was no time. Besides, I dealt with it."

She described what had happened, and suddenly felt vulnerable all over again. She'd never felt scared in her home before, but recent events had changed that. She felt a rush of gratitude that Alex was here. He was solid, reassuring, and as a bonus, a very sexy presence. He was watching her, his hands on his head, which lifted his t-shirt, revealing a sliver of toned stomach, and her own stomach flipped in response.

"In the future, call me. I don't care how busy the pub is, you're more important."

"Thank you," she said softly.

He crossed the room swiftly, pulling her close. "I mean it." He kissed her, and warmth and desire flooded through her until he grabbed her hand and pulled her to the bedroom. "The cards can wait."

A long time later, and after food, Alex and Avery returned to the deck of cards.

"They're just a regular pack," Alex said, examining them and the white linen cloth. "Maybe they weren't hidden, and were just put on the bookshelf for safekeeping."

"Maybe. I think this is a dead end." Avery picked up the book with the witch-mark. "I've double-checked this. There are no other marks in it, or the other books. There's nothing special about them at all."

"Have you checked the box under a witch light?"

Avery looked at him, eyes wide. "No."

He threw a light up above them and turned the lamps off. Within seconds, a series of runes appeared on the inside of the box. "Abracadabra! It's a message."

"Bollocks! Why didn't I think of that?"

He smirked. "Because I'm awesome." He picked up the box, squinting at the rune script. "You got a rune book handy?"

Avery had already opened the book of runes from the House of Spirits. "*Voila!* And a pen and paper."

For the next few minutes they worked through the runes, translating each one for a letter until they had deciphered everything.

The centre of the mysteries is beneath the full moon.

"Well, that's interesting," Alex said. "What the hell's it mean?"

Avery grabbed the pack and shuffled through it impatiently. "Maybe it's the Major Arcana card!" She found the card called The Moon and examined it under the witch light, but there was nothing on it. "Damn it. Why would she leave some random message written in runes in a box?" She looked at the books on the table. "The marked book is called *The Mysteries of the Occult.*" She picked it up again, quoting the line. "'The centre of the mysteries is beneath—'"

She broke off and flicked through the book until she reached the centre.

"And?" Alex asked, leaning over her shoulder.

"The middle of this book falls in the middle of a chapter about demonology, and using demons as spirit guides."

"Really?" he said, tickling her ear with his breath. "Using a demon as a spirit guide sounds very risky."

"And it would take a lot of power," Avery said, lifting the book to eye level. "There's only one name on this page—Verrine." Avery twisted in Alex's arms, turning to look at him. "Okay, this is what I think this means. Madame Charron may have been running scams for ordinary people, but I think she also had a gift. She really could summons spirits, and liked to experiment with using spirit guides. I think at one point, and maybe lots of times, who knows, she used this demon as a guide. Maybe she delved too deep and found something she didn't want to? Maybe that's why she had to stop her business. Perhaps she woke a v ampire?"

Alex frowned as he thought. "It sounds crazy. Do vampires even have spirits to wake?"

She shrugged. "I don't know. But if you're roaming the spirit world, talking with demons, you're risking all sorts. Demons are there to tempt and trick."

"You're presuming it was an accident. She might have done it deliberately. She could be evil to the core."

"But why retire and lock yourself away? Perhaps she had to control whatever she'd unleashed. Maybe it scared her so much that she could never be a medium again, real or fake."

"Hopefully we'll find something out tomorrow."

The next morning, the journey to West Haven was slow. The roads were covered in snow, and although the main streets had been cleared and gritted, the smaller side roads were less accessible. Alex and Avery had opted to travel together in Alex's Alfa Romeo Spider, because Briar informed her that Hunter had arrived that morning, and Reuben and El were picking them up.

"I knew he'd come," Avery said, excited. "Apparently, he arrived at about ten last night, after an epic trip on icy roads. That's dedication."

Alex grinned at her before turning his attention back to the road. "You're such a matchmaker."

"I want Briar to be happy, and I think Hunter will do that. Newton will certainly not. And Caspian just texted. He'll meet us at the House of Spirits, too."

"Full house, then. Let's hope Rupert really has gone away for the day, or this will be one big, fat waste of a trip."

Alex and Avery arrived at the same time as Eve, and she greeted them with a grimace. Her long, dark dreads were wrapped up under a thick wool scarf, and her eclectic clothes were bright against the snow. "I wish I was seeing you guys under better circumstances."

"Me, too," Avery said, hugging her. "No Nate?"

"Not today, but he'll help when needed."

Ben ushered them inside, and the smell of coffee hit them like a wall. "Hey, guys. We're in the séance room," he said, after greeting them. "Come on up. We've got plenty of coffee."

"They've definitely left, then?" Alex asked, shaking snow from his boots.

"Bright and early!"

Avery looked around, admiring the high ceilings edged with elaborate cornices, and the decorative architraves around the doors and windows. She watched Alex as he closed his eyes and concentrated. She knew he was feeling for any signs of spirits, or a presence of any sort, but he took only a moment before following Ben up the stairs.

With everyone seated around the table, it looked as if they were about to have a real séance. Alex and Avery were the last to arrive, and they acknowledged the others with a brief nod. Avery could feel Hunter's Alpha male presence resonating across the room. He wore his black leather jacket and dark jeans, and radiated testosterone.

Hunter sat next to Briar, and he could barely keep his eyes off her, although he did meet Avery's gaze and grinned, a flash of victory lurking behind it. Briar looked flushed and slightly furtive. Avery glanced at El, who raised her eyebrow speculatively, and Avery tried hard to subdue a smile. Looking around the room, Avery saw that only Jasper, Eve, and Caspian were there from the other covens.

Genevieve, also present, caught her questioning glance. "I told Rasmus, Oswald, and Claudia that they didn't need to come today. I'll update them later." She turned to Jasper. "Do you want to start?"

Jasper cleared his voice with a cough. "It was difficult to find out some of the more colourful history of the House of Spirits until I resorted to magic."

"You make it sound like that's a bad thing," Caspian noted curiously.

"No, not at all." Jasper shook his head, and pulled his notebook onto his lap. "It just meant I had to use subterfuge and engage in a rather risky break-in to the council buildings."

"Good work," Reuben said. He leaned back in his chair, his long legs stretched out in front of him. "Didn't think you were the breaking and entering type, Jasper."

Jasper shuffled uncomfortably. "I'm not, but it was important. I needed to find out who had owned that house before, and they're not public records." He gestured to Dylan. "We've both been busy. Tell them what you've found, first."

Dylan flipped open a small notebook, too. "The house was built in 1810 and was originally a large private house with extensive gardens that took up most of the existing street. The family must have been pretty wealthy, but a chunk of the grounds were sold off in 1854, and that's when some houses were built along the street. Fifteen years later more land was sold, and more houses were built. By the time the First World War rolled around, the house belonged to another family, and the road appeared much as it looks today." He paused and looked up. "Before the land was divided up in 1854, there were a couple of deaths in the area. Two female bodies were found close to the grounds. There were also a number of disappearances, men and women, whose bodies were never found."

Caspian edged forward on his seat. "When they built on the grounds, did they ever find any remains?"

"No. But," Dylan pointed out, "it's remote, and the land is surrounded by trees and fields. There was a lot of speculation in the press, but they never found out who did it."

"What years were the deaths and the disappearances?" El asked.

Dylan consulted his notebook again. "On and off over forty years, between 1820 and 1860, approximately."

A collective murmur ran around the room. Avery was astonished. "That long!"

"I know. And this isn't something *I* discovered," Dylan said. "I found this out from a book on unexplained Cornish deaths. It's pretty old, written in the 1960s, and it saved me a lot of work. The author, some guy called Ralph Nugent, speculated it was a local serial killer, and that the disappearances and murders stopped when the killer died. Of course the police never connected them, and perhaps they *weren't* connected, but it's suspicious, especially as they're in the same area." He shrugged. "We'll never know. The murders stopped, apart from the usual ones whose perpetrators were found and arrested. Then time passed and all was well, until—" He paused again, looking at them ominously. "In 1938, a spate of unexplained disappearances started again, lasting just over a year. And of course World War II started in 1939, bringing chaos and disruption."

"Evelyn bought the house in the 1920s and retired from the world in 1938," Alex said. "Everything adds up. So, who owned it originally?"

"And that's where I come in," Jasper said, placing his coffee cup down. "The first owner, the one who built it, was from Eastern Europe—Romania, in fact."

"As in Transylvanian Europe? Dracula-land!" Reuben declared, incredulous.

Jasper didn't even laugh. "I can't give you specifics, because the owner didn't provide them, but Transylvania *is* in Romania."

Once again the room fell silent as everyone glanced nervously at each other and Jasper continued. "His name was Grigore Cel Tradat. Other than the fact that he arrived with his wife and four children, and owned a successful business, I know very little about him. He rented for a while, and then built the house. He traded silks and other materials and did very well, but when he got older he made some bad investments and had to sell some land. According to my notes he'd have been 84 at that point. His wife was much younger. She was not the children's mother, or certainly not of the oldest ones. She would have been too young."

Alex leaned forward on his chair, listening intently. "How old was the oldest child?"

"He was a young boy of sixteen when they arrived. Grigore's wife, Sofia, was only ten years older."

"And the other children?"

"A girl of fourteen, and then two younger girls, aged five and two."

"So the two youngest must have been Sofia's children. It was a second marriage," Genevieve said.

"Well, that's all very interesting," Caspian said dryly, watching Jasper, "But was there anything suspicious about them? Anything other than they built the house that links the family to this current nightmare of vampires and death?"

"Other than the deaths around where they lived? No. But," Jasper's eyes held a gleam of excitement. "The oldest boy was called Lupescu, and he was never seen *anywhere*. He didn't join the family business, not that I could find, anyway, and I checked the census several times. I found the other children, but not him. He never married. He never had children. It's as if he never even existed."

Ben had been watching and listening, frowning between Jasper and Dylan until he finally spoke. "You think it's him, don't you? Our mysterious killer. The vampire."

Jasper spread his hands wide. "It would make sense. Although in Romania, the more common name for vampire is Strigoi. Their mythology describes them as troubled spirits that cause havoc when they rise from the grave. They can become invisible, and transform into an animal. They are what Bram Stoker took his inspiration from. The word is fascinating," he went on, revealing his love of research. "It has also been associated with witches, through various etymological means, and is linked to the word *striga*, meaning scream."

"What about Vlad the Impaler?" Reuben asked. "I thought he was part of the legend too?"

"Ah yes, Vlad Dracule," Jasper replied, nodding. "A man known for his cruelty to his enemies. His reputation was conflated with the vampire myths. Dracul means the devil, or dragon in old Romanian."

Eve looked at them as if they'd gone mad. "As fascinating as that is, Jasper, and great job on finding all this out, nothing about this makes sense. You're suggesting that Grigore brought his vampire son to Cornwall. Why? To hide?"

"Perhaps. Why not? He was a wealthy businessman with a reputation to protect, and his son has become a Strigoi. He needs to get the family out of Romania, and go where no one knows them."

Eve just looked at him. "This is pure speculation!"

"Eve, we're just reporting what we found in the records," Dylan explained. "It's dry—words and records only. Yes, we're speculating, but the missing son is weird! Oldest sons don't just disappear. And there's no record of his death. Grigore died in 1859, and his wife inherited the house. And if you remember the date, that's when the disappearances stopped."

Eve still looked confused. "So you think Grigore had something to do with the deaths, too?"

Dylan leaned forward, his eyes bright, and he raised his index finger to emphasise his point. "No, I think his death freed Sofia to do what Grigore couldn't or wouldn't let her do. She was able to stop Lupescu."

As the events started to slide into place, Avery smiled. "Of course. Grigore wanted to protect his son, despite the fact he was a vampire. Or else why bring him here, where no one knew him?"

"And he built this house to protect him," Caspian said darkly.

"But how did Sofia stop him?" Avery asked.

Jasper shrugged. "That is still to be determined."

"Don't forget the witch-bottle," Caspian said. "You said it was old. That would fit the time period."

Avery nodded slowly as she added things together. "She hired a witch to help, and the witch-bottle was part of that. But who?"

Caspian looked across to Alex. "Your family's magic is the strongest as regards controlling spirits and demons, and they weren't linked to the Cornwall Coven. It's most likely to have been one of them, and that's why we have no knowledge of it. And they would have been close by."

Alex leaned back in his chair, his eyes staring blankly into the middle distance until eventually he looked at Caspian. "You're right. Maybe my family did help. I'll see if there are any clues in my grimoire."

"But there's more," Dylan added. "The children all married and moved out, and then had their own children. But they stayed close." He looked at Jasper. "Do you want to tell them?"

Jasper grinned. "Evelyn...aka Madame Charron, was Grigore's great, great, something granddaughter. When she bought this house, she was going home."

They stared at each other, mute with shock, the silence so great that Avery wondered if she'd gone deaf until Alex groaned. "Now it makes sense! Evelyn was trying to contact the spirits of her ancestors. She was in the house where they had lived for years!"

El nodded in agreement, excited. "Her husband was ill, probably unrecognisable after the war, and she wanted to be somewhere safe."

Cassie frowned as she glanced at the notes Dylan had made. "Do you think she knew about the mysterious Lupescu?"

"Maybe, maybe not," Reuben said, reaching for a pastry from the table next to him. As usual, nothing dented his appetite. "It's hard to know at the moment. You would have hoped she wouldn't have gone poking about with that family history, though."

"We found something else last night," Avery said, placing the box-book on the table, and the book called *Mysteries of the Occult*. "I found these. They're from this house." She outlined everything that had happened, including the attempted break-in. "There's a message in this, written in runes, which says, 'the centre of the mysteries is beneath the full moon.' We think it points to the centre of this book—there's a witch-mark on the cover. The chapter is about using death deities and demons as spirit guides. The page focuses on demons of the First Hierarchy."

"The first *what*?" Ben asked, perplexed.

"According to demonologists of the 16th and 17th century," Avery explained, "there was a hierarchy of demons, much as there was a hierarchy of angels.

There's a first, second, and third hierarchy, as well as many lesser demons. The hierarchy denotes importance and power, and they have traits."

"Christian theology," Caspian said disdainfully.

"There are many belief systems in this world," Jasper admonished him. "Any demon in particular, Avery?"

"Verrine, who tempts men with impatience—apparently."

Reuben snorted. "What kind of demons did we face in the summer?"

Avery stared at him, incredulous. "I have no idea! If you remember, we really didn't have time to ask."

"I think demons are demons are demons," Alex said contemptuously. "I don't hold with this hierarchy crap. As Caspian said, it's Christian theology, and was designed to aid with hunting witches—that was the original reason to name them. In my opinion, Evelyn was looking for a spirit guide, and she found one. And a malevolent one, by the sound of it."

Briar looked thoughtful. "But the runes say beneath the full moon. Is it a reference to vampires? They don't need a full moon, do they? Is it relevant?"

"There's more to this, I'm sure," Genevieve said, worried. "Madame Charron's name is a play on *Charon*, the ferryman who takes souls to the underworld in Greek mythology. I'm sensing a deep obsession."

Hunter finally spoke. "We still don't know if she really was genuine though, do we?"

"There's only one way to know for sure. I aim to try contacting some spirits myself, preferably Evelyn's," Alex said, resolutely.

Nineteen

While Alex set up his crystal ball, remaining in the séance room as he tried to detect the presence of ghosts, the others split up to look around before Ben showed them the tower room.

Avery wandered through the ground floors of the house, checking for signs of spells or magical protection, but she felt nothing untoward, which reassured her. Rupert puzzled her, but she thought it unlikely that he had any magical ability.

The first time she visited the house, she had been taking in so much that she failed to see details in the decor, but now that she had time to look, Avery observed many occult symbols. This included a large sigil embedded in the plaster above the front door, small symbols in the cornices of the ceiling, and the roses around the light fittings.

The rooms on either side of the hallway were large and imposing reception rooms that stretched to the rear of the house. The one on the left of the main entrance had symbols and sigils around the fireplace, and even the paintings were occult in nature—dark, brooding fantastical landscapes. They were symbols she was familiar with, but for anyone coming into the house for a séance, they would have been striking, and probably intimidating. They suggested a house of power and mystery. Perhaps this room was intended for those participating in séances, while the other room was for daytime visitors. The colours were lighter, and decorated with nothing occult at all. No doubt she would find more as they explored.

Avery paused in front of the fireplace and looked up at an oil painting hanging above it. The subject was a striking woman, dressed in velvet and silk, all purples and reds. Her black hair was arranged in an elaborate chignon, and her dark eyes stared down at Avery, imperious and challenging. *Was she Madame Charron?*

Avery found Cassie in the kitchen, pulling the EMF metre out of their equipment bag, and asked, "How long did you say they'd be away for?"

"Overnight. Back by midday tomorrow." She looked annoyed and slammed the metre on the table. "Rupert is getting pretty cranky. He wants to know why we can't find the spirits that he *knows* are here. I've told him we don't raise spirits, just read them! He's being really unreasonable. We're as frustrated as he is that we can't identify whatever it is in their bedroom."

Avery stood by the window, gazing out across the large garden, currently covered in snow, as she listened. At the end of the garden was a brick wall, and beyond was a thick strand of trees that must lead to the reserve. On the far right of the wall was a wooden gate, padlocked. She could see it glinting in the weak sunlight from here.

"I'm still wondering why he hired you in the first place," Avery said, turning to face Cassie. "Everything this man does confuses me. Why is he so obsessed with spirits? It makes me wonder if he's toying with necromancy. A weird hobby."

"No weirder than ours," Cassie said with a wry smile.

Avery heard Eve and Caspian's voices in the hall, and went to join them, leaving Cassie to finish setting up her equipment.

"Interesting place," Caspian noted, looking around, his gaze finally falling on Avery. "It's quirky. I like it."

Eve moved past him, staring at the architraves, as Avery had. "I'm surprised. You don't strike me as the quirky type."

A smile crept over Caspian's face and his gaze swept down Avery from her head to her toes. "Quirky is growing on me."

Is that directed at me? Avery thought, feeling her face flushing with annoyance. Fortunately, no one seemed to notice as Jasper and Genevieve came down the stairs to join them.

"First impressions?" Jasper asked them eagerly.

"Fascinating," Briar said as she exited the room on the other side of the hall with Hunter, El, and Reuben. "And creepy."

Avery caught Hunter's eye. He looked a lot better since the last time she'd seen him. The cuts and bruises he'd received from his fight with Cooper, the old Pack Alpha, and from his encounter with the Wild Hunt had healed. He looked strong and his usual cocky self. "Hey, Hunter. Good to see you back here. I didn't think you were coming until after Christmas."

He smiled, his eyes mischievous. "Good to see you too. When Briar called I grabbed my bag, jumped in the car, and drove like the clappers. I don't like the thought of her being alone with a vampire on the loose."

"How long you staying?"

"At least until the New Year." His gaze followed Briar's retreating back. "Maybe longer."

Avery grinned. "What about work?"

"Josh and the girls can handle it for a while."

Reuben was close, listening to their conversation, and he lowered his voice. "Staking your claim?"

"Something like that," he murmured, watching her as she chatted with Eve. Briar definitely had a glow that morning, Avery decided. Briar looked up and saw Hunter watching, their eyes locking for a moment as something unspoken passed between them.

"Come on, guys, time for the tower room," Ben called from the first floor landing. Alex was standing next to him, looking distracted.

"Hold on," Avery replied. "Can I ask you about this painting?"

She led the way to the left reception room, the rest of the group following, and pointed to the picture above the fireplace. "Is that Madame Charron?"

"Wow," Eve said, softly. "She's impressive."

Ben laughed. "Yes, glad you reminded me about this. It is her. Charlotte found it in an upstairs room and decided it belonged here instead. She's imposing, isn't she?"

"She's in her full regalia, too," Genevieve observed. "It's good to see her in colour. Many of the photos from that era are in black and white."

"I like her," El declared. "She's got a lot of style. The whole room has. It's so dark and mysterious. Do you think that knowing what she looks like will help you find her spirit, Alex?"

"Let's hope so," he said, continuing to examine the picture minutely. "She's holding a card in her hands. You can just see the edge of it. Is that The Moon card?"

Avery stepped closer. "I think it is. How amazing."

"Will you tell Rupert what you've found?" Caspian asked Avery.

She squirmed. "Eventually."

Ben turned away, ever the tour guide. "Come on. Upstairs is more atmospheric."

The group trailed behind him as he showed them the other rooms, many of which Avery and Reuben had seen before.

They lingered in the master bedroom for a few minutes. "This is where we've been filming," Dylan said, heading to one of the windows. "And this is the window Charlotte opens, letting her blood-sucking visitor in."

Briar looked down to the garden. "He'd have to scale the wall. But I guess we know that's not a problem."

"What a stunning room, though," Eve noted.

Briar shuddered. "Beautiful or not, I wouldn't be sleeping in here knowing that something was standing over me at night."

"Let's have a look at the tower," Alex said, already heading to the door.

Cassie had been standing in the doorway watching, and she spun on her heel and led the way down the passage, stopping at a dead end. A panelled wall was in front of them, a series of carvings around the edge. She reached to the side, pressing an ornate moulding of the moon, and the panel popped open, revealing a door. She turned to look at them, a wry smile hovering on her lips. "It's only just registered that it's the moon carving that releases the door." She headed through, leading them up a long narrow staircase. She called back over her shoulder, "There's a third floor for servants and storage. The rooms are much smaller and quite bare, as you can imagine. We'll show you them later. But this set of stairs bypasses that floor and leads you to the square tower you can see from outside."

The stairs turned on to a small landing, and Cassie pushed the door open into the tower, lit from above by a dusty sky light. They all crowded in, hot on each other's heels, and Avery gasped and shivered. She was not the only one.

"Holy crap. This is creepy," Reuben exclaimed.

The room was lined with long, dark wooden panels, making the room circular in design. Nothing could be seen of the square brick bones of the tower. The ceiling was vaulted with an ornate, circular glass pane at the apex. But it was the decoration on the wooden panels that was so chilling. Paintings of demons filled some of the panels, with glowing eyes, horns, and hooves. Spectres and ghouls also jostled for space, and there were several depictions of Major Arcana cards, including The High Priestess, The Moon, The Tower, Death, The Devil, and The Hermit. The floor was decorated with a large pentagram, and surrounded by various runes and sigils, the edges crowded with candles. A small, round table covered with a long, black velvet cloth that reached the floor sat in the middle of the space, a chair on either side.

"Wow," Jasper exclaimed. "This room radiates power."

"I agree," Genevieve said, her hand stroking one of the panels. "This suggests she had real ability. Look, that's her image again as the High Priestess."

Caspian grunted. "I'm not so sure. She seems to be trying very hard to impress."

"But you'd need to surely, for your customers," El reasoned, her eyes narrowed.

If some of them were baffled, Eve was pleased, grinning with delight. "These paintings are stunning. Look at the detail, and the light. I admit, some of the subjects are gruesome, but they're good! Someone spent a lot of time on them."

"Can you imagine seeking a private audience with Madame Charron?" Briar said, turning slowly. "You're probably paying good money, and you're brought *here*! I've got chills just looking at the pictures, and I'm a witch. I know magic and power. But if you didn't—"

"You'd be overawed and seriously impressed," Hunter finished, moving next to Briar, his hand resting on her lower back.

"And impressionable!" Caspian added. "You'd believe anything."

Cassie was staring up at the glass roof, grinning broadly. "Has anyone noticed what the inscription on the glass says?"

"What inscription?" Dylan asked, looking up.

"There, all around the edge. It's hard to make out because of the italics."

Avery's mouth fell open as she deciphered the writing. "Bloody Hell. It says '*The Centre of the Mysteries.*'"

Alex laughed. "The runic script!"

Avery swivelled towards the panel with the moon on it. "And a full moon panel."

"Another hidden doorway?" El asked. "The door release mechanism downstairs was a moon."

"And one of the symbols on the paper found with that witch-bottle was a moon, too," Reuben added.

"So," Genevieve said, hand on hips. "Time is marching on. What first? I suggest that Alex, you try to reach Madame Charron, or Felicity, or whoever else may want to say hello, and that we try to find out if there really is a hidden door in here."

"I wonder if Rupert thinks there is?" Briar mused.

"I guarantee you," Ben said, starting to test the panels for release catches, "that Rupert and Charlotte will have tested every single panel in this room, because they did the same all over the house. That's how they found this attic room in the first place."

"Jean didn't tell them, then?" El asked.

"Nope."

"It would explain why he wants to find the books," Avery said, placing her hand on one of the panels. "I bet he thinks there are instructions somewhere."

"Well, there is, just not the type he probably expected," El answered.

"I have a feeling this may be the best space to try to connect to a spirit," Alex said, "but I agree, you should focus on that door. I'll use the séance room on the first floor."

"Can we film you?" Ben asked.

"Sure," Alex nodded. "But at this stage, I'll work better without any other witches. If something starts to happen, I trust you to get someone, sound good?"

"Perfect," he and Dylan said together, both looking excited.

"I'd like to explore the house a bit more, if that's okay," El said, shouldering her bag. "I would hate to think we'd missed something."

"Good idea," Genevieve said, already looking weary at the task ahead of them.

"I'll come with you, El," Reuben said.

Eve nodded. "Me, too. This place is fascinating. It's like a time capsule. Nothing seems to have changed—not obviously, anyway."

"Rupert has been very keen to preserve it," Ben told them. "At least until he unlocks its secrets. I'd love to talk to Jean, the cleaner who inherited it."

"Remind me to ask Newton about that later," Avery said. "I'll stop here and help with the door. And call me if anything happens to Alex!" She said this specifically to Ben and Dylan. "*Anything*!"

"We will, don't worry," Dylan reassured her.

Alex kissed the top of her head. "Be careful."

"You, too." She leaned into him affectionately.

Eve was already heading out the door. "And call us when you find something!"

Twenty

Caspian, Genevieve, Briar, Avery, and Jasper stared at the panels, and started to discuss their options. Hunter and Cassie stood back, watching.

"We should try some opening spells," Caspian suggested.

"But that would suggest that Madame Charron was a witch," Briar pointed out. "We're pretty sure she's a legitimate psychic, but that doesn't mean she's a witch. Those are two very different things."

Jasper shook his head, frustrated. "This house was constructed long before Madame Charron took up residence. She is not responsible for these panels. She may have painted them, she may have found out this room's secrets, and she may have left clues to find them, but she didn't make them or conceal the room." Jasper's eyes now burned with excitement. "The tower is separate from the rest of the house, the access hidden behind a panel. And there are more panels, one of which must be a door. Grigore did this to hide Lupescu. This *has* to be the way to his hiding place. Grigore would have wanted to protect him from being hunted, and his family from Lupescu's blood lust. As he grew older, he would have grown stronger."

Caspian frowned. "Good point, Jasper." He spun on his heels, looking around the room. "And if I wasn't a witch, I wouldn't want a door to be sealed with magic so that I could never access it. I'd want a mechanism. Where would I choose?"

Avery's head hurt with the layers of time and complexity. "But there *was* a spell at some point—the disappearances stopped."

"True." Briar stared at the panels intently, as if they would reveal their secrets under scrutiny. "But somehow we think the spell, or whatever you want to call it, was broken, because of the deaths in the late 1930s, the 1970s, and the ones that have started now."

"Deaths that coincide with the homeowner dying," Genevieve reminded them.

"Maybe a binding spell of some sort, something to bind the vampire to the owner?" Cassie suggested. "Is that how they work?"

"A binding spell can work however you want it to," Caspian said, looking at Avery. "As we know only too well."

She met his eyes briefly and looked back at the panels, puzzled. "We're missing something. Grigore dies, his wife, Sofia, takes over the house, the deaths stop. And when she dies, *nothing happens*. No resurrection of the vampire until Madame Charron disturbed it in the 1930s."

Genevieve sat on one of the chairs next to the table in the middle of the room, her fingers drumming the surface. "We think she broke the spell that trapped the vampire using Verrine, the demon spirit guide, and then had to trap the vampire again."

Briar nodded. "Two different spells, then. One cast by Sofia, or the witch she employed, and whatever means Madame Charron and her daughter used. A binding spell of sorts, linked to their lives, broken by death."

Cassie frowned, marched over to the panel, and started feeling the edges again. "So, in theory, we're back to square one. If one of these panels is a door, it should just pop open with a mechanism."

"In theory," Jasper echoed, joining her in the search. He ran his hands over the surface, his palms flat, moving in an orderly manner, left to right, right to left, as he moved downwards.

Caspian brushed his fingertips across his lips. "Maybe we need a full moon to see it? Or it could be a play on words." He looked around the room again, scanning the other panels. "There are a least three other panels with moons on them. The High Priestess, The Tower, and The Hermit. The verse could refer to those." He strode across to the closest one, The High Priestess, and started to examine it.

Avery became excited as an idea began to form. "The Major Arcana representations here aren't typical of any particular style of deck. They're rich in symbolism, of course, but look at what's at the feet of The Devil. Normally, there's a male and female figure at its feet, but on this one, there's only a man."

Genevieve frowned as she stared at the painting. "You're right. A man dressed in black and wrapped in chains, with blood on his face." She turned to Avery, a smile spreading across her face. "Well spotted. What else?"

"The Tower is normally depicted with flames coming from the roof, and lightning striking it. That one is set against a night sky with a full moon above it, and there's a cave of some sort, a dark hollow beneath it."

Hunter had been watching and listening, hands thrust into his jeans pockets as he leaned against the door frame, but now he came to life, stalking across the room. "Holy shit! You're right. Does that mean there's a cave beneath this one? Well, the house?"

Avery raised her eyebrows. "Perhaps. It fits our theory."

They were all paying close attention now, glancing back and forth between Avery and the paintings.

Avery continued, "The Hermit is numerologically linked to The Moon. He's an old man, as commonly depicted, but his guiding light is the moon in his lantern, not the star as it normally is. The Hermit shows thought, introspection, isolation...like Madame Charron." She turned to the High Priestess image. "The face is already Madame Charron, we can see that. She depicts wisdom of the world beyond the veil. But again, a full moon hangs above her, which isn't normally represented in many standard decks, and this card is astrologically linked to the Moon, too."

"And Death?" Hunter asked.

Avery exhaled heavily. "Death is normally depicted as a soldier, with a skull for a head. He charges into battle, usually on horseback, so the imagery is medieval, one of the Four Horsemen of the Apocalypse. Sometimes people are at his feet, as he brings judgment to all. But the card doesn't mean actual death; it represents a spiritual death and rebirth. There's usually a setting sun in the background—the end of day, the end of life, or a time in life. In this panel, he stands on a bloodstained field, a tower in the background, but the sky is dark, and it's a moon rising, not a sun setting."

"Wow!" Cassie said, looking at her in shock. "How do you remember all of that stuff?"

"I read the cards," Avery explained. "They are old friends that whisper to me, revealing past, present, and future. Not all witches use them, but I always have."

Genevieve watched her speculatively, and said, "I rarely use them."

Cassie frowned. "Do they predict things—like this?"

Avery frowned, trying to explain. "It's not that straightforward. They offer a personal reading, not broad predictions. In the summer, I certainly read there was a change coming to me, danger that threatened my life in some way, but it depends what you ask them. I certainly haven't predicted *this*!" She spread her hands wide, encompassing the room and the house.

Briar studied her for a moment, frowning. "Do these images match the ones in the deck you found?"

"Shit! I don't know." Avery reached into her bag, pulled the book-box out, and rapidly thumbed through the pack. While she looked, there was a flurry of activity, as Briar, Hunter, Cassie, and Genevieve started to examine the other panels, leaving Jasper to finish examining The Moon panel.

Avery was annoyed with herself, because she knew when she found the pack that they weren't a typical deck, but she hadn't stopped to examine them properly. She'd assumed they were an old design, one she'd not seen before. She found the cards represented on the panels and laid them out in a line on the table. *Damn it.* They weren't the same at all. Not even close. The pictures on the panels told a story, certainly, of a vampire bound in a cave beneath a tower, a High Priestess who navigated worlds beyond the veil, and who sat in lonely contemplation. *But why paint them?* A warning maybe, or perhaps a clue, in case things went wrong, as they have done now. A way to track the vampire. *Bollocks! I'm missing something!*

Avery stared into space, watching shadows move across the room. It brought her back to the present. Time was passing. She looked up at the glass pane set into the roof. The light coming through was muted, filtered by a covering of snow, which earlier had given the room a weird, spectral light. Now it seemed darker, as if the clouds were once again gathering outside. She stared at the words painted on the glass, pondering their many meanings. *The centre of the mysteries lies beneath the full moon,* she repeated to herself. In this light, the circular glass roof looked like a full moon. *The floor!*

Excited at her discovery, she examined the runes that circled the pentagram beneath her feet. The design was painted on, the paint now a faded white, almost yellow, but it was relatively undamaged, sealed beneath a layer of varnish. She couldn't see images of moons, full or otherwise. And then she turned and stared at the table in the middle. What was that hiding? She removed the cards and candles, placing them on the floor by the door, and then pulled the heavy velvet cloth away, dust rising in clouds and making her cough.

"What are you doing?" Caspian asked, turning to watch her. He funnelled the air away with a gesture, and it streamed out of the door and down the stairs.

"I think we're looking in the wrong place. Can someone help me move the table?"

Hunter shooed her out of the way, lifting the table up on his own, and moving it next to the door. By the time he turned round, Avery was already on her knees. In the centre of the pentagram, woven discreetly into other symbols, was the sign of the Triple Goddess, with the waxing, full, and waning moons next to each other.

Briar crouched next to her, watching Avery run her fingers over it. "This must be it. Can you feel anything?"

Avery touched it gently, terrified she might do something before they were ready for it, and then looked at Briar, triumphant. "I can feel a faint line all around the full moon."

They both twisted to look up at the others who surrounded them in a tight circle.

"What now?" Avery asked. "Do I press it?"

But before anyone could answer, they heard footsteps racing up the stairs. It was Dylan, breathless with excitement. "Alex has found Madame Charron! Come quickly."

"Go," Genevieve said, assuming control. "I'll wait here until you're back. No one is pressing anything until we're *all* ready."

Avery rose to her feet, and ran to follow Dylan. "Thanks!" she called over her shoulder.

"I'm coming, too," Briar said, trailing her out the door. Without hesitation, Hunter followed.

They skidded to a halt in front of the door to the séance room, and Dylan paused, hand on the handle. "You should know that he was about to use the crystal ball when he started to examine the large, full-length mirror that rests on the floor against the wall."

"I remember it," Avery said, barely containing her impatience.

"It has an ornate frame. Alex noticed arcane symbols around the edges, a sigil denoting a doorway. He decided to try mirror scrying."

Without another word he pushed the door open, and they entered silently, Dylan shutting the door behind them.

It took a moment for Avery's eyes to focus, because the room was as dark as night. They had drawn the heavy curtains, and the only light was from the fire in the fireplace and a single, black pillar candle placed on the floor in front of the mirror. The room was warm, adding to the sense of claustrophobia. The candle flame burned with unnatural stillness, and behind it, staring into the mirror, sat Alex, cross-legged and immobile. He was oblivious to their arrival.

It was hard to see his face at first, only his deeply shadowed reflection, all hard angles and planes from the firelight. They moved closer, behind and to his right, careful not to disturb him.

His lips were moving, and Avery could hear him murmuring, but was unable to make out the words. She was focused so completely on his face and the flame that it was with a shock that she realised the rest of the mirror was completely black. Nothing of the rest of the room was reflected at all. It was a void. A chill raced down her arms and she shivered, despite the heat.

Avery lowered herself to the floor, staring at the mirror intently. She slowed her breathing and stilled her mind, willing herself to focus. A figure emerged from the darkness. A woman, her face pale and thin, the rest of her body swathed in layers of voluminous clothing. Her lips moved in response to Alex's murmurings. Back and forth they went, their conversation impossible to follow. It seemed to last an age; her face became impassioned, and then furious. And then her eyes widened with shock as a huge, clawed hand appeared on her shoulder, dragging her backwards. She vanished in a cloud of billowing smoke.

Another face appeared, and Avery jumped, suppressing the scream that bubbled in her throat. A demonesque figure filled the mirror, huge and terrifying, and she felt a ripple of fear run through the room. It was nothing like the formless, writhing shapes filled with flames they had encountered in the summer. This assumed a man's shape, but its face was a skull from which thick, grotesque horns protruded. Fire burned from within, lighting his eye sockets and jaw with flames. It fixed Alex with a questioning glare and started to speak, and the most hideous, unearthly sound boomed around the room. This time Avery yelped, jerking back in shock. Her heart pounded so hard she thought it would leap out of her chest.

Simultaneously, a howl filled the room, emanating from behind her. She turned, dreading what she would see, but found that Hunter had changed into a wolf, partially ripping his clothing in the process. He snarled, head lowered, glowering at her, but Briar intervened, a hand on the wolf's head, utterly fearless. Hunter dropped onto his belly, his head in Briar's lap, and she stroked him, her hands buried deep in his soft fur. She met Avery's gaze, eyes solemn.

Avery glanced at Dylan and Ben, and saw them both sitting on the floor, transfixed on the mirror; reassured that they were okay, she turned her attention back to Alex.

He was still immobile, sweat beading on his brow as he murmured a response to the demon. It didn't seem to like what it heard, because it threw back its head, opened its jaws wide, and shot flames out into the void, until nothing could be seen except fire; then it was gone, and the mirror was just a mirror again.

Alex fell backwards onto the floor with a *thump*, and the candle extinguished, a thin stream of smoke rising into the air. Avery untangled her legs and crawled to him. She couldn't have walked if her life had depended on it.

"Alex! Alex, are you all right?"

Fear gripped her like she'd never experienced before. It wasn't like the terror of facing the Wild Hunt. This was something deeper, more personal. *What had he done?*

He stared vacantly at the ceiling for what seemed like endless moments, and Avery was aware of the deep silence around her. She reached forward, wanting to shake him, but knowing that might shock him too much. "Alex! Please speak to me."

And then he blinked, the trancelike state leaving his eyes, and he turned his head towards her and smiled weakly.

"Thank the Goddess," she whispered.

"*Water*," he croaked.

She looked around, and Dylan's hand appeared, thrusting a water bottle in her face. She took it and passed it to Alex, and after taking a deep breath, he eased himself upright and took a long drink, before finally meeting Avery's stare. "Well, that was pretty fucking scary. Remind me not to meet Verrine again."

Thankful he still had a sense of humour, Avery laughed, and the tension in the room dropped.

"Can I open these curtains?" Ben asked, his voice shaky. "I'd really like to see daylight."

"Me, too," Alex called over his shoulder. "Go ahead."

"In a moment," he answered. "I've just realised my legs won't move."

Avery raised her hand, twitching back the curtains with a gesture, revealing the three long windows backed by swirling snow. She then turned her attention to the fire, where the flames had burned down to embers only, and with a word, she reignited it.

Light and heat flooded the room, and Alex sighed.

"Please tell me you didn't promise that *thing* anything?" Avery asked, fear coursing through her again as she remembered their exchange.

He smiled, her usual, adorable Alex, his jaw covered in stubble, his hair falling around his face, and his dark eyes holding her with warmth she never wanted to lose. "I'm not a nut job. He didn't like the fact that I was talking to Madame Charron. Apparently some secrets should stay hidden. I was warned off, and told not to contact her again. I told him I'd do what I wanted and he could get lost. He didn't like that."

Relief rolled through her, and she felt weak all over again. Just as she was about to ask more, she heard the sound of thudding feet as if a herd of elephants was stampeding down the hallway, and the door flew open, Reuben standing at the head of the group. His hands were raised, fire balled in his palms. His eyes swept the room, and when he registered they were okay, he lowered his arms. "What the hell have you been doing? We heard a howl—and we were down in the cellar!"

"You got into the cellar?" Dylan asked, incredulous. "It's out of bounds for us. What's down there?"

"Necromancer shit. What have *you* been doing?"

"Raising demons," Alex answered. "Do you think someone can make some coffee before we get into it?"

Twenty-One

A very leaned against the window frame, holding a hot cup of coffee, and watched the snow. In the last fifteen minutes, since Cassie had made coffee and tea and rustled up a pack of biscuits, the snowfall had become thicker, muting the outside world. Avery felt that some time in the last hour she had stepped back in time. The house was getting to her. Its layers of history and secrets lay on her spirit as thick as the snow on the ground.

She turned away, watching Briar lean against Hunter, his arm protectively wrapped around her. Hunter had returned to human form looking shocked and unsettled, his clothing ripped, and told them that the demon Verrine's voice had literally forced the change to his wolf. "That has never happened to me before, and I hope it never happens again. That was *horrible*."

"Are you sure you're okay?" Briar had asked him, her eyes roving over him as if he was nursing a hidden injury.

"I'm fine. Lying in your lap was worth it."

Briar had flushed with pleasure.

Avery allowed herself a smile. It was good to see Briar happy. She turned her attention to the roomful of people as they listened to Genevieve finish telling them what they had found in the attic.

El whooped. She was sitting next to Reuben, her short sword on the table next to her, glinting in the icy cold light from outside. "Well done! So we've found a way to open the hidden door."

"In theory," Caspian said in his low drawl. "The proof is yet to be found."

As Genevieve finished pouring her second cup of tea, she said, "You better tell us what happened here, Alex."

Alex was still sitting on the floor in front of the fire, sipping on super strength coffee. "I was going to try to reach Madame Charron with my crystal ball, as I said, but before I started, I decided to check the room again. I realised that the mirror had symbols all around the frame that reference doorways and safe passage. I had an idea that perhaps she used this mirror to talk to spirits. Mirrors are a popular way to enter the spirit world. I hoped this would be a hotline to her. I was right." He paused, taking another sip of coffee. He still looked pale, as if the communication had taken much of his energy. "Within only a few minutes of me searching the void, I found her. It was as if she was waiting for me—well, someone. But she was nervous, her spirit flitting away and back again. Anyway, long story short, she confessed that she was told by her mother about how her family had arrived here from Romania, and how Grigore had built the house, and that there was a dark and terrible family secret. But she didn't know what it was. She thought it was related to her own psychic abilities that had been passed down to her. Her mother and her daughter had them, too. She thought that maybe something had gone horribly wrong and that someone's spirit was trapped in the void, so she decided to investigate, like a spiritual detective. She became frustrated with her failure, and in her effort to succeed, she reached too far. She found Verrine. He promised to help her."

Verrine. Avery shivered again. His unintelligible, screeching voice still echoed in her head, and his appearance... She doubted she'd sleep well for a while.

Alex continued. "By then, Madame Charron was an accomplished medium, but she also embellished her séances by either toning them down or enhancing them, depending on the group. She was confident in her ability to manage spirit guides, and had used them before. But Verrine was different. He certainly didn't present himself to her as he appeared to me. Not at first, anyway. He offered to show her the family's dark secret, and he led her to Lupescu's chained spirit—metaphorically speaking. He encouraged her to set him free, so she did."

"And unleashed a monster," Eve said. She sat at the table, watching Alex with fascination.

Genevieve edged forward in her seat. "So that's how the witch did it. They *chained* his spirit. That would have meant separating it from his body." She looked astonished. "That's hard, dark magic."

"And surely," Caspian asked, also leaning forward in anticipation, "that means Madame Charron broke a spell, without having magical ability. As you said, she's a medium, not a witch."

"She broke it because Verrine helped her," Alex explained. "I have no idea about this hierarchy of demons crap, or whether it really exists, but he's powerful, able to transform himself into any feature he chooses. He saw what she needed and manipulated her. A witch chained Lupescu's spirit, but he helped her break it."

"So, Verrine couldn't break it free on his own?" El surmised.

"Perhaps the original spell bound it to a family line. Maybe that's why when Sofia died the spell remained, passing down the generations, until Evelyn broke it, and his dark and twisted spirit fled back to his body. And the deaths started."

Jasper nodded solemnly. "Demons love chaos. They would love the chaos that a vampire would bring."

"When did she realise what she'd done?" Avery asked.

"As soon as she released him. She saw Lupescu for what he was. From that point on, she had to try to find a solution."

Dylan was sitting at the table, fiddling with his camera while he listened. "It took her a while, obviously—over a year, during which time Lupescu ran rampant."

Alex nodded. "She had to find a witch to help her, and it wasn't easy. Let's face it—you can't exactly advertise that sort of thing."

Caspian asked the question that everyone was thinking. "Did one of our ancestors help her? And if so, why don't we know about it?"

"White Haven again," Eve suggested. "The witches that were isolated from the rest of the coven. There was no one to tell—except descendants."

Alex, Reuben, and Avery all snorted, and Reuben said forcefully, "No one told us!"

Genevieve shuffled impatiently. "Did she tell you who she used, Alex? It may help us now."

He grimaced. "No, I'm afraid not. But it was another sort of binding spell. They bound him to her, but she was bound to the house. And when she died, Lupescu was released and went on the rampage again until Felicity contained it. Don't ask me any more details, because I don't know them. I don't know what Felicity did, or who with. She was about to tell me more—I asked about the hidden panel—but Verrine dragged her away before she could answer."

Reuben started drumming his fingers on the table. "We can debate this later. Can we get on with opening this door?"

"Not yet," Genevieve said, as everyone started to rise. "What did you find in the cellar?"

El answered that as she slid her short sword in to its scabbard. "A necromancer circle to summon spirits, and a demon trap. That's why Rupert kept the door locked. It's pretty fresh, drawn in chalk, salt circle and the works. We can show you later."

"Good," Genevieve said, rising to her feet. "Let's get on with this, then. Grab whatever vampire-killing kit you need. This could get ugly."

The group assembled in the tower room, and Avery pressed the moon symbol in the centre of the floor, depressing it by a couple of inches.

Nothing happened.

"Bollocks. What now?" she asked, looking around at the others.

"Maybe it's a double mechanism?" Eve suggested. "You always need someone else to help."

Jasper looked weary and frustrated as he rubbed his hands across his short hair. "Let's check the other moon images again."

"It's pointless," Cassie said, echoing his frustration.

"We haven't checked the rising moon image of Death, have we?" Caspian pointed out as he strode to the panel. He examined the half-moon visible over the tower on the horizon, and ran his fingers over the edge. He turned to them and grinned. They didn't often see Caspian grin; it transformed him, making him look ten years younger. "Bingo. On the count of three, Avery? One, two, three!"

They both pressed the images together and with a loud *click*, the panel of The Moon swung outwards, revealing a passageway.

Whoops of joy filled the room, and Caspian rolled his shoulders and stepped inside first. "Here goes," he murmured and threw a couple of witch lights ahead. "There's a passage running between the panelling and the wall for a few feet, and then it disappears into the wall."

They filed in after him, and he led the way through the musty, cobwebbed passage, dust rising around them. It was narrow, with just enough width for one person to pass comfortably. The wall was straight on one side, and the curved panelling lined the other. A dark opening appeared in the wall and they turned into it. Immediately, a set of steps appeared and ran downwards, turned left and then heading down again.

Caspian called back over his shoulder. "We must be next to the outside wall, and I think this goes directly to ground level."

The stairs were steep, the steps small and slippery underfoot, and Avery started to sweat. It was hot in here, stuffy, and the dust kept rising, getting in her hair, her eyes, and up her nose. She sent a waft of air around them, and immediately felt better. Eventually, they reached a small landing on what they estimated was the ground floor, and the stairs turned again. Avery was now completely disorientated, unable to work out whether they were at the front, middle, or rear of the house. The air became damp and musty and Caspian stopped, causing everyone to stumble into each other.

"A little warning, please," El grumbled.

"Sorry. I think we're under the house now. We've reached a flat area."

Avery was at the back, still on the steps, and light bloomed down below as Eve and Alex immediately threw more witch lights above them, throwing the room into stark relief. Avery stumbled down the last few steps, glad to be out of the narrow passage.

The room they were in was made of stone, plain and unadorned, and the floor was packed earth. On the far side were two heavy wooden doors, enormous bolts keeping them locked.

Caspian strode toward them, rattling the wood. "These are still solid."

"Do you have to do that?" Ben asked, looking horrified. "You might wake what's behind it!"

Cassie visibly shivered and gripped her stake hard. "Don't say that. Do you really think the vampires are there?"

Genevieve stood next to Caspian, her pupils huge in the low light. "If we're in luck, they will be. We can kill them and get this over with. Are we ready?"

"No," Cassie answered.

"You can leave if you like," Genevieve said. "I understand."

Cassie shook her head. "I'm just nervous. I have a few spells in my pockets, as well as my stake. I'll be fine."

Eve patted her arm. "I am, too—you're not alone."

Everyone was nervous, it was obvious from the general air of tension in the room, and level of fidgetiness that everyone exhibited as they readied themselves, Avery included. She hadn't forgotten how quick the vampires were when they'd encountered them before, and she took deep breaths to calm herself.

Genevieve looked them all in the eye. "Are we ready?"

Reuben pulled a torch from his backpack and lit his face up from under his chin, pulling a ghoulish expression and announcing in his best Vincent Price voice, "Time for the crypt! Ha ha ha!"

"You're such a doofus," El said affectionately.

"I'll take that as yes," Genevieve said dryly.

"Wait!" Jasper called. "What's the time?"

Alex checked his watch. "Half past three, why?"

"Not long until sunset," Jasper noted. "If they're in there, they should be sleeping, but we're cutting it close."

"I'm not turning back now," Genevieve said, and together she and Caspian released the bolts and pulled the doors open.

It was pitch black beyond them, and they launched a flurry of witch lights, illuminating another passageway, but this one was as wide as the double doors. At the far end was another set of doors.

"It seems Grigore was keen to keep the vampire from his own door," Hunter said, wryly. He started to shed his clothes. "I'd rather proceed as a wolf from now on."

Within seconds he changed into a larger than average wolf, and he loped to the passage entrance, Briar next to him, her hand buried in the fur of his neck. She'd slipped her shoes off, and she wriggled her toes in the dirt. "I can't feel any magic ahead."

"Me, neither," Caspian agreed.

The passage was again lined with brick, and they progressed slowly, as if they were expecting booby traps. Avery felt like she was in an Indiana Jones film.

Alex nudged her. "You okay?"

She nodded. "I think so. You?"

He raised an eyebrow. "As I'll ever be."

The next set of doors was as solid as the first, but they were ornate, covered in sigils.

Genevieve ran her hand over them gently. "These had a spell on them once. There's just a trace of it now, but the sigils warn against intrusion."

Once again, everyone raised their weapons or their hands, magic summoned, as she and Caspian released the bolts and opened the doors, sending witch lights through at the same time.

They illuminated a bedroom. This time, the walls and floor were made of large stone blocks, and it was filled with wooden bedroom furniture—an ornate, four-poster bed, a chest of drawers, a mirrored dressing table, and a wardrobe. But it was an imitation only. The place was a wreck, the furniture broken, as if smashed in a rage, and the mirror shattered. The bed was the only intact item in there, but it was covered in rumpled and rotten linen that tumbled onto the ground, and it was soaked with stiffened, dark blood. But worse was the pile of bones that lay ankle deep in places, and the skulls lined up along the deep shelves cut into the wall; the stench was horrific. On the far side of the room was the entrance to another passage.

Avery heaved, and she heard a few others doing the same.

Briar's hand flew to her mouth, and she said a quick spell; within seconds, the smell disappeared, replaced by the scent of roses and honeysuckle.

For a second there was silence as they all stared aghast at what lay before them, and then Hunter headed in, padding stealthily towards the bones, the rest of them fanning out as they explored.

"Over a century of death," Jasper said solemnly as he looked at the devastation. He raised his hand, and immediately the candles placed around the room flared to life, and if anything, the warm light made the horror of it all so much worse.

Alex advanced slowly, the stake raised in his right hand, a ball of fire in his left. He kicked at the bones by his feet. "But nothing recent, by the look of it. These bones are old."

"No wonder they never found bodies," Dylan said as he swept his camera around the room. "He brought them all here. What an animal."

The room fell silent as they advanced, and Avery shivered. Although Briar had disguised most of the stench, it was still there, faint and rancid, and Avery sent a gentle wind ahead of her, carrying it away. She reached out a hand to touch the broken mirror. "Grigore must have been trying to make his son more human."

"Well, that was a big fat failure, wasn't it?" Cassie said. "I can't believe what I'm seeing."

El extended her sword ahead of her as she looked around. "Well, it's clear there's nothing here. So where are they now?"

"The recent bodies, or the vampires?" Avery asked her.

"Both."

Genevieve rubbed her face with her hands, her lips pinched tightly together. "I can't believe we haven't found them. Where the hell do we look now?"

Caspian pointed to the passageway ahead. "We keep going."

Hunter was still sniffing around the room, and he jumped on the bed, his head lowered as he sniffed the sheets. A snarl rumbled in the back of his throat, and he snapped at the sheets, grabbing them between his strong teeth and pulling them back. Before he could do anything else, an arm emerged, knocking him off the bed and sending him crashing into the wall.

Everyone whirled around, as Reuben yelled, "Shit!" One of them's here!"

Instantly everyone was ready, and Alex raced towards the bed, stake raised. Before he could get close, the vampire sprang up to the ceiling, its long, claw-like fingers grasping a wooden beam. It hung upside down, and still looked dazed, if that's what you could call it, struggling to open its eyes against the daytime pull of sleep. The struggle didn't stop its strength or viciousness, though. Its eyes were completely black, skin grey, and its teeth elongated and sharp, dried blood already crusted around its mouth.

For a second it seemed everyone was frozen in shock, and then Reuben and Ben raised their water guns and blasted the vampire. It screamed as its skin blistered, but it barely slowed it down. It dropped to the floor and charged Reuben.

Before he could take more than a few paces, Hunter leapt towards it, jaws wide. The vampire raised its arms, stopping Hunter from reaching its throat, and he bit hard on the vampire's arm instead, his weight carrying them both to the floor.

With superhuman strength, the vampire tossed Hunter aside, though Hunter took a good chunk of its arm with him.

Once again the vampire sprang to its feet, but a powerful blast of magic swept it back against the wall and pinned it there.

Half a dozen stakes were raised, ready to attack, but Dylan was closest, and he charged, leaping over the piles of bones and driving the stake into its chest. The vampire roared, the noise terrifying. The stake was only partway in.

Dylan looked around wildly, desperate for something to hammer the stake in with as the vampire struggled to break free, but instantly every single witch sent a wave of magic that pushed the stake home with such force it went straight through its chest and cracked the wall behind it.

The vampire went limp, but Alex took the sword from El's hand and decapitated the body, as well. "Just making sure," he said, grimacing.

The room fell silent, and then Reuben quipped, "Holy shit. Who would have thought this lurked beneath West Haven?"

"Is everyone all right?" Genevieve asked, arms still raised and magic dancing at the tips of her fingers.

She was answered by groans and nods, but Caspian and Alex were silent, both of them standing at the entrance to the passage on the other side of the room. Alex turned, his finger to his lips gesturing silence, and Caspian sent half a dozen witch lights ahead, illuminating another narrow passage.

They all listened, and Hunter padded forward, sniffing the air.

After a minute of absolute silence, Alex said, "I think we're okay. The others aren't here. Hunter?"

Hunter looked at them and gave what could only be interpreted as a nod, and then he padded forward again, ears pricked.

"I think we should get out of here," Jasper said, looking worriedly at the others. "His death may have alerted the others, and they could be on the way right now."

"But we may not have the opportunity to come down here again," Caspian pointed out. "Let's press on, at least see what's down here. We have the chance to end this. *Tonight.*"

He was right, and everyone knew it, but nobody liked the idea.

He marched on regardless, Alex at his side, as Hunter led the way, and they hurried behind him, their footsteps echoing around them.

The passage was narrow, carved out of natural rock, the ground a mixture of earth and sharp stones. After a few minutes they came across a ladder leading up to a heavy metal door.

"Let me," Reuben said. He clambered up and inched the hatch open, allowing a sliver of dim light to illuminate his features. "We're in the wood behind the garden. I'm going out."

Alex leapt onto the ladder. "I'm going, too."

Avery followed, eager to see where it led, Genevieve right behind her. They emerged into undergrowth, trees growing closely around them, the ground speckled with snow and thick with leaves and rotting vegetation.

Reuben stood nearby, peering through the bare tangle of branches. "This is a natural dell," he said. "Kids might use it for a camp, but probably not in years."

Avery walked over to his side, and squinted through the trees, noting that there was nothing else in sight. "This was how he hunted then. No one would find him in here."

Snow was still falling, and it was almost fully dark.

"Damn it," Genevieve said, hands balled at her sides. "Let's get back inside. There's nothing else we can do here."

The group was arguing when they joined them, Jasper annoyed. "It would be madness to continue. We have no idea how long this passage is, or how many vampires we may find at the end of it. There are definitely two, and one is older and much stronger than the other."

"Agreed," El said, raising her sword and watching the white flame flicker along its blade. "As much as I want to finish this, when we encountered them the other night at the docks, they were too strong for us. We got away only because Avery got the upper hand."

Avery nodded. "El's right—I was lucky."

Caspian glared at her. "But there are more of us now! This is our chance."

Genevieve intervened. "Not our only chance. The entrance above means we don't need the house. We could come back tomorrow in the daylight."

Caspian's expression was bleak. "And what if there are more deaths tonight?"

She looked away, her expression conflicted, and Avery knew exactly what she was thinking. As much as none of them wanted to continue now that it was dark, Caspian had a point. She'd never forgive herself if someone else died, and from her quick glance at the others, despite their misgivings, she knew they thought the same.

But Genevieve was their coven lead, and she didn't want to argue with her again.

Fortunately, Alex was prepared to. "I hate to agree with Caspian, but he's right. We have the chance to end this. Now."

Caspian glanced at him with the barest flicker of appreciation, and maybe annoyance.

Reuben added his support. "I agree. Those who don't want to come should leave now. I won't hold it against anyone. Especially you three," he said, looking at Cassie, Ben, and Dylan.

"Not a chance," Dylan said, squaring up to him. "I staked the last one, didn't I ?"

Reuben high-fived him. "Yes, you did!"

"I'm staying, too," Cassie said, dropping her shoulders as if preparing for a fight. "Don't you dare tell me to go!"

"Genevieve?" Caspian said softly. "I know you don't want to lose anyone like Rasmus did last time, but we have to move, now!"

Hunter changed into human form, completely naked but seemingly impermeable to the biting cold around them. "I got a good scent of Lupescu. It was the strongest scent in there, which makes sense. I can smell him now—it's faint, but there. I'll lead you straight to him."

Genevieve smacked her hand against the earth wall, a wave of magic punching a hole into it. "Damn it! When did you get to be so rational, Caspian?" She turned to the others. "All right. Let's do this. Who wants to leave?"

Jasper sighed. "If you insist on this madness, of course I'm coming."

Everyone nodded, resolute, and Genevieve sighed. "Let's get on with this then, before we freeze to death down here."

Twenty-Two

H unter turned back into a wolf and led the way again.

El was just behind Avery. "I don't like this. It's too narrow. If anything happens, those at the front are on their own."

"As are those at the back," Avery said softly. She could see Ben ahead, but not the other paranormal investigators, and she looked back over her shoulder, hoping it wasn't one of them, but she couldn't quite see. She raised her voice. "Who's at the end?"

"I am," Jasper called back. "All good so far."

"Thanks," she shouted, relieved, and then fell silent, concentrating on the path ahead.

After endless minutes they reached an intersection with three passages running off in different directions, and they waited while Hunter sniffed the ground. Avery was now completely disorientated. She had no idea where they were, or what direction they were heading in. After a moment, Hunter headed down the right-hand passage, and Eve marked their path with a streak of white luminescence against the wall. "Just in case," she said to no one in particular.

Several more times they encountered other passages, some wider than others, some with the distinct stench of sewage emanating from them. They would never have done this without Hunter, Avery reflected. His nose was saving them hours.

As they hesitated for a moment at another crossroads while Hunter sniffed the ground, they heard a skitter of footsteps behind them that immediately stopped when they fell silent. They turned as one.

We're going to die down here.

A blast of fire hurtled down the passage from the direction they had come from, briefly illuminating the people behind her, and Jasper yelled. "Get a bloody move on!"

Hunter howled and raced ahead, and they ran, too. A scream echoed around them, and Avery stopped to look behind her. El was sprinting away. *Shit.* Avery followed, and almost stumbled over figures wrestling on the ground.

Jasper was pinned down by Bethany, her teeth inches from Jasper's throat. Cassie clung onto her back, desperately trying to pull Bethany's head away. Eve was lying dazed on the floor, a cut on her head, and Dylan was nowhere in sight.

"Move!" El yelled at Cassie, and with a well-timed blast of magic, propelled her away from the vampire. Bethany's head lifted, her lips peeling back as she snarled at El, fire blazing behind black eyes. El bounded forward, sword ready, and sliced with clinical precision, beheading Bethany in an instant.

The body slumped on Jasper, and thick, viscous blood pumped over him, and spattered across the wall as Bethany's head rolled away into darkness.

"Where's Dylan?" Avery yelled. She threw up another witch light, showing Cassie, insensible against the wall, and Dylan another few feet beyond.

Leaving El to help Jasper to his feet, she raced to Dylan's side, her heart pounding in her chest. *Please be alive.*

His left arm was lying at an odd angle, but his neck was unmarked, and he was still breathing. She heard running from the other direction, and saw Alex and Reuben in the dim light.

"Avery!" Alex shouted.

"I'm okay," she called back. "Dylan's unconscious and I think his arm's broken, but he's alive."

Avery held her hand against his head, feeling for bumps or cuts. She whispered a healing spell that Briar had taught her, and Dylan's eyes flickered open.

He groaned. "What the hell..."

"Careful," she warned him as he sat up.

"Bollocks, my arm." He cradled it, stiffly.

"You need to leave."

She turned and saw El helping Cassie to her feet, Eve and Jasper already standing.

"What the fuck happened?" Reuben asked, walking over to examine Bethany's head.

"She snuck up on us, even through the fire ball," Jasper explained. "She moved too quickly, and took me down first, but Dylan jumped on her, and she threw him like he was nothing. She leapt around the walls like a damn spider."

"Where are the others?" Avery asked, looking behind Alex and Reuben.

"We told them to go on. We'll catch up."

"They won't," Avery said. "Everyone's injured, especially Dylan."

"I'll be fine," Eve reassured them. She brought her hand to her cheek and wiped away the blood, healing the cut as she did so.

"But Dylan won't be. Or Cassie. She smacked her head against the wall, too."

"Sorry," El said to Cassie. "My fault."

She grimaced. "At least I still have my head. Poor Bethany. What an end."

El wiped her sword on a cloth from her pack. "Better dead than killing us."

Jasper watched Avery help Dylan to his feet. "I'll escort them out, and get Dylan to a hospital."

"No!" he protested weakly.

Cassie looked defeated. "You can't fight like this. Neither can I—I can barely focus."

"That settles it, we're going." Jasper looked at the other witches apologetically. "I'm sorry; we'll leave you short-handed."

Avery brushed off his concerns. "There are still plenty of us, but one of us needs to go with you. What if you're attacked by other vampires? You'll all die."

"I'll go with them," Eve said decisively. "You guys should stick together. I have a plan, but it will get hot. I'll surround us with fire for the entire journey. If I make it big enough on either side, they won't be able to penetrate that."

Alex frowned, looking between her and Jasper. "It's a long way to hold that spell. You'll be exhausted."

"But we'll live, hopefully."

Avery hugged Eve. "Stay safe, and we'll see you soon."

The White Haven witches watched them walk a safe distance away and fire ignite around them, and then they ran to catch up with the others.

The group raced through the twisting passageways, and after a few minutes heard shouting and the familiar blasts of magic.

"What now!" Alex said, sprinting ahead.

They burst into a low-roofed cave, and Avery's feet immediately crunched into old bones that littered the floor. At least a dozen vampires were fighting with the three witches, the wolf, and Ben. It was mayhem, and without hesitation, they dived in to help.

Genevieve, Caspian, and Ben, were back to back, fighting furiously, battling either hand to hand or with magic. Ben kicked, punched and rolled to defend himself, swinging an axe viciously as one vampire tried to get close enough to take him down. Another scuttled over from above, clinging to the roof like a spider, and Avery picked it up in a flurry of wind, smacking it repeatedly against the far wall until it fell, unconscious. Alex readied his stake and ran to it, plunging it into his chest. Avery directed the wind to another vampire and smacked it so hard against the cave walls that it was almost swallowed by them. Ben threw his axe and it embedded into its chest with a *thunk*. But it wasn't enough, and it struggled to break free, ripping the axe out. But Ben hadn't finished. While Avery still had it pinned to the wall, Ben grabbed a stake and drove it into the vampire's chest, then picked up a heavy rock and smacked the stake, forcing it deeper. The vampire fell to the floor, dead.

At the same time, Briar had opened the earth beneath a vampire and it sank into it, desperately trying to free itself, but it was waist-deep, and although its arms clawed wildly, it couldn't move. Hunter raced forward, and ripped out its throat, and then followed that up by ripping her head off.

El and Reuben were together, both wielding swords as they attacked two vampires with grace, severing limbs as they went, but although that slowed the attack, it didn't stop them. The witches were quick, but the vampires were quicker.

One vampire had Caspian cornered, and he was losing the fight. The vampire's long, talon-like nails had sliced Caspian's chest open, and the smell of blood enraged it. Just as the creature was about to sink its teeth into Caspian's neck, Caspian disappeared in a whirl of Air, appearing right behind it, and he plunged his stake through its back, into its heart.

Genevieve was fighting her own battle, fending off a vampire with fire streaming from her fingers.

They must have found their main cave.

"Ben!" Avery yelled, "Did you bring the spells I gave you?"

Ben was busy fighting yet another vampire. He ducked, swung his axe, missed, and rolled to face the vampire again. "The bag at the side," he yelled back breathlessly.

Avery turned swiftly, spotting his rucksack near the entrance. Only days ago she had made the sunlight spell. She hoped they'd brought it, and she hoped it would work.

She was steps from the bag when a vampire attacked from above, lifting her off her feet, its teeth inches from her neck. Avery was so annoyed, she didn't hesitate. She punched him and his head snapped back, and then she pressed her hand into his ice-cold skin and burned through his flesh, hearing it sear and pop beneath her fingers as its eyeballs exploded. He screamed and dropped her, and she used Air to cushion her fall. The vampire fell at her feet, blind and vulnerable, and she plunged the stake through its heart, and set fire to it at the same time.

Avery ran to the bag, fumbling through the contents, vaguely aware of the mayhem around her. She found bottle after bottle and cast them aside, until she found the right one—a black bottle, sealed with yellow wax.

She needed to be in the middle of the room for the best effect, and she used wind to lift her to the roof, rising above the carnage. She uttered the simple words of the spell and smashed the glass against the roof.

A wave of energy knocked her to the ground as sunlight streamed through the cave, bringing with it screams, fire, and then silence. For a few more moments the sunlight warmed them, cleansing the cave of vampires, and then it was gone, leaving them with only the pale, white witch light.

Within seconds hundreds of candles were burning as someone's magic lit them, and the witches, wolf, and Ben stumbled to their feet. Avery could see Alex, covered in blood, but he was standing, and seemed otherwise okay.

"What the hell was that?" Genevieve asked. Her clothes smoked from the fire spells she had been casting.

"My sunlight spell. It worked better than I thought," Avery confessed.

Reuben looked around warily. "Let's talk about that later, and instead get the hell out of here."

Caspian stumbled, and Briar ran to him. "You've lost a lot of blood."

"I'll live," he said. "I'm just dizzy." Blood poured from the wound down his chest, and he winced. "It's burning."

As Briar pressed her hand to it, Hunter growled softly at her side, and she glanced at him. "Behave." He sat and watched, his eyes boring into Caspian.

Avery surveyed the room. "How many do you think were here?"

"Probably a dozen." Genevieve shrugged. "More or less. I didn't see Lupescu, though."

Reuben twirled a sword like a Samurai and looked appreciatively at El. "But Bethany's dead. El killed her."

Genevieve suddenly realised the others weren't there and she looked panic-stricken. "Where is everyone else?"

Avery tried to reassure her, hoping that what she was about to say was true. "They're okay. Dylan's broken his arm, and there were some minor head injuries, but hopefully they're all safe now. We need to get out, too." She looked around for the closest exit, but there were too many; at least half a dozen passageways left the cave.

"We'll go back the way we came," Alex said, already striding towards it. "Quick, in case reinforcements come back."

It was relief to be out of the dark, narrow tunnels, although the house felt strange, somehow expectant. They shut the hidden panel, and left the tower room as they had found it, and after gathering their gear, they congregated in the hallway, ready to head their separate ways.

"Wait," Reuben said, halting by a small door beneath the stairs. "I need to show you the cellar, Alex. I'm pretty sure it's all hooey and no doey, but I'd like your opinion."

Alex nodded, weariness etched across his face. "Sure. Let's make this quick."

Reuben turned on the overhead light, and led them down the stairs to a long cellar, lined with brick. Dozens of candles lined the edges of the room, and in the centre of the floor, drawn in chalk, was a rudimentary series of sigils and signs within a circle. The witches walked around it, and Alex crouched, examining some of the signs carefully. Caspian echoed his movements, and Avery remembered that Caspian's family also had a history of demon raising and necromancy, particularly Alicia.

Alex looked up and grinned. "This is useless. A façade."

"I agree," Caspian said, rising to his feet. "It looks pretty, but it has no power. Idiot."

Alex stood, too. "It's a worrying occupation, but essentially harmless."

Reuben looked relieved. "Great. Just wanted to check."

They filed back upstairs, Avery sure her legs would collapse beneath her at any point.

"We need another plan of attack," Genevieve said, her face grim, once they were in the hall again. "Lupescu is still out there. Have we heard from the others?"

Avery nodded. "I spoke to Eve; she's on her way home."

Ben held his phone. "Cassie texted. They're at the hospital. I'll meet them there."

"Maybe have a shower first," Reuben suggested, gesturing at his clothes.

They were all covered in blood.

"Right, shower."

Relief flooded Genevieve's face. "Good. Let's go home, I'm too tired to think now. I need space, and I want to see my kids."

Briar's expression was gentle as she said, "I think we all need space to think. This feels like a house of horrors. I don't know how Rupert and Charlotte can bear to live here."

"Because they don't know what's under them," Alex answered. "I hope. Let's talk again tomorrow."

"It's the solstice tomorrow," El noted. "The longest night of the year."

"Let's hope that's not bad news for us," Caspian said, clutching his coat to his chest.

Briar noted his wince. "Who can heal you?"

"My sister has passable skills. Thanks, Briar."

"Even so, come and see me tomorrow," she insisted. "I'm better than passable."

He nodded, and as Ben locked up, they called their goodbyes.

Avery turned to watch the house as Alex drove away. Within seconds, it was swallowed by the swirling snow, as if wrapping itself in its secrets once again.

Twenty-Three

The Wayward Son was a welcome haven of warmth, cheer, and noise, after a tense journey in heavy snow on hazardous roads. Only the use of magic had helped them get back so quickly.

Once the witches had arrived in White Haven they headed home to shower, and then met in the quiet backroom that overlooked the courtyard. No one wanted to be alone, needing the normality of a crowded pub to cheer them up. And besides, it was still only 9:00pm. They had been in the tunnels under the house for all of four hours, although Avery felt like it had been much longer.

Avery sipped a glass of wine while she looked out of the window. The snow was still falling thickly, which was unusual so close to the coast. She would have enjoyed it, had she not been so worried. She caught her reflection in the glass and wondered how she could look so tired and still be awake. She ran her hand through her hair, trying to look more presentable.

"Cheer up," El said, chinking her glass. "At least we found out a lot more today, and managed to kill some vamps."

Avery turned to face her, amazed that El could still look so cheerful after all they had seen today. Her long, blonde hair was swept up into a messy knot on her head, and her red lipstick was bright against her pale face. "How come you always look so good?" Avery asked her. "Even when we're fighting vampires, you manage to look cool."

El winked. "It's a skill. Besides, you always look pretty good yourself. So do you, Briar." She nodded to Briar who sat next to her, her dark hair tumbling about her face. She was looking particularly pretty tonight, and Avery was sure she knew why. El continued. "Stop changing the subject."

Avery sighed. "Sorry. I'm trying to distract myself from that horror show we've just experienced."

"So am I. Wine helps." She looked behind her to where they could see Reuben at the bar, ordering food. "So does he, even with his stupid water gun."

Briar laughed. "It is stupid, but it works."

"True dat," El said, nodding. "And unfortunately, I'm sure he'll have to use it again."

"We need to tell Newton what we found," Avery pointed out. "There's nothing he can do, but even so."

"There's plenty he can do," Briar said, frowning. "They need to collect all those bones down there and give them a proper burial."

"Not yet he can't," El replied. "It means letting Rupert know what we've found, and we can't let that happen yet. We have no idea whose side he's on, or what he's prepared to do. Finding that necromancy stuff was weird."

The arrival of Reuben, Alex, and Hunter interrupted them, and they all sat down with fresh pints. Alex sat next to Avery, nudging her arm. "Cheer up."

"That's what El said. I can't help it. Lupescu is still running around, and we have no idea where he is."

"I can rip his throat out," Hunter said nonchalantly. "I've got Lupescu's scent now. It will give me great pleasure to hunt him down."

"It's a bit weird that he's called Lupescu," Reuben said. "Is that something wolfy?"

Hunter shrugged. "Maybe. But it's just a name. He sure didn't smell of wolf—just death and rotting flesh." He tapped his nose. "I'll be able to find him again, if we can narrow down where he is."

"How can you distinguish him from the other smells?"

"They may be vampires, but they all have their own distinct scent, beyond the decay."

Avery watched him thoughtfully. "Had he been in that cave?"

He nodded. "Yep, but it wasn't as strong in there as in his 'bedroom,'" he said, making air quotes. "We were close to the sea in that cave, though. I could smell it."

"Smugglers' caves again," Briar said. "As we thought."

Avery persisted. "But how do we find him?"

Reuben took a long drink of his beer, as if bracing himself. "We go back tomorrow, in the daylight, through the hatch in the woods. We don't need the house now."

Avery rubbed her face, annoyed with herself. "Of course. I'm so tired I'd almost forgotten it. Could you find it again?"

"Easily. But I think only we should go. Eve, Jasper, Dylan, Cassie, and Caspian, were injured, and Gen has three kids! She can't risk her life with them at home."

"I'm not sure she'd agree with you," Briar said, glaring at him. "She's our coven's High Priestess, and will want to be there. She saved us on Samhain."

"But that was different," he argued. "It was a huge coven spell. This is us hunting vampires. We have agreed we aren't going to try and bind Lupescu—who it seems is the lead vamp. We're going to kill him, and end this once and for all."

They were interrupted by the arrival of their food, and they fell silent for a moment, as Grace spent the next few minutes bringing their plates. The young blonde woman looked as knackered as Avery felt.

"Anything else, boss?" she asked Alex.

He smiled at her. "No thanks, Grace. You can start taking out the rubbish, if there's time."

She nodded and went back to the bar, and Avery's stomach growled with hunger. No wonder she was tired. She was starving. For a few minutes everyone was silent as they ate, and then Avery asked, "But what if there are *another* dozen vampires?"

"I don't think there are," Reuben said. "I'm pretty sure we killed all of them except Lupescu. It was only just after dark. They wouldn't have had time to leave."

El frowned. "Unless there was another base. There was the last time."

He shrugged. "Maybe, but the deaths and disappearance have all been local, which makes me think they are only based here."

"True," Alex agreed. "But I was wondering where they came from. There were more there than I was expecting."

"I was wondering that, too," Hunter said, pushing his plate away. "They've probably been accumulating over years of disappearances, probably from long ago. I think Felicity's spell not only sealed Lupescu, but all of his progeny. That would explain why they've been inactive for so long. And why they've woken so hungry that they've caused such obvious devastation."

Briar looked at him, admiringly. "Good point. There have only been a few recent deaths that we think have turned. The others are accounted for."

"But there have been quite a few disappearances," El reminded them. "They may not all be dead."

Reuben picked his glass up. "I need another pint. Anyone else?"

The others nodded, and Avery drained her wine. "Yes, please."

He headed back to the bar while they discussed their options, and then a scream sliced through the hum of conversation. Something fell with a *thump* into the courtyard, blood splattering against the windows. They all leapt up so quickly that their chairs scraped back and fell to the floor.

A woman's body lay on the ground of the courtyard, her limbs spread at unnatural angles, her throat ripped open. Blood spread around her, staining the snow. It was Grace.

Without hesitation, Hunter rose to his feet and headed to the back door.

Briar shouted, "Wait! What are you doing? You can't go out there. It's a crime scene! And you'll get hurt."

Hunter's eyes were already developing a molten yellow glow. "I'm going to find him. Wait here!" And then he was gone.

Newton stood over Grace's body, looking furious. The coroner was next to him, and they had a few hurried words before Grace was lifted up and carried out of the side gate. The place had been cordoned off by SOCO, and blue and red lights were flashing, making the blood on the floor look black against the snow. He looked up at them watching through the window, scowled, and turned to speak to Detective Moore.

The Wayward Son was now empty of everyone except the witches and the bar staff, and everyone was upset. The bar staff were sitting together by the fire in the main room, but the witches stayed by the courtyard window, watching the police. For a while, Alex had sat with his staff, but now he sat next to Avery again, looking white faced and grim, his hands clenched. He stared at the blood staining the snow, unmoving.

Avery sat next to him, squeezing his arm from time to time, and feeling ineffectual. She was horrified by the events of the last few hours, worried about Alex, and *very* worried about Hunter. She watched Briar's taut face, and the way she kept looking behind her to the door. El and Reuben sat apart from them, talking quietly, no doubt hatching some plan, but Avery was too tired to think coherently.

Eventually, Newton came in through the rear door, at the same time that Hunter reappeared through the main doors, and their eyes met across the pub, both of them glaring at each other. Newton glanced at Briar and back to Hunter, and his grim expression soured further. Avery noticed that Hunter didn't push it; he just sat next to Briar quietly.

"Where have you been?" Newton asked Hunter.

"I was out, trying to get his scent."

"Really? Because the victim's throat is ripped out, and wolves do that, don't they?"

A low snarl started in the back of Hunter's throat as he said, "I was sitting here when it happened. Everyone saw me. I went out afterwards."

Briar glared at Newton and clenched her fists, and the pot that the indoor plant in the corner was sitting in exploded in a shower of earth and plastic.

Avery spoke quickly before Briar could do anything else. "Newton, Hunter was sitting here with us. All of us were in here for at least 20 minutes, together, when that happened." She gestured to the window, swallowing hard, and then back to him, imploringly. "You *know* the vampire did this. She was dropped from a height."

"And how did she get to the roof?"

Alex looked up at him, finally. "I checked with Simon—he's the bar manager tonight. She was putting the rubbish out, as I asked her to do, heading out the kitchen door to load the rubbish bags in the main bin. It must have been waiting. It would have lifted her up before she could do anything." He paused. "This is my fault. If I hadn't asked her..." He trailed off, unable to finish his sentence.

Avery squeezed his hand. "Stop it, Alex. It's not your fault. It's Lupescu's."

"And who is Lupescu?" Newton asked, seething.

"The vampire we've been chasing. The one who has been responsible for the recent deaths—well, some of them," Avery explained.

"Nice to know you're keeping me in the loop," Newton said, glaring at them all as if they'd betrayed him.

Avery could feel her eyes filling with tears. "We only found out today, and it's been *a very long day*. Of course we would have told you."

Reuben butted in. "Newton, calm down. We'll tell you everything we know. We're not the enemy here."

Newton blinked, with what might have been reassurance, but then he turned to Hunter. "And when did *you* arrive?"

"Last night. Briar asked for my help." He tapped his nose. "This is good for tracking."

"And have you tracked it?"

"I found its scent a few roads down. It took me a while. It must have cut across the roofs. I followed him back out of town, and then lost him—he must be up high again."

Newton stared at him for a moment longer, and then addressed everyone. "I need statements from all of you, and the staff. Moore will take them."

"That's fine," Avery said. "And then is that it for tonight?"

"Yes," he said abruptly. "Where can I find you later?"

"I'll be here, with Alex."

Briar bristled with defiance. "I'll head home. Hunter is staying with me."

They were back to this now, were they? Avery thought, looking between them.

Newton could barely look at her. "And you, El?"

"We'll be at my flat," she answered.

"Fine. I'll be in touch." And then he turned and left, the door slamming behind him.

However, they didn't head home straight away. After they'd been interviewed, and Alex had locked the pub up and ensured the rest of his staff weren't travelling home alone, they all headed to Alex's flat to discuss their options.

As soon as they were through the door, Reuben said, "I need whiskey."

"In the cupboard next to the TV," Alex instructed him. He slumped in the armchair, immobile. "Make mine a large."

"Whiskey all around?" Reuben asked, as he reached for the bottle and glasses.

"Yes, please," Hunter said. He'd never been in Alex's flat before, and he paced around, curious.

Avery declined. "Not for me, thanks. I'll have more wine." She lit the fire and the lamps, and then peeked through the blinds. "It's still snowing. I haven't known it to fall this heavily for years. Do you think Lupescu will hunt again tonight?"

Briar stood next to her, watching the swirling snow. "I hope not, but I doubt snow will stop it."

El was curled in her favourite place on the sofa, her long legs tucked beneath her, and she stared into the fire, swirling the whiskey around the glass. "I feel guilty sitting here when it could be out there now, attacking others."

"Me too," Alex said, as he took his glass from Reuben. "Grace is dead, and more could be tonight, and what am I doing? Sitting here by a warm fire, drinking sodding whiskey." He downed it in one go and held it out again. "Another, please."

"Yes sir." Reuben topped him up, and then stood with his back to the fire, looking at them all. "Let's do something about it!"

El's head shot up. "Now?"

"Yes, why not?"

"Because there's a bloody great blizzard out there, and we can't see Lupescu. The night is *a vampire's* friend, not ours."

"Where's your sense of adventure, El?" he challenged.

"Buried beneath my sense of self-preservation!" She looked at him as if he'd gone mad.

"Just hear me out," he said, appealing to everyone. "I don't mean we run around like loonies chasing him in the snow. That *would* be suicide. And pointless. No, I suggest that we find Lupescu's lair and wait for it, and then when it comes back—*boom*! It will *not* be expecting that! It will think we're lying in terror in our beds."

Hunter had stopped pacing, and he leaned against the wall, sipping his drink. "I could smell Lupescu's scent particularly strongly in one of the tunnels leading away from the main cave, and there were very few other scents with it. I think that particular tunnel led to its very own den of horrors. Lupescu is the head vamp. The king doesn't slum it with the rest of them." His eyes developed a molten glow again. "And we smelt the sea, remember? I bet that his lair is close to the beach for easy access. I've got a very good sense of direction—it's a wolf thing. If you pull a map out, I can tell you which way we were moving underground, and I can narrow down where the cave will exit."

Reuben frowned. "You're saying that we don't have to use the hatch in the wood?"

Hunter shook his head. "No—I don't think so, anyway. Show me a map, I'll show you where we should exit, and you tell me what's there. We'll see if it's possible."

"Hold on," Avery said, confused. "It's probably not in its cave. It's out here, hunting innocent people. And, sorry to keep reminding you of this—it's *awake*! That means it's *dangerous*! What happened to the plan to stake it when it's asleep? And—" she added, "it could well move to another sleeping area. Our scent will be all over that main cave. It knows we've been there. That's why Grace is dead—for revenge!"

"Which is why we should act tonight," Reuben argued. "It could be heading back to grab its vampire backpack of death and escape right now!"

El rolled her eyes. "Now I know you've gone mad. *Vampire backpack of death*?" She looked at Briar and Avery. "When I said earlier that he keeps me sane, I was clearly delusional. Remind me of this in the future."

Reuben batted his eyelashes at her. "I keep you sane? That's so sweet."

"And wrong!" she retorted.

"Actually," Hunter said confidently, "I think Lupescu has no idea that we know where to find it. I sniffed out every single exit in that place, making sure to smear my wolfy scent everywhere. I even started down the wrong passage. I made it seem I was going the wrong way." He grinned, smugly. "And besides, it's arrogant. It underestimates us."

Talk about arrogant. If only Newton could see him, it would be all out war.

Alex was suddenly alert. "I like this idea. I like it a lot. I've got a big map here, somewhere. I know I have. It'll be better than using a phone." He jumped up and ran to the bookcase, shuffling through books and throwing a few on the floor. "Here!" He triumphantly pulled an A4, dog-eared folder out, filled with folded maps, and rustling through them produced one of the Cornish coast. "These belonged to my uncle." He headed to the table and spread it out, turning the overhead light on at the same time, and the others crowded around. He pointed to a spot on the map. "Madame Charron's, and there's the woodland where the hatch is."

They fell silent while Hunter studied the map, running his finger over it while muttering to himself.

Half of Avery wished that he wouldn't have a clue and they'd give up this ridiculous idea, and the other half wanted him to be absolutely sure so they could go and get this over with.

"Look," Hunter said, his finger stabbing the map. "There's the hatch. We continued on for a while, west, then we turned south, then east, then south, and east again. We smelt sewage in a few places here, which would make sense—it's right under the village. Then east, then south again, and that's where I think the main cave is." He jabbed the map emphatically.

Alex frowned. "It's closer to White Haven than I expected. Are you sure?"

"Yep. I'd bet my life on it."

"What's that squiggle under your finger?" Briar asked, as she leaned in closer.

"It's one of the old Second World War bunkers, called a pillbox, I think," Alex answered. "I didn't think those things had tunnels."

"What were they for?" El asked.

"They were part of the coastal defences that were erected when we thought the Germans were going to invade at the start of the war," he explained. "Pillboxes are concrete boxes dug into the ground with slits for weapons. Some were linked together by huge trenches for tanks, but they've long since been covered in weeds and undergrowth. You can't even see most of them anymore."

"Maybe when this one was constructed, it opened up an existing tunnel," Reuben suggested.

Alex nodded in excitement. "Maybe." He looked at Hunter. "You're sure about this?"

The molten glow fired in Hunter's eyes in anticipation. "Yes."

"Are you sure it wouldn't be safer to go through the tunnels?" Avery asked. "We know that way."

"But it's long. This will be quicker," Alex reasoned.

Briar looked worried. "But it will scent us, surely."

Reuben looked exasperated. "We're *witches*! We can disguise our scent, hide ourselves, and set up a trap. We're allowing ourselves to be frightened by this thing! We are stronger combined than Lupescu is." He looked around, appealing to them. "We have stakes, swords, fire, holy water, and magic. We have spells that can immobilise it! Come on! Are we witches or wimps?"

They looked at each other, slow smiles spreading.

Avery felt hopeful once more. "You're right, Reuben. Let's do this."

Twenty-Four

Avery's van crawled along the coastal route towards West Haven, the blizzard ensuring no one else was on the road, and shielding them from prying eyes.

Briar sat up front, next to Avery and Alex, and used magic to clear the snow from their immediate path, creating a pocket of calm in the storm, while Reuben and El erased their path from behind. Alex consulted the map.

"Are we close?" Avery asked, her hands gripping the wheel.

"I think so. GPS says we are, anyway."

Hunter called from the back of the van. "Let me out and I'll check."

Avery eased to the side of the road, and within seconds Hunter had shed his clothes and disappeared, a flurry of snow settling in the van as he left.

Reuben grinned at Briar. "I like your new boyfriend. He's very useful."

She glared at him. "He's not my boyfriend."

He sniggered. "Yeah, right. He thinks so, and so does Newton. He was *not* happy tonight."

"Well, Newton has no say in what I do," she shot back.

Reuben continued, undaunted. "In my opinion, you made the right choice. Newton will never really get his head around witchcraft, no matter how much he likes you, whereas Hunter doesn't give a crap." He smirked as he added, "And clearly can't keep his eyes off you."

El prodded him. "Reuben, behave."

"Just saying! I have a brotherly love for you, Briar. I approve."

"Thanks so much," Briar said, a dangerous edge to her voice.

He grinned again. "My pleasure."

"Could we maybe get back to our plan to kill a vampire?" Alex asked, watching with amusement from the front seat.

Reuben held his hands out, palms up. "We have a plan. Trust me."

They jumped as Hunter landed on the bonnet with a *thump*, and then ran around the side. "He's back," Avery said.

El opened the door and Hunter bounded in, shaking snow from his fur, and then changed back to human form.

"It's bloody cold out there, even with my wolf fur to keep me warm. But I found it. Another couple of hundred metres up the road."

"I don't know how you can find anything in this," Briar said, and even in the tension of the moment, Avery noticed how her eyes travelled across him almost hungrily.

"We have a lot of snow in Cumbria," he answered. "I'm used to it. But someone will have to wipe my prints...I went a few different places before I found it."

Reuben grabbed his backpack. "That will be me. Let's erase those first, and then we'll go."

They both disappeared for another few minutes, and the others waited in anxious silence. Then Reuben stuck his head in the back door. "Ready everyone?"

They nodded, and slipped out of the van and into the night, Avery casting a spell to hide the van, before following Hunter.

Avery's jacket was zipped up tight, and she wore a scarf and a hat, but even so it was bitterly cold. Hunter led them away from the road, a bubble of stillness around them as Briar kept the snow away, and Reuben erased their tracks from behind.

It was hard going despite their magic, and they slipped and stumbled through the deep snow. Avery could hear the sea, the waves crashing onto the beach and the cliffs somewhere beyond them, but she couldn't smell it. The snow blanketed everything. After a few minutes they passed through some scrubby bushes, bent over by years of wind, and stumbled into a ditch. A low, concrete wall appeared in front of them, cracked and pock-marked.

Hunter led them around the small building. The walls were only a few feet high, and at intervals Avery could see long, dark slits in the concrete. They must have been for the lookouts and their guns. The ground dropped as they reached the other side, and a rotten wooden door appeared, partially open. Inside it was pitch black, and a musty, sour smell escaped from it.

Hunter slipped inside and they followed him. Avery hesitated a moment, watching Reuben as he wiped their prints, the snow smoothing under his magic, and then she slipped inside, too, Reuben behind her.

A witch light hung in the air, revealing cracked walls and chunks of concrete on the broken floor beneath them where weeds were pushing through. At the rear of the small room, a black hole yawned in the ground, and Hunter sniffed at its edges, Alex next to him.

Hunter changed back to human form as he crouched next to the opening, shivering in the cold, and once again Avery tried to ignore the fact that he was completely naked. "This is it. The scent is really strong here, only hours old. But I'm pretty sure Lupescu's not here."

Alex nodded. "Good. Are we covered outside?"

Reuben nodded. "All trace has gone, including our scent. Briar will take over in here—she's better with Earth spells."

Briar was already taking her shoes off and putting them in her backpack. "I'm ready."

"Won't your feet freeze?" Avery asked, worried.

"The Earth generates her warmth for me," Briar reassured her. "Go on. I'll be right behind you."

Alex threw another witch light into the hole, revealing a metal ladder set into the wall. It led to a brick-walled room beneath the bunker, but a passageway went out of it on their right and left, running parallel with the coast.

"Was this part of the defences?" El asked.

"Must have been," Alex said. "Storage for weapons, I guess. They must have dug into the tunnel that was already here. Smugglers' tunnels, I bet. They probably link caves to cellars. Like at your place, Reuben."

Reuben nodded in agreement. "This place never ceases to surprise me."

Hunter, already a wolf again, was sniffing around the passage entrances, and led them down the passage heading west. It sloped downwards, and the lower they went, the louder the sound of the sea became, until suddenly the tunnel ended in a small cave.

The ground was a mix of sand, earth and rock, but the roof was high, disappearing into utter blackness. The walls were made of rock, except for the side closest to the sea, which was a jumbled mass of earth and huge boulders of rock with the occasional tree roots thrusting their way through. Another tunnel headed north, away from the coast. But most importantly, the cave had bones in it, blankets on the floor, the remnants of a fire, candles, and the limp but unmistakable form of a teenage girl against the far wall.

Hunter was already sniffing her gently, and Avery ran over and felt her pulse. "She's alive, but only just." Puncture marks scarred her neck, and she was thin and pale. "We need to get her out of here."

"Not yet," Alex said. "Lupescu will know. We have to just try and keep her out of the fight."

Briar pointed to the mass of boulders and fallen debris. "A cliff collapse. This place has probably been hidden for well over a century."

El had already unsheathed her sword. "What now? There aren't many places to hide in here."

Reuben pointed upwards. "There are natural cracks in the rock face...some of them look pretty big. A couple of us can hide in them. The rest can hide down the tunnel."

Alex nodded. "I want to check down there, make sure nothing else is lurking behind us while you investigate the cave."

"I'll come, too," Avery said.

She followed Alex down the narrow passage, which was sculpted by water and difficult to navigate. They had to crouch and wiggle through in places, and Avery hated it. She felt suffocated, and for one horrible moment, thought she was going to be trapped forever. Then it opened out into the main cave they had found earlier that day; it already seemed like a lifetime ago. They spent a few minutes exploring it thoroughly before Alex said, "I think we're good. You?"

"Yep, all good. That's one win for us."

They squeezed back through the narrow tunnel again, and Avery turned to Alex at the entrance to the Lupescu's lair. "Once we cast the shadow spell we'll be completely invisible, but I'm worried we won't have a good view of Lupescu until he's in the middle of the cave."

"But we will," Reuben noted from above their heads. "I'll see it the moment it arrives."

"And once it's in," El said, from the other side of the cave, "I'll seal the tunnel behind it."

Avery looked up to see her lying in another natural rock crevice, almost invisible in the shadows.

Alex still looked worried, but he said, "All right. Where will you be, Briar?"

She stood next to the rock fall. "I'll pull some of this earth and plant debris around me. There's room within the gaps between these boulders...enough for Hunter, too."

"So now we just have to wait," Reuben called down.

"Take your places, and I'll erase our scent again. But we could be waiting some time," Briar cautioned.

"So be it," Alex said. "It will be worth it. Good luck everyone—and let's stick to the plan!"

Once the lights were extinguished, the cave was pitch black. Avery stood immobile for what seemed like an age. She felt utterly alone. The shadow spell was so effective that even though Alex was only a short distance away, she couldn't feel him at all. She started to get anxious, and willed herself to complete stillness, using her magic to help keep her warm. Just when she began to think Lupescu would never arrive and they'd got everything wrong, she heard a noise.

It was the sound of footsteps, slow and deliberate. And then they stopped for a moment, and Avery could sense its doubt and caution. She willed it onwards, and with relief heard the footsteps again. Then there was a *thump* as something hit the floor.

At the same time as the vampire started to light candles, Avery felt the gentle *whoosh* of magic as El placed a protection spell on the tunnel, sealing Lupescu inside. It walked into view in the centre of the cave, dragging a body behind it, then lit the fire, allowing Avery to see its cruel, hard face. The vamp was young looking, far different than the other night when its skin had looked grey and was wrapped tightly around its skull. The blood it had consumed must have plumped up its skin. Its hands were almost elegant, had they not ended with long, curved nails. Lupescu might have been handsome before he became a monster.

As planned, Briar opened the earth beneath its feet, swallowing Lupescu up to its chest, and the fire disappeared with it. It roared, its jaw opening unnaturally wide and showing sharp canines, stained with blood.

Avery was just saying her spell to immobilise it when with unexpected swiftness, it disappeared in a streak of smoke up towards the roof and the tiny vents in the rock.

They had talked about whether it could do this, and they had a plan just in case. Avery and Alex linked hands, sending another protection spell around the cave and sealing it with a rippling blue wave of magic. Lupescu veered course, flashing towards Reuben, who rolled out of his hiding place and sent out a shockwave of power, effectively blocking him again.

Meanwhile, Alex ran out, and he grabbed the unconscious young woman Lupescu had brought in, and pulled her out of the way.

Lupescu remained in smoke form, streaking around the cave, desperately seeking a way out.

Briar and Hunter stayed hidden, biding their time, as did El, but Avery sent a blast of wind around the cave in ever stronger circles, sweeping the vampire up, and herding it into the centre of the room. It landed on its feet, in physical form again, and, full of rage, launched itself at her so quickly that Avery had barely time to react. But Briar did, opening the earth beneath it again, and this time tree roots snaked towards it, grabbing its limbs and pinning them tight.

It smiled at Avery, a terrible, rictus grin that made it look more dead than alive, and spoke with a horribly wheezing, raspy voice that grated her nerves. "I can hear your heartbeat now, witch. You're scared, like they all are. I'll enjoy your blood." It pulled free of the roots, snapping them in seconds, and with superhuman strength, it leapt out of the earth, ready to attack. But she was ready for its speed this time, and didn't hesitate.

She commanded wind and using it like a giant hand she pinned the unnatural creature to the ground, watching it squirm. Roots again sprang from the earth, and Hunter raced across the cave, snarling, his jaws wide, at the same time as Alex raced towards it with his stake raised.

But again, Lupescu changed into smoke, evading all of them. It headed toward Reuben, who stood on a narrow ledge, watching it. Reuben again blasted it with a shield of magic, and Lupescu shied away. El rolled free of her hiding place and raised another magical shied, reducing the places that Lupescu could run to.

Briar stepped out of her hiding spot and placed a silver jar on the ground, covered in runes and sigils. She raised her arms in front of her and started the spell that would bring the vampire down into the jar they had prepared to seal it in. When they had discussed this earlier, they were pretty sure it wouldn't work. It would likely change again before it would risk that happening.

El and Alex closed in, Alex with his stake, and El with her raised sword. They edged closer and closer as the witches closed the protection circle, trapping the creature in an ever-smaller space. It flitted about like a crazed, dying bluebottle.

Briar's spell was working. Lupescu was being pulled towards the jar, the runes and sigils on it now blazing with a white light. Just as they thought they might trap it after all, it transformed into its physical form again, and Hunter launched, leaping metres across the floor and landing with a *thump* on the vampire's chest. He ripped into its skin and took a chunk out before Lupescu flung him off like he was a toy, but El was close now, and she swung with her sword, cutting off its right hand.

Lupescu was enraged, its eyes blood red with fury. It leapt to its feet, snarling and hissing, as black veins rose on its skin. But no matter how furious it was, it was clear that Lupescu was running out of options. Hunter jumped, and his huge paws landed on Lupescu's chest again, propelling it to the ground. But this time as they rolled, the vampire pinned Hunter to his chest with its right arm, and forced its left hand into Hunter's jaw, as if to rip it out. It happened in a split second, and for one heart stopping moment Avery froze, unsure of what to do. But Hunter was as unnaturally strong as the vampire, and he bit down hard on Lupescu's remaining hand and twisted as he leapt free, ripping the hand clean off and leaving a ragged stump. Lupescu fell awkwardly, unable to defend it self.

Alex seized his chance and ran in, plunging the stake into its chest, but it wasn't in deep enough to kill, and Avery used a blast of powerful wind to hammer it in.

Lupescu was motionless on its knees, looking helplessly down at the stake protruding from its chest, its arms ending in bloody stumps. It looked up at them, unnaturally still as it became clear there was no escape.

"Move!" El yelled at Alex, and as he stumbled backward, El swung the sword and cut Lupescu's head off, and its twitching body collapsed to the ground. She raised her hands and cast a fireball at it, consuming the corpse in flames.

The witches and Hunter stood back watching it burn until nothing was left.

"And so ends over a century of violence," Briar said softly, her left hand once again buried in Hunter's thick fur.

There was no quiet moment from Reuben; instead, he whooped. "See! I told you it would work."

El just looked at him. "Oh, shut up, bragger!"

The rest of them laughed as their remaining tension seeped away, and Hunter howled so loudly that Avery winced as her ears protested. And then a groan disturbed them.

Avery whirled around. It came from the young girl Lupescu had dragged into the cave. She ran to her side, Briar next to her, but before the girl could rouse further, Briar cast a spell that sent her to sleep. "Best she doesn't remember this," she said gently, before heading to the other girl.

Alex said, "We need to get these girls out. Looks like the other one is still unconscious."

"That's because she's almost dead," Briar said, her fingers feeling for her pulse. "I can stabilise her, but then we need to drop them somewhere close, where they can be taken to a hospital."

"Why don't we call Newton?" Avery suggested as she hefted her pack. "He can say he'd had an anonymous tip, and he can organise it."

"Great idea," Reuben agreed. "It means they can get into that other cave, too, and hopefully start to identify the bodies."

Briar finished healing the young girl, and as her breathing started to improve, she wrapped an old blanket around her. "She'll need a blood transfusion and lots of fluids, but that should keep her going."

As the witches gathered their things, Avery looked at the cave and the old bones littering the floor, and she shuddered. "I'm glad to see the back of this place. Can you imagine being one of his victims, dying here? Horrible."

"Well, we've ended it now," Alex said, wrapping his arm around her waist and pulling her to his side.

"Are we sure we've killed them all?" she asked, worried.

El walked to the tunnel entrance, ready to leave. "After the noise we made tonight, any other vampires would have rushed in. I'm sure we got the lot."

"If they have any sense, any survivors would have taken off, in my opinion," Reuben said. "But there's nothing we can do about that now."

Avery just looked at him. "Oh, thanks for your reassurance, Reuben!"

He winked. "My pleasure." And then he turned and led the way out of the cave.

When they exited the pillbox, they stopped with surprise. The storm was over; snow lay thick upon the ground, and it was utterly still and silent, other than the sound of the waves crashing onto the beach below them. A full moon was low on the horizon, and the snow sparkled in the light. Hunter howled again, and everything seemed perfect.

Twenty-Five

The solstice parade started at midday and the main road that ran through the centre of the town down to the harbour was lined with excited crowds that had been gathering for the last hour or so. Hundreds of children crowded to the front.

The deep snow, which was unusual in Cornwall, made White Haven postcard-picture perfect, and after the previous week of horror, it warmed Avery's soul. She'd given the shop an extra zing of magic, and it smelt of cinnamon and frankincense. The parade didn't pass by Happenstance Books, for which she was very grateful. Stan and the town council had insisted that the shops open for a few hours, and it would have been madness to close anyway, as it was a good day for business. Although, she had trouble keeping her eyes open. She didn't work well on three hours of sleep.

She'd opened the shop at ten, and Alex had decided to spend an hour or so with her, before he walked down to his pub. Sally wasn't due in for another hour, and Dan had gone to fetch hot chocolate. They were sitting behind the counter, each eating a bacon sandwich and idly chatting, when Stan bounded in. He couldn't have been happier, and he grinned at Avery and Alex with delight. "The gods have smiled on us today! Look at White Haven. It has never looked more magnificent!"

Magnificent was a stretch, but Avery smiled. "It is beautiful, Stan. I'll try and sneak out to see some of the parade. We're going to take it in turns once Dan and Sally are here."

Stan sidled closer to the counter, his voice low. "Is the snow anything to do with you two?"

Avery almost choked on her coffee, and Alex froze. "Us?" Avery said, shocked. "No! How can we make it snow?"

He wiggled his eyebrows. "You know. You have a certain something we've all grown to trust."

She was momentarily stunned into silence and glanced nervously at Alex, but she had to answer his expectant look. "I have many skills, Stan, but I can't make it snow."

"Neither can I," Alex said with a shrug, as if being asked if he could make snow was the most normal thing ever.

Stan's face fell slightly and then he smiled. "Oh, well. We all have our limitations, I suppose."

Avery tried not to laugh. "Are you in the parade?"

"Of course! I shan't be wearing my druid's robe today. Instead, I shall be the Oak King," he said proudly. "I have a cape of oak leaves, an oak crown, and an oak staff to carry."

"Who's the Holly King?" Alex asked.

In Celtic legend, the Oak King and Holly King vied to rule over the year's turn. The Oak King conquered the Holly King at the winter solstice and ruled until midsummer, when the Holly King is victorious and rules until midwinter.

"Phil from accounts. We'll have a bit of banter and fight before I declare victory. I can't wait!"

They laughed, and Avery said, "Fingers crossed I'm there in time to see that!"

"Anyway, I must run," Stan said. "I'm just doing my rounds before the parade begins. Your shop looks great." And with that he was off, leaving just as Dan arrived with their drinks.

Dan joined them behind the counter and sipped his drink, his eyes half closed with pleasure. "This is exceptional. All I need now are Sally's mince pies, and my morning will be complete." He was wearing another Christmas t-shirt, reading

Santa Does It Better. "Now, would you two like to tell me why you look so awful?"

"We had a very busy night killing a vampire," Alex explained. "And day, actually. In fact, there was a lot of vampire killing all around."

"I love how you say that so casually," Dan said, raising an eyebrow. "Like it was just a regular Saturday for you."

"Yeah, right," Avery said, grimacing. "I hope we *never* have to do that again. Although, the way James was talking, it sounds as if vampires are not that uncommon in cities. They can stay there."

Alex grunted, his mouth full of sandwich. "James is full of surprises."

"And what about that Rupert guy?" Dan asked. "Is he something to worry about?"

"I don't think so." Avery pulled a stack of books from under the counter. "I phoned him this morning and told him he can come and get these."

Dan frowned and picked up the box-book. "You're letting him have them?"

Alex shrugged. "They're of no use to us, and to be honest, they belong with the house."

Avery agreed. "He won't be able to read what we can, anyway. There's hidden runic script in the box that he can't possibly see."

"You don't think he's a necromancer?"

"He'd like to be," Alex answered, "but I had a good look at the stuff in his cellar. It looks cool, but it's harmless. He's just a regular guy who's a bit obsessive over the occult. And a bit of a creep."

"A lot of a creep, actually," Avery corrected him. "But essentially harmless."

Alex grinned. "I'd love to see his face when he gets a visit from the police about the crypt under the house."

"Ha! Me too. How much will he love that?"

They were interrupted by the jingling of the bell by the door. Shadow strode in, dressed completely in black, which made the shine of her silvery hair stand out even more. Dan hadn't met her before, and his mouth gaped open.

Shadow was oblivious. She stood in the entrance looking around the shop for a moment, and then marched over to them. "You did not tell me that you had so many books!"

"It's a bookshop—of course I have lots of books!" Avery said, already irritated. Dan was still gaping at her. "Shadow, this is Dan, he's a friend and works here. Dan, Shadow."

She smiled at him, and a strange, otherworldly light seemed to shine from her. She held her hand out, and Dan stood and grasped it as if she was a queen. "Dan. So good to meet a friend of the witches." She was only a fraction shorter than him, and she leaned forward, as if she was going to sniff him. Dan leaned in, too, and Avery wondered if she needed to snap him out of the sort of trance he'd fallen in. "No, you are not a witch. Just human."

"Er, yes, just human," Dan stuttered. "And you are what, exactly?"

Alex seemed to be trying very hard not to laugh, so Avery intervened swiftly. "She's our new arrival, the fey from Samhain."

Dan stepped back in shock. "You're the fey from the Wild Hunt! The one who wants to find all the artefacts and get back to the Otherworld."

Shadow held a finger to her lips. "Our secret." Then she put her hands on her hips and said to Avery, "So, are you going to let me help with the night walker?"

Awkward. "Sorry, too late. It happened quicker than we thought, and we killed it last night."

"Mmm. How convenient. You don't trust me!"

Alex narrowed his eyes. "We don't know you. And you did try to kill us. It gives me trust issues."

She sighed in true drama queen fashion. "So long ago! And I told you, that was Herne's request. I'm a good soldier. Besides, that's over now. I'm going back to treasure seeking."

"To return home?" Avery asked.

"To try to. And to make some money. That's what I used to do."

Dan frowned and managed to speak. "You hunted treasure for a job?"

She wiggled her shoulders. "A sort of job. I teamed up with others occasionally. It could be lucrative. My friend, Bloodmoon, was very good at it."

Dan gaped again. "*Bloodmoon*? Is that the name of a person?"

"A fey," she corrected him. "One of the best thieves I know. In fact, you'll like this story—he helped your old king."

Avery was starting to wonder if Shadow had lost her mind. "What old king?"

"King Arthur. He was a king here, is that right?" They looked at her, baffled, but she carried on regardless. "Bloodmoon actually stole a Dragon Blood Jasper—one of *the* rarest and most expensive gemstones *ever*—from the private collection of one of *the* richest men in Dragon's Hollow for his cousin, Woodsmoke, his friend, Tom, and the displaced King Arthur, to help them break a curse. Now that's impressive!" She looked proud and took a moment to bask in Bloodmoon's glory. "Unfortunately, he's not here to help me now, but Gabe and the others said they can."

Dan held his hand up imperiously. "Wait! You said King Arthur. *The* King Arthur?"

"Your old king, so I understand, yes." She shrugged, in a what-of-it sort of way.

Now they were all looking at her like she was mad, but it was Dan who spoke first. "King Arthur is dead, and has been for well over a thousand years, if he even existed at all."

"Well, he's not dead now. He's well and truly alive in the Other. Now, can you show me the books you have? Avery said you could help." She turned and walked away. "Where do I look?"

Dan stared at Avery and Alex, and said quietly, "Are you sure she's sane? And why didn't you tell me she was so hot!" And then he vanished into the stacks, shouting, "This way, Shadow."

Avery looked at Alex. "*King Arthur*?"

"She's clearly nuts."

"And what about Dan? You'd have thought he'd have learnt his lesson after Nixie."

He looked at her, doe-eyed. "True love knows no bounds."

"You are so full of shit, Alex Bonneville."

"You have no romance in your soul."

Avery was tempted to throw her hot chocolate over him, but it was too good, so she changed the subject. "So, what now?"

He kissed her. "I'm going to the pub, but we're not opening today. I've asked all the staff to come in so I can talk to them about last night, and I'm going to try to speak to Grace's mother. I'm not looking forward to it."

Lupescu's last victim. Avery closed her eyes briefly in regret. "I hope it goes okay. I don't envy you that job."

His eyes darkened. "At least I can tell them it won't happen again."

She nodded. "I'll try and get hold of Newton. And I'd better phone Genevieve, too. All I managed to do was send a garbled text last night to her and Ben. See you at your place later, before we go to Reuben's?"

"Perfect."

He kissed her again, leaving her breathless, and she watched him saunter down the street, wishing they could stay in bed all day instead of having to work. She picked up the phone and started her round of calls, waving at Sally absently as she came in with more mince pies. Genevieve and Ben were predictably annoyed at missing the fight, and relieved at the same time. Genevieve was going to hold a coven meeting in the New Year to update everyone, but was planning on otherwise spending a quiet Christmas at home. Ben told her that Dylan was okay but had broken his arm, and Cassie had mild concussion. She then phoned Eve and Jasper to update them, and was about to call Newton, having left him until last, because she knew he was going to be the most difficult, when Caspian walked in, holding himself stiffly.

"You look sore," Avery told him.

He grimaced. "Never underestimate the sharp talons of a vampire."

"Have you come to see Briar?"

"Yes, she's right. She's much better at this than Estelle."

"I bet Estelle hated hearing that."

He allowed himself a small smile. "Yes, she did. I heard from Genevieve you killed Lupescu last night."

Avery had a flash of guilt that she'd forgotten to call him. "Wow. News does travel fast. You were next on my list to call."

He watched her for a moment. "I think you were mad to go with so few of you, but well done."

"You were injured, so we weren't going to ask you. It seemed quicker to just get on with it. It was Reuben's crazy idea."

He nodded. "Fair enough. Just be careful, Avery." He looked as if he were about to say more when Dan and Shadow arrived at the counter. Caspian's eyes widened as he looked at her, and then he looked quizzically at Avery. She nodded and introduced them, hesitating to announce he was a witch, but Shadow could tell.

The fey's sharp eyes appraised him. "You're the one who Gabe now works for."

"I am. I think we met briefly on the night of the Hunt. You created a lot of damage that night."

She smiled, but it didn't quite reach her eyes. "Herne's orders. That's over now."

His cool, calculating gaze appraised her and clearly found her wanting. "I hope so." He turned back to Avery. "More interesting company in White Haven. See you soon." And then he left, a cold draft swirling in his wake.

"He's a prickly one," Shadow said, dropping a pile of books onto the counter. "Powerful, too."

"Very," Avery agreed, as she started to charge the books. "Interesting selection you have here."

"Dan's been very helpful." She flashed him her biggest smile, and Dan grinned goofily back. She continued, "I have much to study before I start my hunt. I may need your help."

Avery considered her next words carefully. "If I can, I will, but I am very busy in White Haven. The Nephilim will be of far greater help I'm sure."

She pinned Avery under her intense stare. "Maybe. But they aren't witches. See you again soon."

Avery watched her leave, then looked at Dan and said, "Bollocks."

White Haven glistened in the winter sunshine. The main street was shut off from traffic, and crowds thronged the pavements. The sound of drumming filled the air as the parade made its way down to the harbour. The participants were dressed in all manner of strange costumes; the Holly King and Oak King led the way, but behind them were adults and children all dressed and masked as various woodland creatures, goblins, elves, and a man dressed up with huge antlers on his head—Herne, the winter king. He looked far less terrifying than the real one. Jugglers and fire-breathers strolled along the edges, and Avery could smell hot chestnuts and mulled wine from the various street stands that had been set up. She smiled and clapped in time with the drums, feeling the beat in her blood.

She watched for a short time before heading back to her shop, and was almost there when Newton fell into step beside her. He looked shattered. "I've been looking for you."

"I've been trying to call you," she explained.

"Can we have coffee before you go back to the shop?" he asked her. He pointed to a cafe on the opposite side of the road.

"Sure." She followed him in, and sat at a small table in the corner. He spent a couple of minutes ordering coffee and food and then he slumped into the opposite seat. He looked pale, his shirt was rumpled, and his hair was messy. "Long night?" she asked.

He grunted. "Exhausting. All those bones, and those two girls." He shook his head. "It will take weeks to go through. Probably more. The forensic team have barely started."

"But at least they are found now," she said, trying to comfort him. "That's a huge amount of cases you can close. All those people will be able to be buried properly, and all of their loved ones will know what happened to them."

"Thank you, again. And sorry about last night. I was angry."

"It's okay. You're allowed to be."

He rubbed his face. "I know this is a good thing, but it's been an exhausting night. It's been an exhausting few weeks, actually. Are you sure it's over?"

"Yes. We watched him burn, and the others—including Bethany." She filled him on the details of the night, and the history they had found out about the House of Spirits. "Some of those bones will be very old. Did you find the other room? The crypt with the smashed furniture?"

He nodded. "Only a few hours ago. I'm paying a visit to Rupert and Charlotte tomorrow. I know they aren't a part of this, but we have to interview them, anyway. And then of course, search the whole house."

"I bet Rupert will love it," Avery said thoughtfully. "But how will you explain the deaths?"

"Serial killer, probably. It seems to be my only recourse when these weird deaths happen—although, I have no idea who we'll blame it on." He paused while their coffees were delivered, and a huge plateful of English breakfast was placed in front of him. He had a few mouthfuls, and then asked, "How long's Hunter here for?"

Avery sighed. She knew he'd ask this. In fact, it was probably his only reason for wanting to see her. "I'm not sure, but he'll be here over Christmas, maybe longer. Why do you care? It's not like you and Briar are together."

He tensed slightly. "I know, but I like her. I don't want her to get hurt."

Avery wanted to throw something at him. "The only person who's been hurting her is *you*, Newton."

He glared at her. "That's bullshit."

"Is it? You like her, that's clear, but you can't get around the fact that she's a witch. You've admitted it yourself."

"I don't have a problem with witches. I'm sitting here with you, aren't I? You're my friend, so is Alex, Reuben, and El. I respect what you do. I helped you recover the grimoires!"

"I know that, and I know that you keep our abilities a secret. But you still struggle with the decisions we make sometimes—especially about the Nephilim. And that's okay. You're a detective. Your priorities are different from ours. But Briar is a witch, to her core, and you clearly can't handle that in someone who might be *more* than friend," she said abruptly. "So, she's moved on, to someone who can deal with that. He'll make her happy, so you need to get used to it." Newton grunted again and continued to eat, refusing to meet her eyes. "Newton, seriously, stop it. You can't have it both ways, with her waiting and waiting until you change your mind—which you will never do. If you want to keep her friendship, respect her decision."

He grunted again, and she finished drinking her coffee in silence. *Men!*

The full moon shone over Old Haven Church, and snow glistened around the old headstones spread across the cemetery.

The witches and Hunter sat around a brightly burning fire in the cleared space in front of the mausoleum steps, wrapped up in layers of jumpers, coats, and scarves. They had placed rugs, cushions, and fur blankets on the ground to sit on, and Avery sipped a mulled wine, heated with a spell. She smiled at Reuben. "This was a great idea."

"Thanks, Avery. I've been thinking about Gil a lot lately. He was with us on the summer solstice, when we were attacked by demons in your garden. Remember?"

"Of course. I don't think I'll ever forget it."

"Although I am trying to," Briar put in with a shudder. "I hope we don't have to face those again in the coming year."

El nodded. "It has been pretty eventful. Sad at times, but also good." She squeezed Reuben's arm. "At least this place feels much better than the last time we were here."

Instinctively, they all looked up and across to the wood at the rear of the grounds where Suzanna had summoned the Wild Hunt.

Hunter stretched his legs out, wiggling his toes in front of the fire. "The pack enjoyed that story!"

"And now you can tell them about vampires!" Briar said, smiling.

"You can tell them yourself," he said, with a cheeky grin.

"What do you mean?" she asked, and even in the firelight, Avery could see Briar's cheeks flushing.

"We have a wild party on New Years! In the Castlerigg Stone Circle. You have to come." He watched her, his eyes molten gold again, and not with anger this time. They challenged her to refuse.

"I might be able to spare a few days away from my shop," she said hesitantly.

"Good," he replied, and looked back into the fire, a ghost of a smile on his face.

Avery grinned at El across the fire, which she swiftly hid when Briar scowled at her. She decided to change the subject. "At least James is happier now—well, since Samhain."

"Have you seen him today?" Alex asked.

"No, but I'll try and see him tomorrow. I thought today would be too busy for him. At least he doesn't have to worry about vampires in White Haven any longer."

"None of us do."

"For now," Reuben added ominously. "We might have them again. I'm still sure there'll be another one or two out there."

"Preferably not half-starved, vengeful ones," El said grimly. "I wonder if Charlotte will be okay. Hopefully her neck will heal and her weird dreams will stop. I wonder why he didn't kill her."

"Convenience," Avery suggested. "For when you don't want to go on a killing spree for food."

Alex sighed. "Today was horrible for me. The bar staff are shaken up and upset. But Simon is a good manager, and Zee's been pretty good, too. I think his sheer size is a comfort. I can't help but wonder, if Zee had have been working last night whether that would have changed anything. If he'd have gone outside instead of Grace, Lupescu wouldn't have been able to kill him."

"You can't start the what-if thing," Briar told him. "That will take you down a rabbit hole you'll never get out of."

"Are you open tomorrow?" Hunter asked.

"Yeah, life goes on, and the staff need to get paid. We'll go to Grace's funeral, though."

"I'll come, too," Avery said, nudging him gently. "I have news. Shadow came to visit today. She's borrowed a load of books to start her artefact search. She's going to be trouble."

Reuben laughed. "Sounds fun to me."

"We can handle her," Alex said, wrapping his arm around Avery and pulling her to his side.

El agreed. "We can handle anything together."

"True," Avery murmured, looking around at her friends. Six months ago she wouldn't have dreamed that she'd be such close friends with all of them, and that she and Alex would be together. It had been quite the journey. Avery smiled, raising her glass to the group. "Here's to the next six months. Happy Solstice!"

Thank you for reading *Undying Magic*. I hope you enjoyed it. I'd love it if you could leave a review here.

Book six, *Crossroads Magic*, is out now. You can buy it here: https://happ enstancebookshop.com/products/crossroads-magic

Read on for an excerpt.

Newsletter

If you enjoyed this book and would like to read more of my stories, please subscribe to my newsletter at tjgreenauthor.com. You will get two free short stories, *Excalibur Rises* and *Jack's Encounter,* and will also receive free character sheets for all of the main White Haven witches.

By staying on my mailing list you'll receive free excerpts of my new books, as well as short stories, news of giveaways, and a chance to join my launch team. I'll also be sharing information about other books in this genre you might enjoy.

Ream

I have started my own subscription service called Happenstance Book Club. I know what you're thinking! What is Ream? It's a bit like Patreon, which you may be more familiar with, and it allows you to support me and read my books before anyone else.

There is a monthly fee for this, and a few different tiers, so you can choose what tier suits you. All tiers come with plenty of other bonuses, including merch for the top two tiers, but the one thing common to all is that you can read my latest books while I'm writing them – so they're a rough draft. I will post a few chapters each week, and you can read them at your leisure, as well as comment in them. You can also choose to be a follower for free.

You can comment on my books, chat about spoilers, and be part of a community. I will also post polls, character art, and some of my earlier books are available to read for free.

Interested? Head to Happenstance Book Club.

https://reamstories.com/happenstancebookclub

Happenstance Book Shop

I also now have a fabulous online shop called Happenstance Books where you can buy eBooks, audiobooks, and paperbacks, many bundled up at great prices, as well as fabulous merchandise. I know that you'll love it! Check it out here: https://happenstancebookshop.com/

YouTube

If you love audiobooks, you can listen for free on YouTube, as I have uploaded all of my audiobooks there. Please subscribe if you do. Thank you.

https://www.youtube.com/@tjgreenauthor

Read on for a list of my other books.

Excerpt of Crossroads Magic

A fire blazed brightly at the centre of the clearing, and figures weaved a dance around it as they passed candles between them. The light cast a warm, gentle glow on the faces of the participants, many of whom were laughing as they trod the well-known path in the centre of the woods.

It was midnight at Imbolc, and the entire Cornwall Coven was celebrating the festival together.

Avery was there with the White Haven witches, all of whom had travelled together to Rasmus's estate on the edge of Newquay. After the horrors of the vampire attacks before Christmas, they hadn't seen the coven since, so it was a chance to celebrate the festival and their victory over Lupescu, the Romanian vampire who had caused so much destruction only weeks before.

However, it was freezing cold. Imbolc fell on the second of February, and frost lay thick upon the ground. When the coven completed the circle, they stopped and turned to watch Genevieve, their High Priestess, raise her hands to the sky. She invoked the Goddess, giving thanks and asking for protection for the months to come, and then she turned to kiss Rasmus gently on each cheek, and handed him a besom broom. Rasmus accepted it with a small bow, and then walked around the circle, brushing it along the ground as he did so, symbolically chasing away the old in a cleansing ritual. Once completed, he gave it back to Genevieve, who invited the others to join in, and then there was a frenzied few minutes as they all grabbed their own brooms and repeated the ritual.

Avery laughed as she furiously swept the ground. It was an old rite, but fun, and the symbolic cleansing really did feel as if they were getting rid of the toxic time they had all experienced. *And at least the snow had gone,* she reflected, as she swept past Reuben and laughed even harder. He looked so out of place with a broom in his hands, but he participated with good grace, even though he had moaned about it on the way over.

When they all finally stopped, they were breathless and hot. Genevieve clapped her hands, her smile beatific, and called a halt to the proceedings. She said a few final words before lifting a chalice of wine from the altar next to her. "And now, it's time to eat and drink!" She gestured to the table on the far side of the clearing, filled with food, and with that the circle broke apart and they headed to fill their plates.

Avery fell into step next to Nate and Eve, the two witches who lived in St Ives on the north coast of Cornwall. Both were artistic and unconventional. Nate was dressed in scruffy combat trousers and an old flying jacket, and Eve had long dreads. "How have you been?" Avery asked them.

"Pretty good," Nate said. "Better than you, by the sound of things."

Avery shrugged. "At least I didn't get a head injury like Eve. Are you better now?" she asked her.

"I'm fine, thank you," Eve answered, with a rueful rub of her scalp. "It soon healed. It was scarier getting out of those tunnels surrounded by fire. I was more worried I'd burn us all. No more news of vampires though, I hope?"

They had all been worried that some vampires had escaped, but if they had, they'd been quiet, and there were no other disappearances or strange deaths that had been attributed to them. "No, fortunately, which is good because we now have a headstrong fey on our hands."

They arrived at the long table, and Avery filled her plate as Nate frowned. "Ah yes, the survivor from the Wild Hunt. I'm intrigued."

Avery laughed, or at least tried to laugh. "Her name is Shadow, and she's driving us mad, the Nephilim included. She's an absolute force of nature! She's using Dan, who works in my shop, as her own personal myth-ometer." She rolled her eyes. "He loves every minute of it. I guess it's good that someone does!"

Nate studied her for a moment. "Eve mentioned her to me, but what's Shadow trying to do? Get back to the Otherworld?"

"And treasure hunt at the same time. You know, find ancient artefacts and sell them for a high price."

"And will the Nephilim help her?"

"I think so. They're trying to find their way in our world, and to make money. They think this will be lucrative. And let's face it, they're supernatural creatures. They have a natural interest in this sort of thing."

Nate looked troubled, and Eve said, "Nate's worried, because he thinks she could find things that are best left hidden."

"You're probably right, Nate," Avery said, worry stirring within her again. "But there's little we can do to stop them. I think we'll just have to manage the consequences."

"But those consequences could be big," he pointed out. "Any black market for art, drugs, or guns will always attract the worst kind of people. A market for mythical objects won't be any different—except for maybe having supernatural buyers. She may even want to steal what's already been found for her own uses."

Avery had a sudden image of Shadow breaking into museums and raiding their displays. Nate was right. She could definitely see that happening.

"Although," Eve countered, "the Nephilim and Shadow are very capable of looking after themselves. If you ask me, anyone who takes them on would be an idiot."

Avery sighed. "True. An even better reason for us to remain on their good side."

Avery spent the next hour or two mingling with the other witches, glad of the chance to talk to Ulysses and Oswald, and then Jasper, Claudia, and a few others. The fire was now blazing, and they sat around it on old deck chairs and logs in an effort to keep warm. They were nearly ready to return to the warmth of Rasmus's house when Caspian arrived at her side. Caspian lived in

Harecombe, the town next to White Haven, and like Avery was an elemental Air witch. His relationship with their coven had started badly, but over time things were improving.

"Avery," he murmured, his dark eyes appraising her. "How are you?"

"Pretty good," she replied. "How's your wound?" She was referring to the deep cut on his chest caused by a vampire.

He rubbed it absently. "Better now, thanks to Briar. It felt like it had poison in it for a while—maybe it had. Let's face it, we don't know much even now about vampires, do we?"

"No, and if I'm honest, I'd like to keep it that way." She remembered that Gabe was now working for Caspian. "How's it going with the Nephilim as security guards?"

"Good, but I'm not surprised. Gabe has a strong work ethic, and they're imposing. No one argues with them."

Avery was curious. "Your company doesn't work with occult goods, does it? Why did you want Gabe?"

"We hide enough of ourselves in everyday life, don't we? I thought it would be good to have honest conversations with as many people as possible. Life can be lonely otherwise." He held her gaze for a moment before returning back to the fire.

Avery knew Caspian seemed to have developed an interest in her, but she refused to be drawn in, instead deciding to tease him. "You need to find a girlfriend. You're a catch, surely, with your wealth and big house. I'd have thought you'd be battling them away."

"Is that all I am? Money?" he asked, his eyes narrowed.

Avery had been flippant, and certainly hadn't meant to cause offence, but this was a topic she wanted to steer clear of. "No, of course not. And anyone who is interested in only that clearly isn't worth your time."

"You don't care for money, do you?" he asked, watching her.

"Not particularly." Avery started to get annoyed. He was being a flirt, and she didn't like it. "And stop it, Caspian."

"Stop what?"

"You know what. I'm with Alex. I love Alex." As she said it, she glanced up and saw Alex across the fire, deep in conversation with Genevieve. As if he sensed her looking, he glanced her way and smiled, before turning away again.

Caspian stared at his feet. "I know."

Immediately, Avery felt terrible, which annoyed her even more. "Maybe you should turn your attention to someone who's free."

"But where's the fun in that?"

Now she knew he was baiting her. "I'll stop talking to you if you keep this up."

"Oh, please don't, we have so much fun!"

She was about to say something unpleasant, when she felt a tap on her shoulder, and she turned to see Reuben's large frame looming over her. "We're heading back to the house, and then home. Coming?"

"Sure," she said, grateful for the interruption, and swiftly rose to her feet. "See you soon, Caspian."

He nodded and turned back to the fire, and Avery fell into step beside her coven, feeling Alex's arm slide around her waist. Alex's strength was spirit-based, and he was able to banish demons and ghouls, and use his intuitiveness to scry, spirit-walk, and communicate with ghosts. He was also skilled with elemental Fire, and as an added bonus for Avery, he loved her, despite all her quirks.

Reuben and El, both tall and fair-haired, walked just a few steps ahead. Reuben was an elemental Water witch, who was still coming to grips with his powers after neglecting them for years. It had taken the death of his brother, Gil, to bring him back to magic. El was skilled with fire and metal work, wore lots of jewellery, and like Reuben, had several tattoos. Briar, the fifth member of their coven, was petite, with long dark hair, and a natural affinity for Earth magic and healing. She was a caring, gentle soul, who had just started a relationship with Hunter, the wolf-shifter who lived in Cumbria, and she was keeping very quiet about it.

Being with them brought Avery more pleasure than she could describe. She had resisted joining a coven for so long, but now these four amazing people were family. They completed her. She smiled and nestled against Alex, feeling a sudden flash of guilt about Caspian's behaviour, even though she hadn't done anything wrong.

"What's Caspian done?" he asked. It was as if he'd read her mind, and she loved him for it.

"Nothing, really. Just flirting, even though he knows it's useless."

A trace of annoyance flashed across Alex's face. "Doesn't stop him trying though, does it?"

Avery hugged him harder. "I ignore it, and so should you."

"I try. Don't worry, I'm not about to get violent."

He pulled her to a halt and kissed her, and Reuben grimaced as he glanced at them. "Oh, you two, get a room."

Alex flipped him off. "Sod off, Reuben."

Reuben just laughed, and El punched his arm. "Stop being naughty."

"You normally like it," he teased, as he increased his pace.

The house came into view, as did Rasmus, greeting them on the broad patio that stretched across the back of his old home. His place wasn't as old as Reuben's, and it was made of faded red brick rather than mellow stone, but it was eccentric, just like he was.

Avery broke away from Alex and went to his side, hugging him. "Thanks, Rasmus. It was great to finally be here and celebrate Imbolc with you. You have an amazing home."

Rasmus smiled, his old face dissolving into wrinkles. "Thank you, Avery. You're welcome anytime. Are you sure you don't want to stay? I have room."

When she'd first met him, Avery had thought him gruff and quite scary, but now she was incredibly fond of Rasmus, especially knowing now what she did of his past. "No, it won't take us long to get home. And besides, we all have to work in the morning." Newquay was on the north coast of Cornwall, and their trip to White Haven on the south coast would only take about 45 minutes.

Briar hugged Rasmus, too. "I'm sure after having to put up with us all, you'll be glad to have the place to yourself."

"I wouldn't offer if I didn't mean it," he remonstrated. He turned to Alex and gripped his proffered hand. "Alex, thank you. The White Haven witches have been a welcome addition to our coven."

"And we're glad to be part of it," Alex replied.

While the others talked, Avery looked back towards the trees, noting the feeling of peace and gentle magic that came from them. Rasmus's family and the Cornwall Coven had celebrated there for years, and the wood seemed to have absorbed the positive energy. A line of lanterns lit the way to the clearing, but the fire itself was lost to view. She was about to turn away when she felt a prickle run down her spine, as if she was being watched. She stared into the darkness and saw a figure standing a short distance away from the path, just at the edge of the wood. Avery blinked. She could have sworn the figure hadn't been there a second before. She stared on, waiting for whoever it was to come fully into view. It must be one of the other witches; although, it was odd that they wouldn't have followed the path. The undergrowth was thick in places.

The figure didn't move. Whoever it was just stood there, watching her. Avery could see a pale face, but it was impossible to tell if it was male or female. And then, as quickly as the person had appeared, the voyeur went. Avery squinted and blinked again. *Was she seeing things?*

"Are you okay?" Briar said to her, following her eye line. "What are you looking at?"

"I could have sworn I saw someone at the edge of the trees, but they've just vanished!"

Briar frowned. "It's dark, and the lanterns throw uneven light, or maybe it was one of the witches enjoying the solitude."

"Maybe." Avery finally turned away. "And it's late and I'm probably over-tired."

But as they said their goodbyes and finally left, Avery couldn't help but look over her shoulder again, convinced that someone had been silently watching them all.

If you enjoyed this excerpt and would like to read more of my stories, please visit tjgreenauthor.com.

Author's Note

Thank you for reading *Undying Magic,* the fifth book in the White Haven Witches series. I thought it was about time to introduce vampires to the White Haven paranormal world. However, as you can see, I wanted to keep them inhuman and inherently evil; I hope you like my version.

As usual, I have mixed myths and legends into my fictional world, and of course kept my focus on the witches. They are the heart of this series, and I love them all. I try to represent witchcraft honestly and positively, but of course, I have taken some liberties with facts.

Witch-bottles really exist, and there was a news article about one quite recently. It's also true that mediums and séances were very popular in the 1920's and '30's. Arthur Conan Doyle was a huge fan and an ardent believer in spiritualism. It's also true that vampires are called Strigoi in Romania, and that Bram Stoker took his inspiration from them.

I'm now working on book six in the series, and mulling over spin-offs, which will probably start with Shadow and the Nephilim. And I'm working on some short stories. I need more hours in the day!

Thanks again to Fiona Jayde Media for my awesome cover, and thanks to Kyla Stein at Missed Period Editing for applying her fabulous editing skills.

Thanks also to my beta readers, glad you enjoyed it; your feedback, as always, is very helpful!

Thanks also to my launch team, who give valuable feedback on typos and are happy to review on release. It's lovely to hear from them—you know who you are! You're amazing! I love hearing from all my readers, so I welcome you to get in touch.

If you'd like to read a bit more background to the stories, please head to my website, where I blog about the books I've read and the research I've done on the series—in fact, there's lots of stuff on there about my other series, Rise of the King, too.

If you'd like to read more of my writing, please join my mailing list at www.tjgreenauthor.com. You can get a free short story called *Jack's Encounter*, describing how Jack met Fahey—a longer version of the prologue in *Call of the King*—by subscribing to my newsletter. You'll also get a FREE copy of *Excalibur Rises*, a short story prequel.

You will also receive free character sheets on all of my main characters in White Haven Witches and White Haven Hunters—exclusive to my email list!

By staying on my mailing list you'll receive free excerpts of my new books, as well as short stories and news of giveaways. I'll also be sharing information about other books in this genre you might enjoy.

I look forward to you joining my readers' group.

About the Author

I was born in England, in the Black Country, but moved to New Zealand in 2006. I lived near Wellington with my partner Jase, and my cats Sacha and Leia. However, in April 2022 we moved again! Yes, I like making my life complicated… I'm now living in the Algarve in Portugal, and loving the fabulous weather and people. When I'm not busy writing I read lots, indulge in gardening and shopping, and I love yoga.

Confession time! I'm a Star Trek geek – old and new – and love urban fantasy and detective shows. Secret passion – Columbo! Favourite Star Trek film is the Wrath of Khan, the original! Other top films – Predator, the original, and Aliens.

In a previous life I was a singer in a band, and used to do some acting with a theatre company. For more on me, check out a couple of my blog posts. I'm an old grunge queen, so you can read about my love of that here. For more random news, read this.

Please follow me on social media to keep up to date with my news, or join my mailing list—I promise I don't spam! Join my mailing list here.

f facebook.com/tjgreenauthor/

𝓟 pinterest.pt/tjgreenauthor/

♪ tiktok.com/@tjgreenauthor

▶ youtube.com/@tjgreenauthor

g goodreads.com/author/show/15099365.T_J_Green

instagram.com/tjgreenauthor/

bookbub.com/authors/tj-green

https://reamstories.com/happenstancebookclub

Books by TJ Green

Rise of the King Series

A Young Adult series about a teen called Tom who's summoned to wake King Arthur. It's a fun adventure about King Arthur in the Otherworld.

Call of the King #1

The Silver Tower #2

The Cursed Sword #3

White Haven Witches Series

Witches, secrets, myth and folklore, set on the Cornish coast.

Magic Unbound #2

Magic Unleashed #3

All Hallows' Magic #4

Undying Magic #5

Crossroads Magic #6

Crown of Magic #7

Vengeful Magic #8

Chaos Magic #9

Stormcrossed Magic #10

Wyrd Magic #11

Midwinter Magic #12

White Haven Hunters
The action-packed spin-off featuring Shadow and the Nephilim.
Spirit of the Fallen #1
Shadow's Edge #2
Dark Star #3
Hunter's Dawn #4
Midnight Fire #5
Immortal Dusk #6

Storm Moon Shifters
Paranormal Mysteries set around the the wolf shifter pack, Storm Moon.
Storm Moon Rising #1

Moonfell Witches
This series features the mysterious and magical witches who live in Moonfell, the sprawling Gothic mansion in London. They first appeared in Storm Moon Rising, Storm Moon Shifters Book 1, and then in Immortal Dusk, White Haven Hunters Book 6, and features characters from both series. However, this series

can be read as a standalone.

The First Yule #0.5 Novella